THRESHOLD

THRESHOLD

G.M. Ford

THOMAS & MERCER

Published by Thomas & Mercer, Seattle
www.apub.com

Amazon, the Amazon logo, and Thomas & Mercer are trademarks of Amazon.com, Inc., or its affiliates.

ISBN-13: 9781477822173
ISBN-10: 1477822178

Cover design by Kerrie Robertson

Library of Congress Control Number: 2014951149

Printed in the United States of America

1

Her silver hair brushed against the young man's cheek as she whispered into his ear and gently traced the outline of his body with her hand. "This is where the universe ends and where Joseph begins," she said, in the smallest of voices. When her hand had found its way back to the top of his head, she began again. Whispering still.

On the third time around his outline, Joseph's right hand twitched. On the seventh, his eyelids began to flutter like the wings of small birds. He was close. She could feel his presence now. Feel his fear and confusion.

A sudden change in air pressure pulled her attention toward the door. Joseph's father, Paul Reeves, stood in the opening. "They want to move him," he said.

The young woman shook her head. "If we let him go now, we may lose him. I need more time."

"Is he . . . ?"

"He's coming," she said.

Reeves pointed a stiff finger. His hand was shaking. "Keep going," he said. "You just keep doing what you're doing." He slipped back through the opening and disappeared.

She made three more circuits of Joseph's outline, whispering all the while, and then got to her feet and crossed to the door, where her jacket hung from a hook. From the inside pocket, she pulled a small package wrapped in tissue paper and then returned to Joseph's bedside. Carefully, she unwrapped the bundle. Inside was a small leather-bound book, badly burned. Flames had devoured the corners and part of the binding, leaving only the soot-encrusted center. As she opened the book and carefully picked her way to the page she was looking for, her hands became soiled by the black ash, the residue of which was transferred to Joseph's sheet as she began working her way around his body once again. "This is where the universe ends and where Joseph begins," she whispered.

Joseph coughed. She began to read aloud from the book.

. . . .

The police negotiator brought the bullhorn to his lips.

"Unlock the door, Mr. Reeves. Drop your weapon and come out. Let us see your hands." The amplified voice ricocheted off the hard surfaces like small-arms fire.

Nothing.

A SWAT officer duck-walked across the floor to the negotiator's side. "How long's he been barricaded in there?" he asked.

"They're not sure. At least two hours."

"We know who he is?"

"Guy's name is Paul Reeves. His son Joseph's a patient here. Joseph's in there with him."

"What sort of weapon?"

"No idea. Last nurse in the room said she thought she saw a gun."

"Thought?"

"That's what she said."

"Long gun? Short gun? What?"

"She wasn't sure."

"That makes it tough."

"Yeah."

"Where is she?"

"She was upset. They sent her home."

The officer shook his head in disgust.

"What's this guy's beef?"

The negotiator set the bullhorn on the floor, pulled an old-fashioned white handkerchief from his pants pocket, and mopped his brow. "The kid's been in a coma for the better part of a year. Seventeen years old. His mother wants to pull the plug. Says all they're doing is prolonging the boy's agony." He motioned with his head. "Mr. Reeves in there doesn't want to hear about it." He wiped beads of sweat from his upper lip. "They've been duking it out in court for the past year or so. As I understand it, an appeals court is supposed to render a final decision this Wednesday. The legal eagles seem to think Mom is going to get the nod." He shrugged. "Apparently Mr. Reeves thinks so too."

The SWAT officer mulled it over. "How many ways in?" he asked after a long moment.

"Two. These doors here and there's an entrance on every floor that connects to the emergency stairwell. And, of course, the elevators, but they don't count because Reeves shoved hospital beds into both door-ways and shut everything down."

"I'll send a team up the back stairs."

"It's not that simple."

"Why not?"

"Joseph's room . . . that's the only room in that wing that's still in use. The five others are all under construction. There's construction material all over the place. He's got some sort of steel I beam wedged through the door handles. Worse than that, the construction crew brought one of those little front-loader things . . ."

"A Bobcat?"

"Yes. They brought it up in the freight elevator. Reeves parked it in front of the stairway door."

SWAT took about five seconds to shuffle his options. "We'll come down from the roof," he said.

At the nurses' station, several voices rose simultaneously. While the speakers were too far away to make out the words, a sense of urgency suddenly spread through the air like smoke.

A moment later, the squeak of rubber-soled shoes pulled their attention in that direction. A middle-aged nurse in green scrubs was coming their way at a lope.

"Get down! Get down!" SWAT hissed, motioning toward the floor.

The nurse ignored him. Just kept coming. The second she came within reach, the SWAT officer pulled her into the alcove where he and the negotiator were crouched.

He opened his mouth to admonish her, but she beat him to the punch.

"Joseph's monitors have gone down," she announced. "We think his ventilator has been unplugged."

"Which means what?"

"Joseph doesn't breathe on his own. Never has."

"How long have we got?"

"Six minutes at most."

SWAT began shouting orders into his shoulder radio. Within thirty seconds, every doorway on the opposite side of the hall was filled with a black-visaged SWAT officer brandishing an automatic weapon.

SWAT leaned back against the wall. "Team's on its way to the roof," he said.

An eerie silence crept in. It was like nobody was breathing.

Another minute passed. Somebody coughed. And then another forever minute.

The double doors quivered. A scraping sound grated through the hallway.

The SWAT team members shouldered their weapons.

A loud clang sounded from inside F Wing.

The right-hand door opened a foot.

"I'm coming out," a man's voice said.

"Throw the gun out," roiled from the bullhorn. "Keep your hands where we can see them."

"There's no gun," the voice said.

"Hands on top of your head," the bullhorn blared.

The door eased open wide enough for him to step through. Bald guy in a business suit. Oddly, he was smiling like he'd won the lottery.

"Hands on top of your head."

Reeves complied. "There's no gun," he said again, shuffling forward.

Four officers moved in his direction behind ballistic shields.

Inexplicably, the smile got wider.

Within five seconds the officers had him spread-eagled, face down on the floor, as they searched him for weapons. "Clear," one of the officers said.

And then it was as if everyone finally exhaled at once.

In that moment of shared relief, a young woman appeared in the doorway. The overwhelming impression of her was of something tenuously held together, as if only the stillness of the air allowed her to remain intact, and even the slightest breeze could scatter her like wind-blown leaves. Her pure white hair hung to her shoulders. Her eyes seemed to have no color at all.

The apparition settled a brown leather jacket around her shoulders. "Joseph's awake," she said. "He's breathing on his own."

· · · · · · · ·

Chief of Detectives Marcus Nilsson had a sign on the wall behind his desk that read: *You can always tell a Swede, but you can't tell him much.*

"Ah . . . Mickey. Come in. Have a seat." He gestured toward the red leather chair to the left of his desk. "Can I get you a bottle of water or something?"

Detective Sergeant Mickey Dolan shook his head and then slid into the chair. Back in the ice age, Marcus Nilsson and Mickey's father, Jack, had spent several years riding around in a patrol car together. As a result, in the decade since Jack's death, Nilsson had taken a paternal interest in Mickey's career, which was a good thing. Dolan had no illusions. Without Nilsson covertly covering his ass, he'd probably be working at a Taco Bell by now.

Nilsson rocked back in his chair. "How you feeling?" he asked.

Mickey Dolan mulled it over. It wasn't something he asked himself much lately. Mostly he just got up, went to work, and then got up and did it again.

"I'm here," he said finally. "Everybody still looks at me like I'm growing an extra head. Other than that, things are peachy."

Nilsson heaved a Hollywood sigh. "This is a station house, Mickey. Man's wife walking out on him is not exactly news. Happens all the time. Probably to cops more often than anybody else. Man's wife leaves him for *another woman*. And the local *news anchor*, no less . . . and then goes on the television every fifteen minutes advocating same-sex marriage . . . that's news most everywhere." He gave a rueful shake of the head. "I don't have to tell you, Mickey. The job lends itself to a certain kind of gallows humor. Kinda warped sometimes."

"Like the old, *how do you make a lesbian?* joke."

"Yeah . . . like that one."

Nilsson was meeting his gaze now. He sat forward and leaned his elbows on the desktop. "I've got a new assignment for you," he said.

"What's that?"

"Series of assaults."

"Whose case was it originally?"

"Terry Quinton's."

Dolan rolled his eyes. Terry Quinton was the size of a rhinoceros and about six months from retirement. As far as Mickey was concerned, taking over a case from Quinton was akin to replacing Edward Smith at the helm of the *Titanic*.

"Howsabout I just keep on chasing bicycle thieves," Dolan said. That's where Nilsson had assigned him, giving him a little break while he got his personal shit back together after the divorce and letting the stationhouse chatter subside to a dull roar.

What everybody in the department knew, though, was that Dolan had picked up two excessive force complaints in a five-week span. Even his union rep was talking anger management classes. Without Nilsson's intervention, he'd have ended up in front of the civilian review panel, several members of which favored *a kinder, gentler police force* and might well have insisted on Dolan's dismissal.

"This one comes from upstairs. The mayor's office. I need to put an experienced man on this. I've gotta look like I'm giving it the old college try."

It pissed off Nilsson, too. Dolan could tell. The C of D wasn't the kind of guy who liked being told what to do . . . especially by civilian pencil pushers. Dolan watched in silence as Nilsson walked across the room and closed the office door.

"You know Edwin Royster?" Nilsson asked.

"Used to be a big-time shyster, ambulance chaser. Graduated to bigmouth asshole on the City Council. What about him?"

"He's up the mayor's tract over this thing. His family's been missing for three days. He wants immediate action."

"I thought you said it was a series of assaults."

"The latest assault victim is some slimeball named Donnely Kimble. Sheet as long as your arm. Mostly petty shit."

"What's he got to do with Royster?

"He's good for the probable cause."

"For what?"

"For a search warrant on something called the Women's Transitional Center, which is who these assholes are *really* looking to fuck with."

"How's that work?"

"This Kimble fella was following somebody come out of the Women's Transitional Center when somebody kicked the living bejesus outta him and left him in an alley downtown."

"What's the Women's Transitional Center?" Dolan asked.

"Their mission statement says they help women who might otherwise stay in abusive relationships, because they don't feel like they have the resources to leave. You know—provide a safe haven, someplace where hubby can't get at them. Get them started on a new life. That sort of thing."

"Sounds admirable enough," Mickey said.

"They seem to have taken things one step further, this time."

"How's that?"

"Family court ruled Royster's wife to be an unfit mother. Said she was nuts. Awarded the kids—a couple of little girls—to Royster. Instead of handing over the kids, she packed up the tykes and disappeared into the ozone."

"And Royster thinks the Woman's Transitional Center is responsible?"

"Yep."

"So what do you want from me?"

"I want you to handle the victim interview and then roust the broads hard."

"Why me?"

Nilsson set his jaw like a largemouth bass. "Recess is over, Mickey. It's about time we find out if you still got what it takes to be a good cop." He clapped a big hand on Mickey's shoulder. "I think you do."

Sure hope you're right, Dolan thought as he got to his feet.

He'd had a lot of time to think lately. Probably too much. Lots of time to wonder about what had happened to his life. About how he'd never actually decided to be a cop. His *father* was a cop. *His* father was a cop. It was what the men in his family did. He'd walked out of college, straight into the police academy, and the rest was history. Same thing with Jennifer. She'd sat behind him in the fifth grade. They were high school sweethearts and then one day it was like everybody in their little world just sort of assumed they'd get married. It was simply what came next. So they did it, and right from the beginning, something was missing. By the time it was over, Dolan felt as if he'd watched the whole thing from the bleachers.

Nilsson slid back behind his desk. "See Joan on your way out. She'll find you a desk," he said. "Milton will have a search team ready for you at four thirty. Meet 'em in the garage. Report to me first thing Monday morning."

. . . .

A pair of green-clad nurses came out of Joseph Reeves's room with their arms looped around one another, as if for support.

They stopped in the doorway and stared blankly at the room full of cops.

Judging from her facial expression, the one who spoke first didn't believe what she was about to say, but had decided to say it anyway.

"Joseph's conscious and breathing without a ventilator," she said.

"It's a miracle," the other nurse said. "I don't know what else to say."

"We need the police to unseal the area," the first nurse said to no one in particular.

"So we can get his doctors in there," added the second.

. . . .

Detective Sergeant Mickey Dolan straightened his tie and leaned as far back as the padded hospital chair would permit. The septic smell of the place brought back unpleasant memories of the nursing home where his mother had spent her final frantic days. The place had always smelled like everybody was breathing everybody else's last breath.

"Let me see if I've got this right," he began. "What you're telling me is it was a couple of nuns who kicked your ass."

The victim slowly nodded and then turned what was left of his face toward the window. A muffled groan escaped his chest.

Dolan stifled a grin. Apparently, getting your clock cleaned by women of the cloth was considered poor form in low-rent loser circles. Kind of like wearing a balloon hat to a board meeting.

This particular bottom-feeder's name was Donnely Kimble. Unlicensed gumshoe to the poor and obscure, skip-tracer, bail agent, process server, and all-around dipshit for hire, he'd been on the outer rings of the police department's rectum radar since he arrived in town from Toledo, Ohio, about ten years ago.

Patrol officers had found him purblind, crawling on his hands and knees, searching for his front teeth in a cobblestoned alley off North Tremont Street. His face looked like he'd been threshed and baled. One crushed testicle, two missing teeth, assorted contusions, lacerations, and an upper lip the size of a pot roast.

"They wasn't really nuns," Kimble mumbled.

"That's sure as hell how I'd play it," Dolan assured him.

Kimble turned his angry face back in Dolan's direction. Glared at him with a single bloodshot eye. "Wasn't really women neither," he said.

Dolan maintained a straight face as he liberated his notebook from his jacket pocket and flipped to a blank page.

"Tell me about it."

· · · · · · ·

Roberta Reeves stared down at her ex-husband. He sat, looking at the floor, with his hands manacled behind his back and a storm trooper hard by each elbow.

"My God, what have you done?" she demanded of him.

Paul Reeves looked up and grinned. "Joseph's conscious."

"Don't be ridic—"

Mercifully, something in the collective consciousness prevented her from launching into an all-too-familiar tirade. She stopped herself. Stiffened. And then looked questioningly down the hall toward her son's room.

"Mrs. Reeves," a familiar voice called.

She turned toward the sound. It was Pamela, a registered nurse she knew well.

"It's true," Pamela said. "He's awake."

Roberta's lower jaw began to quiver uncontrollably.

"I don't remember who," her ex-husband said, "but somebody once said that, in the end, we're defined by our sins."

Without another word, Roberta Reeves hurried across the floor. The sound of her jackhammer heels filled the air. She disappeared into the room.

What seemed no more than an instant later, she came rocketing back out, clicking over the tiles, carrying a little burned book out in front of her, like an offering. She kept her nose in the air and her eyes locked in the forward position as she marched from the room and disappeared into the elevator.

"What's her problem?" someone asked in a low voice.

. . . .

They'd suckered him. That much was obvious—even to a dim bulb like Donnely Kimble. First couple of times he'd showed up at the Women's Transitional Center, the "lesbo central" staff had been patient with him. They'd buzzed him in, offered him a seat and a beverage, and explained that, although Grace's mother Eve was indeed the center's founder and executive director, Grace Pressman herself was in no way affiliated with the center. They explained that they'd necessarily developed a rather draconian method of ridding themselves of adventurers, a method to which they would prefer not to resort, as it diverted resources from the valuable work they were doing on behalf of battered women. So nice to see you. Don't call us; we'll call you.

True to their oath, they'd been calling the cops on him for the past two weeks. Every time their security cameras captured his image, they'd lodge a formal stalking complaint with the city police department, who'd dutifully send a cruiser down to cuff him and stuff him, and drag him to the station house for a couple of hours of slap and tickle before dumping him back on the street.

So, by the time the cops dropped him on the same corner for the fifth or sixth time, the dykes were ready with Plan B. No sooner had his shoes hit the pavement when the elusive Grace Pressman came walking out the front door of the place, turned left, and started hoofing it up South Harvey Boulevard in a light rain.

At least Donnely Kimble thought it was her. As far as he knew, there was only that one photograph. The one where she was being led out of court by a couple of corrections officers; she was staring at the pavement, with her pure white hair hanging down over her face like a bridal veil. But, you know—how many six-foot albino women could there be in one town? Had to be her. He figured for once in his life, he'd gotten lucky.

He crossed the street, bobbing and weaving among the parked cars, trying to stay unobtrusive, as she hurried up the street. The neon green outline of a crouching cat adorned the soles of her tennis shoes, blinking in and out of view, as she strode along.

By the time they'd covered three blocks, and turned left onto North Winslow Street, Kimble was beginning to suspect that stealth wasn't necessary. She never once looked back to see if she had a tail. And, as nearly as he could tell from that distance, she wasn't checking her back in the store windows either. That's when his internal dive-horn should have sounded, when some alarm should have assaulted his consciousness and refused to let him continue. Anybody with as many people looking for her as Grace Pressman should have been warier than a Haitian chicken, but she wasn't. She and the cats were just bopping along the sidewalk, like they were out for a Sunday stroll.

Two more blocks, and the rain began to thicken just as Grace Pressman slid between cars and slipped out into the street. Kimble watched as she walked through the ornate wrought-iron gate and started across the wet parking lot toward Union Station.

The train station was hopping, the parking lot jammed beyond capacity. A steady stream of vehicles crept along the aisles, joined hood to trunk like elephants, brake lights casting long red arrows across the wet pavement as they crawled along, hoping to be johnnie-on-the-spot should someone abandon their much-coveted parking slot. Above it all, the big brass clock in the tower read four-o-seven.

He hit the big set of brass doors at the north end of the building in time to see Grace Pressman duck into the ladies' room. He breathed an inward sigh of relief and found himself a seat about twenty yards away, over by the newsstand, where the damp gray light never ventured.

By the time twenty minutes had passed, Kimble had worked himself into a lather. Thinking maybe there must be another way out of the ladies' john. That he'd somehow lost her, and once again fucked up his big chance. That's when they came out of the ladies' room. The nuns, a pair of them, like they were joined at the hip or something. He watched as the long black robes and ornate headpieces made a beeline for the great outdoors. His first thought was that they must have been in the john a hell of a long time, 'cause they hadn't gone in since he'd been sitting there, and that was the better part of twenty minutes now.

Then he figured taking a leak in those nun getups was pretty much bound to be a pain in the ass. Probably had to get right down to their skivvies before they could do their business, which got him to wondering what nun skivvies looked like. Probably had padlocks on them, and that's how come they were in there so long.

They were about halfway across the polished stone floor when those neon green cats began flashing at him from beneath the robe on the left. That's when they set the hook. Got him thinking what a smart guy he was to have noticed such a thing. How a regular guy would have let them march right out the door, but not Donnely Kimble. No sir. Ol' Donnely was way too slick for that.

The air smelled of transience and wet gravel. He hung back and watched as the sisters of mercy marched single file down the metal walkway that ran parallel to the train tracks, watched until they disappeared into the black mouth of the railroad maintenance tunnel that ran under Tremont Street, and then slipped off his shoes and followed them inside.

He still had his loafers pinched between his fingers when he reached the far end of the tunnel. Instinctively, he stopped in his tracks, then sidestepped quickly to his left, pressing his body behind a humming electrical transformer. The vibrating cylinder of metal was cold and damp against his cheek.

Ten yards ahead, one of the sisters stood with her back to him. Just standing there. Doing nothing. Like she was praying or something. Kimble held his breath and frowned. Why had she stopped there? Where the hell was the other one?

Donnely Kimble had just begun to wonder how anybody could get lost in a tunnel when sister number one suddenly took off her nun hat and dropped it onto the sidewalk. Her pure white hair seemed to glow in the gloom.

Donnely Kimble smiled. It was *her* all right. And it was then, in that final self-congratulatory moment, when things went completely to shit.

The nun now reached up and pulled the white hair from her head, revealing a shiny bald pate, with some kind of geometric tattoo at the crown of the skull. As Kimble was busy collecting his lower jaw and trying to process the information, the scrape of a shoe jerked his attention back toward the tunnel entrance.

That's when somebody kicked him in the nuts so hard his ears popped. Just like on an airplane. One second, everything was a dull, muddy roar and then bingo—everything crackled, crisp and clear. The hiss of the rain. The buzz of the electrical transformer. All of it. Except, on this unfortunate occasion, every muscle in his body cramped simultaneously. He blurted out a great whoosh of breath, bent at the waist and tried to gulp oxygen, all in the half second before something metal hit him flush in the mouth, and the force of the impact turned his world to red.

He felt his front teeth drop onto his tongue, but couldn't bring himself to remove either hand from his crotch. He bubbled out a mouthbreather groan, spit his bloody teeth onto the ground, and dropped to one knee. After that, they were on him like wolves, punching and kicking him from all directions at once.

Next thing he remembered, a couple of firemen were loading him onto a stretcher. Donnely Kimble still had both hands welded to his crotch when they closed the ambulance doors and rolled off down the alley.

. . . .

"Arrest him for what?" the Deputy Assistant DA asked. "Negligent Barricading?"

"He had himself locked in there—"

"The clinic's not pressing charges. He's the kid's legal guardian. He has his son's medical power of attorney."

"What about the mother? I'm telling you, she was none too happy about this whole goddamn—"

"They share custody. They *both* have medical power of attorney. It was part of their divorce settlement. As I understand it, they were in the process of settling the matter this week in court."

"He put a lot of people in danger."

The Assistant DA leaned in close to the officer's ear. "Have you thought about the political component of this thing?"

"What political component is that?" the cop sneered.

"Guy finds a way to bring his son out of a coma—where the kid's been for nearly a year—and what do we do? We arrest him? How's that scan?"

"What about the woman?"

"What woman?"

The officer turned toward the chair where the blond woman had been seated. The chair was empty.

"She *was* right there," the cop said.

"The operant word apparently being *was*."

The officer clamped his mouth so tight, the muscles along his jaw-line writhed. "What do you want us to do?" he asked through clenched teeth.

"Turn him loose," the DA said.

. . . .

"It's the cops," Indra whispered. She was tall, sturdy, and quite dark-skinned, for a Sikh woman.

Eve Pressman stopped writing, snapped the top back onto the fountain pen, and frowned. "Officer Quinton?" she asked.

"Uh uh. A new guy." Indra flashed a rare smile. "Real good-looking."

"Send him in," Eve Pressman said disgustedly.

Indra was right. The lead cop was good-looking. Early thirties. Six three or four. Even features, wavy ginger-colored hair, and the sort of solid build that made him either a football coach or a cop. A trio of uniformed officers fanned out on either side of the front door, checking the place out and awaiting further orders.

"Good morning," the cop said as he crossed the room and stuck out his hand. Eve met his hand with hers. "Sergeant Michael Dolan," he said.

"Won't you sit down?" Eve said, nodding at the nearby leather chair. She knew he'd rather stand; cops were like that. They liked to loom above you in the power position.

"I prefer eyes on a level with mine," she said evenly. "I'm sure you understand."

"Thank you," he said as he folded himself into the chair.

"Where's Officer Quinton?" Eve asked.

"He's been reassigned."

"What can we do for you, Sergeant?" Eve asked, after an uncomfortable moment.

"I have a warrant to search these premises."

"Search away," she said. She held out her hand. Dolan leaned forward and dropped the warrant into her palm.

Dolan waved the uniforms forward, then sat back as the room slowly filled with the sounds of the search. Metal file drawers rolling in and out. Rifled folders and the clunk of furniture being turned upside down, as the uniformed officers checked to see if anything was taped to the bottom.

The better part of ten minutes passed, until the officer in charge aimed his upturned palms at the ceiling. "The place is wired for sound and pictures. Other than that, it's cleaner than Nancy Reagan's ass. Not a scrap of paper. Not a matchbook. Nothin'."

"Alright," Dolan said. "I'll meet you back at the precinct."

By the time Indra had locked the front door behind them and returned to her desk, Eve Pressman had finished reading the search warrant.

"Who's this Donnely Kimble?" she asked finally.

"A local creep you or someone in your organization has repeatedly had arrested for stalking and criminal trespass."

"Really? When was that?"

He checked his notes.

"Last Friday. Three p.m." He flipped a page in his notebook. "The previous Wednesday. The Monday before that." He rolled his wrist as if to say, "and so forth, and so forth."

"You've quite obviously done your homework, Sergeant."

Dolan suppressed a smile. "Yeah—the homework. Now that's where this got interesting." He waved a hand. "Usually you do a little work on people's pasts, you come up with pretty much the same old mundane stuff. Love, hate, lust, greed, stupidity. But with you . . ." He waved the hand again and chuckled. "With you, it's more like a soap opera. Like something straight out of the movies."

When she remained silent, Dolan segued.

"The Women's Transitional Center is quite unpopular in certain circles."

"What circles are those?"

"Social Services circles."

Eve gave a nearly imperceptible shrug. "Like most governmental bodies, they're a least common denominator, Sergeant Dolan. They do the best they can, for as many as they can."

"Child Protective Services asked me to inquire as to the where-abouts of"—he checked his notes again—"the Royster family. They seem to think your organization had something to do with their disap-pearance and subsequent failure to appear in family court on Tuesday."

"I'm sure I have no idea," she said.

Dolan snapped his notebook closed. "They think you do. They think you're running your own little underground railway system here."

She gave him a razor-thin smile.

"Edwin Royster isn't somebody you want for an enemy," Dolan said.

"Edwin Royster is a homicidal, wife-beating alcoholic and sexual predator who has put his wife Cassie in the emergency room on four separate occasions." Dolan started to speak, but Eve cut him off. "But because he was very well off, and knew how to work the system, and because Cassie was being treated for bipolar disorder, Child Protective Services awarded custody of their two daughters, Maddy and Tessa, to Mr. Royster, who continued to beat and sexually assault the girls for the next eighteen months."

She anticipated Dolan's next question. "Cassie reported the abuse to every social service organization in the city. To the police. To the mayor's office. And you know what happened?" She didn't wait for him to answer. "Nothing. That's what happened. When Royster put Cassie in the hospital again, CPS sent the girls to foster homes. Royster and his legal team demanded their return. The law says that unless and until Mr. Royster was proved in court to be an unfit parent, he retained custody of the girls. So, when the system returned his daughters to him for the umpteenth time, Cassie Royster did what she had to do."

"I take it the girls reported the alleged sexual abuse to Social Services," he said.

"Under oath. In court," she said. "At which point the powers that be concluded the girls had been coached by their unstable mother and sent them right back to live with their father. Since then, they've been too terrified to talk about it."

An uncomfortable moment passed.

"Royster's a city councilman," Dolan said. "He's got a lot of juice. Friends in high places. People who owe him favors."

"I'm aware of that."

Dolan abruptly changed the subject again.

"I understand you were a victim of domestic violence," he said.

"My ex-husband threw me down a flight of stairs," she said, after a pause.

"Put you in a coma for twenty-seven months."

"You *have* done your homework," she said with mock admiration.

"You have a daughter, Grace." He phrased it as a statement rather than a question.

"I thought you were here about this Kimble fellow," Eve countered.

"There seems to be a persistent piece of urban folklore that says your daughter has . . ." He chose his words carefully. "They say she's got special powers. That she can pull people out of comas. People the medical establishment says aren't going to come around. That she figured out how to do it by waking you up. They've even got a name for her. They call her the Silver Angel."

"How prosaic."

"Mr. Kimble claims he was assaulted while following your daughter"—Dolan made a pained face—"or what he thought was your daughter."

"I fail to see how we can be held responsible for Mr. Kimble's delusions."

"He's not the first guy to be deluded like that," the cop said.

Eve Pressman looked away.

"I checked Officer Quinton's field notes, and made a few of my own," Dolan said. "Over the past three years five different individuals claimed to have been assaulted while trying to make contact with your daughter." He read a list of names and dates and injuries. "And that's just the people who filed a complaint. And considering what slimeballs most of them are, it kinda makes me wonder how many others there might be."

"Does it now?" she said.

Dolan read from his notes. "Linda Karston, Barbara Davinci, Raymond Williams, Shirley Bossier, Merla Fritchey, Andrew Wright, Lutz Kramer, Mary Rose Ross. That's a partial list of the people who your daughter Grace has supposedly awakened from trauma-induced comas."

She shrugged as if to say, *Whatever.*

"They say there's some guy in the Midwest, with a wife in a coma, who's offering a hundred grand for anybody who could put him in touch with Grace Pressman. Is that true?"

"At one time it was," Eve Pressman admitted.

"But not anymore?"

"We sued him, and he withdrew the offer."

Dolan got to his feet and pocketed his notebook.

"I'm guessing Mr. Kimble didn't get the memo," Dolan said.

Eve Pressman rolled herself out into the middle of the room.

"Are we finished here?" she asked brightly.

"I'd like to talk with your daughter," Dolan said.

"I'm afraid that won't be possible," she said, turning her back on him, rolling all the way over to the front door and pulling it wide open. "My daughter doesn't appear in public these days."

"Why is that?"

"My daughter suffers from albinism. A recessive gene she inherited from my first husband, Ronald. Bright lights are quite hard on her eyes and even the briefest exposure to sunlight puts her at risk for skin cancer."

"I wasn't looking for a day at the beach. I just want to talk with her. We can do it inside, at night."

She was shaking her head. "Grace is—how shall we say—fragile."

"Aren't we all?"

"Some of us are already damaged," she said. "What about you, Sergeant Dolan? What condition are you in?"

He thought it over. "Dented," he said, after a moment.

"Married?"

"Not anymore."

"Let me guess. It was"—she made quotation marks in the air with her long fingers—"it was 'the job' that tore you apart."

"Happens to a lot of cops," Dolan said defensively.

"Hence the cliché."

Dolan felt his blood begin to rise. Felt the urge to reach down and pluck her from the wheelchair and shake her like a maraca. The words were out of his mouth before he realized he was about to speak. "Why you?" he asked.

"Why me what?"

"Why you? How'd you end up being everybody's keeper? You're running interference for your daughter. Getting between families and the social service system. Who died and made you boss?" He didn't wait for an answer. "I see people doing things like that, it's usually because they're trying to make up for something. What is it you're trying to atone for?"

"I want to do everything I can to keep women from suffering the same fate I did."

"And being a martyr to the cause didn't have a thing to do with it? 'Cause, you ask me, you seem to be getting a hell of a lot of mileage out of this thing."

"I don't think I like you."

"Join the club," Mickey snapped.

"So nice to have met you, Sergeant Dolan," she said with a brief, insincere smile.

. . . .

"I've got a bad feeling about this one," Grace Pressman said.

She stood with her back to the room, gazing out across the river, into another world, watching rainy Strander Avenue fill with cars and hunched, hurrying figures, as the bars emptied for the night. Between the vast puddles on the pavement and the beads of rainwater covering the windowpane, the scene was reminiscent of an Impressionist painting, smears of overlapping color skittering and glittering over the surface, like glaucoma through glass.

Her mother wheeled her chair over to Grace's side.

"How so?" she asked.

"I brought him back to complete chaos," Grace said. "Joseph was just about to surface when they said they were going to move him to another room, on another floor."

Her mother winced. "And?"

Grace rolled her nearly colorless eyes. "That's when the father barricaded us inside. Told me he'd keep everybody out for as long as it took me." She waved a hand. "It was completely over the top."

"It always is," her mother said.

Grace shook her head. "I know. But not like this. When I met with the father, for coffee, before we went to the hospital—he gave me a little book, with a leather cover. It was all burned on the edges, like somebody had tried to destroy it."

"A diary."

Grace shrugged. "But you couldn't really read anything. Just a few words here and there. Parts of sentences. Parts of poems." She waved a hand again. "The minute I started to read from it—just snippets, you know—Joseph started coming back to me. Almost like that was what he'd been waiting to hear."

"What did his father say about it?"

"When he gave it to me in the coffee shop, he said we could talk about it later, but we never got a chance. There were cops everywhere. SWAT teams. I thought I was going to get arrested."

"That wouldn't be good," Eve said. "We don't need any kind of undue attention, right now."

Grace caught an edge to her mother's voice. "Why right now?" she asked.

"We had a visit from the police today."

"Nothing unusual about that."

"A new cop," Eve said. "A dangerous cop."

"Why dangerous?"

"He's looking for the Roysters, and, unlike Officer Quinton, he's good at his job."

"Which means what?"

"It means we're going to have to move the family."

"Where?"

"I'm waiting for a call from Mr. K."

Absentmindedly, Grace used her finger to draw in the condensation on the inside of the window. A heart. Then an arrow through it. "I never wanted any of this," she said.

Eve nodded. "I know."

"I just wanted the regular stuff. What everybody wanted. The house, the husband, the kids, the picket fence, minivans, PTA meetings . . ."

"You have a gift," Eve said.

Grace sighed. "Feels more like a curse. Like, from the moment I was born, I was paying for somebody else's sins."

"Probably mine," Eve said.

Grace pulled her sleeve over her hand and wiped away the heart and arrow.

. . . .

"How's your weekend?" Nilsson wanted to know.

"Quiet," Mickey Dolan said. "Real quiet." Truth be told, despite being on call, Dolan had turned off his phone and spent the weekend playing video games. No TV either, for fear of seeing his ex-wife Jennifer and her *life-partner* Joanna doing one of those same-sex marriage ads that seemed to be broadcast every thirty seconds lately. The marriage referendum went to the voters in two weeks. Dolan planned to stay subterranean until then.

"Wish I could say the same thing," the Chief of Detectives growled. "Wife dragged me to IKEA on Saturday. Looking for a crib for the new grandbaby." He shook his big bald head in disgust. "Like goin' on a friggin safari," he said. "Time we got out of that place, I felt like I'd run a goddamn triathlon."

Dolan watched as Nilsson pulled his day planner from his briefcase and sat down behind his desk. "Well . . . let's button this Women's Transitional Center thing up and hand it back to the mayor."

Dolan half rose out of the chair and dropped his report on the Chief's desk. "We've got absolutely nothing," Dolan said. "Nothing on their phone logs. Nothing in the file cabinets. Nothing on the computers. Only thing on the security tapes was us. The office is just a front."

Marcus Nilsson had his fingers steepled over his belly and his chin on his chest.

Dolan went on. "The office was leased by something called Hallinan and Associates. Far as I can tell, there's no Hallinan, and no associates. Paid the lease in cash and in advance. They pay for everything that way. Folding money up front. No paper trail whatsoever."

"You pay that way," Nilsson said, "people don't ask a lot of questions."

"They don't own or rent any property or cars. Don't pay utility bills. At least not in their own names. As far as the system is concerned, they're nothing more than a pair of social security numbers who don't make enough money to pay taxes."

"Anything else?"

Dolan thought about it. "If you ask me, Chief, this Donnely Kimble guy was worked over by professionals. This wasn't kids doing a beatdown or somebody rolling him for his wad. These were people who knew what they were doing. People who'd had a lot of practice busting heads, and knew just how far to go."

"Interesting."

"The Pressman woman who runs the Center—Eve."

"What about her?"

"She's got a daughter named Grace. Grace Pressman."

Nilsson's four acres of forehead wrinkled. "Where do I know that name from?"

"Several years back, she did a year and a half in juvie for negligent homicide."

"Killed her father. Hit him with a bat. Pushed him down a flight of stairs," Nilsson said, nodding. "Real tall, real blonde."

"That's the one."

"What about her?"

"Supposedly . . ." Dolan hesitated. He raised his hands in mock surrender, as if to indicate that this was merely what he'd *heard*, not necessarily what he personally *believed*. "Street talk is that she has these special powers. That she can wake people from comas. People the medics say aren't waking up, now or ever."

The Chief made a rude noise with his lips. "Bunch of crystal-gazing bullcrap is what it is. Some kind of goddamn scam."

Dolan nodded and kept his mouth shut.

"So," Nilsson said, lifting the flimsy report off the desk. "We did what we were asked to do." He let it drop. "They want to take it from here, that's up to them."

"Yes sir."

"I made some calls," the C of D said. "See what maybe we had that was open and we could ease you into. Get you back up to speed."

"And?"

"Worsley in the Southwest Precinct's got a Major Crimes opening."

"You do realize . . . bicycle theft stats are bound to spike," Dolan said.

Nilsson actually smiled. "You sure you're ready for this?"

Truth was, Dolan wasn't sure about much these days. For the first time in his life, he found himself unable to assume that the world was as he saw it. Suddenly there was another voice in his head. Reminding him that other folks, looking at the same picture, probably saw something completely different.

Not only that, but his first attempts to get back into the dating game had turned out to be spectacular flops. Whatever inner reserves were required before one could roll around naked with strangers had deserted him, on both occasions, leaving him frustrated, embarrassed and, at least for the time being, unwilling to give it another try.

"I need to put all this behind me," he said. "Get on with my life."

Nilsson's smile was more like a wince. "I told Worsley you'd be down at Southwest right after lunch. He wants to have a little chat first." He shrugged. "Before he commits to anything."

"I'll be there," Dolan said. "Is there—"

His inquiry was lost in a sudden volley of raised voices from the other room.

A woman's voice rose above the din. "Captain? Captain!"

Marcus Nilsson was on his feet and moving around the desk when the office door burst open, thumping hard against the wall, sending the old-fashioned blinds clattering against the glass like out-of-tune wind chimes.

The guy came into the room like Caesar entering Gaul. Dolan had seen Caesar's face on television often enough to know who it was. Edwin Royster was an overripe, pear-shaped specimen, with a big wet mouth and a thinning head of hair slicked straight back. The overwhelming impression you got from being up close to him was of sheen. It was as if he'd been sprayed with a light coat of machine oil and left to steep.

Another guy sporting an elegant haircut over a thousand-dollar suit slid unobtrusively into the office. Dolan had seen him before, too, but couldn't put a name on him.

Nilsson's secretary shouldered this last intruder aside far enough to poke her head into the room. "I'm sorry, Captain Nilsson. I told him you were engaged . . . he wouldn't . . ."

The C of D held up a restraining hand. "It's alright, Joan," he assured her. "I'll handle it." An angst-filled moment passed before she shot the uninvited guests a vaporizing glare and exited the scene.

"You find my family yet?" Royster demanded of Nilsson.

The Chief of Detectives ignored him, and instead directed his attention to the guy in the good suit. He held out a hand. Good Suit took it.

"Marcus," the guy said, with a wan, apologetic smile.

"Deputy Mayor Browning," the C of D replied. "To what do we owe—"

"Did you hear me?" Royster demanded. "Where the hell's my family?"

Nilsson finished his handshake before turning Royster's way. "Detective Sergeant Dolan has just now submitted his preliminary report," the Chief said, evenly.

"Why haven't I got a copy?" Royster demanded.

"Because police reports are confidential, and the sergeant doesn't report to you," Nilsson said in his best Mr. Rogers voice. "He reports to me."

Royster strode across the carpet and stood face to face with Dolan. "Well . . . where are they?"

"I'm afraid I can't comment on an ongoing investigation," Dolan said.

"I asked you a question, Sergeant. Where the fuck is my family?"

"I suggest you get out of my face," Dolan said in a low voice.

"Dolan . . . Dolan . . . you the one with the dyke wife?"

"Excuse me?" Dolan said.

"Yeah . . . the one on the tube with her gap-lapper buddy, trying to ruin the sanctity of Christian marriage."

Despite the better part of a decade sitting behind a desk, Nilsson's cop instincts remained intact. By the time Dolan had screwed his right foot into the carpet and taken a half step back, the Chief of Detectives had inserted himself between the two men.

Dolan was quivering with anger. His eyes were locked on Royster like a Rottweiler ogling a chuck roast.

"Don't," Nilsson said, then turned to the Deputy Mayor. "I'll have the report over to the mayor this afternoon."

"I want those dykes arrested," Royster bellowed.

Dolan and the Chief watched in silence as the Deputy Mayor managed to get Royster moving toward the door. At the last moment, Royster turned and pointed a finger at Marcus Nilsson. "You can't do your job, I'll find somebody who can," he promised, as the Deputy Mayor eased him through the doorway.

A moment later Browning poked his well-coiffured head back through the doorway. "Find them, Marcus. The mayor will get you anything you need in the way of subpoenas or warrants." He checked over his shoulder. "We won't forget this," he said with a degree of ambiguity available only to prostitutes and politicians.

Nilsson gritted his teeth and did his Mount Rushmore impression as the pair made their way through the outer office and disappeared from view. Apparently satisfied they were unlikely to return, Nilsson banged himself down into his chair, slapped the flat of his hand on the desk, and pointed a big blunt finger at Dolan.

"Nice to see you've regained your composure," he said with all the sarcasm he could muster. "I'd hoped your little vacation would have calmed you down a bit. I know this has been tough on you—woulda been tough on anybody—but we can't have any more excessive force complaints, Mickey. Union or no union, you don't get control of yourself, you're gonna find your ass out on the street."

Dolan turned away and folded his arms over his chest.

"Goddamnit. Mickey, what the hell were you thinking?"

Dolan shrugged but didn't say anything.

"I asked you a question, Sergeant."

Dolan turned slowly back toward the Chief of Detectives.

"I was thinkin' I'd kinda like to find out whether or not Royster's wife is really nuts," Dolan said. "And whether or not he's abusing his kids." Dolan waved a disgusted hand. "That part bothers the shit out of me, Chief."

Nilsson dropped his finger to his lap and nodded in silent agreement. Child abuse wasn't one of those things you could go easy on. Or even *appear* to go easy on. If anything, you wanted to err *way* over toward medieval retribution, a fact not lost on the political side of Marcus Nilsson.

So Dolan kept talking. "I'd like to know whether this Women's Transitional Center is really involved in the disappearance of Royster's family, and how the woo-woo daughter and her supposed superpowers factor into it. I was also wondering how a woman's shelter gets access to the kind of professional muscle that messed up our friend Donnely Kimble. Stuff like that. That's what I was thinking about."

Nilsson rocked back in his chair.

"I'll call Worsley at Southwest, tell him you're not going to report for a while."

Dolan started for the door.

"And Mickey . . ."

Dolan looked back over his shoulder at the Chief of Detectives. Nilsson's face was set like concrete. "Try not to hurt anybody," he said.

. . . .

The cop computer geeks were housed in the basement of the Public Safety Building, the rationale being that it was cheaper to keep the computers cool down there, and that underground installations were more likely to survive a disaster, natural or otherwise. These days, life was cheap, but information was not.

Dolan rode the elevator to the bottom, credentialed his way through the security checkpoint, and then hoofed it over to the door marked INFORMATION TECHNOLOGY. Originally, the section had been named CRIMINAL INTELLIGENCE, an oxymoron if ever there was one, but saner heads had prevailed and bestowed its present moniker.

Dolan knew the drill. He headed right over to the side table, found an *Information Request* form and filled it out. He copied the names from his notebook. Linda Karston, Barbara Davinci, Raymond Williams,

Shirley Bossier, Merla Fritchey, Andrew Wright, Lutz Kramer, Mary Rose Ross. Everything they had on everybody. See what the Feds had too. Under "Authorization" he wrote the Chief of Detective's name and extension.

The beehive of activity buzzed for a full minute before anybody spotted Dolan standing at the counter. A stocky African American officer finally ambled his way. Her name tag read H. Jenkins.

Dolan watched her mental computer reset itself as she read his ID badge and recognized the name. Or at least, he thought she did. It was hard to tell. He'd reached the point where he was perfectly capable of imagining such things. When that happened, he reminded himself that just because you're paranoid, it doesn't mean they're *not* out to get you, and he somehow felt better.

"Whatcha need?" she asked affably.

Dolan handed her the Information Request. "Expedite it, if you can."

She barked out a single-syllable laugh. "Feds are three weeks out, unless it's terrorism. Then they're five weeks out."

They shared a chuckle.

"Put the C of D's name on it." Dolan said. "Maybe that'll light a fire under them."

She eyed him closely. "You sure you want to do that?"

Dolan understood her reluctance. The Chief of Detectives seldom . . . read never . . . got directly involved in investigations. Dolan showed two fingers. Scout's honor. "Feel free to call upstairs," he said.

"Man's got friends in high places."

Dolan's turn to laugh. "And it's a good thing, too."

· · · · · · · ·

As Dolan walked the three blocks to the City Administration Building, boxcar clouds rumbled across the horizon. He'd convinced himself he could use the exercise. Not only that, but walking that far took about a third of the time needed to sign a car out of the police garage and about one-eighth the time required to find a parking space in that part of town.

Half a block from his goal, his cell phone began to buzz in his pants pocket. Reminded him of that old Rodney Dangerfield line about how if it wasn't for pickpockets he'd have no sex life at all. He kept walking as he fished for the phone. He winced at the sight of Jennifer's photo on the screen. He held down the power button until the phone cycled off, and stuffed it back into his pocket. She'd leave a voice mail. She always left a fucking voice mail.

Social Welfare had the sixth floor to itself. Family Court and Child Protective Services were side by side on seven. Since Royster's main bone of contention seemed to have been the children, Dolan opted for CPS.

Dolan shared a manly cop nod with the security guard sitting on a chair in the hallway and stepped inside. The old-fashioned Roman-numeral clock on the back wall read twelve-o-five. A petite woman in a tan Hillary Clinton pantsuit was working feverishly at the counter. Stuffing things back into folders. Tamping everything down. Getting the edges all neat and tidy. She looked up myopically at Dolan, realized her glasses had migrated to the end of her nose, and pushed them back up where they could be of service. She smiled.

"Oh, hello," she said. "How can I help you, Sergeant?"

"I need to see some Family Court files."

"Parties' names?"

"Royster. Edwin and Cassie Royster."

Didn't take Dr. Phil to see he'd hit some kind of nerve. No, as a matter of fact, Little Miss Paperwork suddenly looked as if Dolan had just tried to hand her a dog turd. She took a step back from the counter, squared her shoulders inside the jacket and said, "You'll have to talk to my supervisor."

"Okay," Dolan said affably.

"I'll see if she's available." She threw a hand in the direction of the chairs lined up along the wall behind Dolan. "Perhaps you should have a seat," she suggested.

"I'm fine," Dolan assured her.

He watched as the young woman started off and then suddenly changed her mind. She walked back to her desk, pulled a key from the top drawer, throwing a glance back in Dolan's direction, as she walked over and locked the second filing cabinet.

Dolan watched as she picked her way through the maze of cubicles, stopping once to whisper in another woman's ear and then continuing on, all the while checking back over her shoulder, as if the hounds of hell were nipping at her *Manolo Blahniks.*

The sitting-down thing turned out to have been good advice. They kept him cooling his heels for twenty minutes before she reappeared with a pair of scowling civil servants in tow.

The woman was maybe fifty-five or so, salt and pepper hair, good haircut, and a flinty gaze that exuded all the warmth of a wrecking ball. She introduced herself as Janice Robertson. The rat-faced guy was ten years younger and already going threadbare at the cuffs.

"All Royster files have been sealed by the court," Robertson said.

Over Ratface's shoulder, Dolan watched as the younger woman returned the file cabinet key to the desk drawer.

"Why's that?" he asked.

"Judge Nalbandian deemed it to be in the best interest of the children."

"Why was that?"

The guy piped up. "You'd have to ask her," he said.

"And who might you be?" Dolan inquired.

"I'm Robert Piper, Judge Nalbandian's clerk," he said.

"How do I get them unsealed?"

"You'd need a court order," the Robertson woman said.

"I can probably manage that," Dolan said.

Piper smirked. "Somehow, I don't think so," he offered.

The woman checked her watch. "It's a Family Court matter. Since Judge Loomis retired, Judge Nalbandian is the only sitting Family Court judge. The request would automatically come right back to her, and I seriously doubt she'd consider vacating one of her own judicial orders."

Before Dolan could decide what his next move was, the woman said, "I'm afraid you're going to have to leave."

"Don't be afraid," Dolan quipped. "I'm armed."

That's when the recorded message began to play through the overhead speakers. *"Ladies and gentlemen, by order of the mayor and the City Council, this office closes every day between 12:30 p.m. and 2:00 p.m. If you will come back at that time . . ."*

Dolan remembered now. The city's austerity program. Shorter work hours, monthly furloughs. Shit like that. The unions had gone nuts, but when you're broke, you're broke, so the program had gone into effect.

The clock on the wall read twelve twenty-eight. Everyone in sight was packing up and getting ready for their fiscally forced midday furlough. Behind the deadly duo here, Little Miss Paperwork shouldered her purse and started for the door.

"Alright if I use the men's room?" Dolan inquired.

"You'll have to hurry," the woman said, as she turned and walked away with Piper the court clerk in hot pursuit.

Dolan wandered down the narrow corridor, found the facilities and stepped inside. It looked like an old-fashioned train station bathroom. An ocean of little white octagonal tiles, urinals along one wall, stalls along the other, a couple of sinks, and a pair of those hot-air hand dryers. Dolan walked over and pushed the chrome button. The machine began to roar.

It was still roaring as he stepped back into the hallway and noticed a door to his left. Must lead back into the central hallway. Backward, through the etched glass, he read the words: No Admittance.

"Sir."

The security guard from the hall was coming his way. Gold name tag read D. Williams. "Sorry, Sergeant, but you're gonna have to go. I gotta lock up."

"No problem," Dolan said. "Just needed to tap a kidney."

As he started for the front door, he glanced back in time to see the guard kick open the door to the restroom, throw a cursory glance inside, and then follow along as Dolan headed for the door.

. . . .

The man in the passenger seat pushed the green button and spoke into the microphone. "Subject has exited the building," he said. "Looks like he's headed back to the cop shop."

The dashboard speaker squawked, "Roger that."

His counterpart in the driver's seat straightened up and started the car.

He pushed the green button again. "Richard."

"Here." A new voice from the speaker.

"You and Jerry station yourselves on Hobart Street, facing north, just in case he gets a car, we'll have somebody in place."

"Got it," came back.

"Let's go," he said.

. . . .

Mickey Dolan was lost in thought. Driving on radar, seeing nothing but the blips inside his own head as he tried to decide whether or not everybody in the DA's office had known *exactly* who he was and *exactly* what was going on with Jennifer, because it sure had seemed that way to him. Seemed like everywhere he went, conversations stopped in mid-sentence, and the carpet suddenly became interesting. He had to keep reminding himself that there was a decent chance he was making it all up. Maybe better than decent. He silently cursed the uncertainty.

Either way, he'd struck out. What he'd hoped would be a simple, straightforward investigation, destined to make him look good and get him back on regular duty, was proving to be gnarly. Despite the Deputy Mayor's assurance that his office would get them whatever they needed, *whatever* apparently didn't include any of the paperwork connected to the Royster family. Not the court records, not the family's medical histories, not the girls' report cards, not Bobo the dog's veterinary records. Nothing. Judge Nalbandian had sealed all of it, and according to the DA's office, short of divine intervention, it was very likely to stay that way.

So, on one level, at least, it should have come as no surprise when Dolan failed to notice the red light on the corner of Hobart and West Twelfth Street and damn near plowed his unmarked car into the back of a DEX van.

Wasn't till his world turned bright yellow that Dolan snapped out of his stupor, swerved violently to the left to avoid tagging the van, and then fishtailed back and forth through the six-lane intersection three or four times, dodging cross traffic like a drunken matador, leaving a chorus of angry horns howling in his wake, and his arteries filled with enough adrenaline to float a canoe.

The rhythm of his heart thumped in his ears; his stomach was lodged somewhere high in his throat. Reflexively, he threw an apologetic glance at the rearview mirror. The sheepish grin, however, quickly disappeared. Unbelievably, he hadn't been the last car through the intersection.

A gray Lexus, with two guys hanging on for dear life, had rolled through after he had, bobbing and weaving through half a dozen lanes of road rage and obscene gestures before emerging unscathed on the far side.

Dolan took several deep breaths, trying to get his heart rate down to something manageable, then turned left on Strander Avenue, heading south into the city's Gaslight District, a part of town where the traffic didn't thicken until after dark.

When he made another turn, and the Lexus stayed right on his tail, Dolan was certain. He grabbed the radio.

"Lemme have patrol dispatch," he said into the microphone.

Five seconds later, "Dispatch" crackled through the speaker.

"This is Sergeant Michael Dolan." He gave his badge number.

"What can we do for you, Sergeant?"

He told the dispatcher.

"On the way, Sergeant."

. . . .

"I'm going to see Joseph," Grace said, zipping her jacket and turning up the collar.

Eve arched an eyebrow. "That may not be a good idea."

"It's a rotten idea, but I'm going to do it anyway." Grace heaved a sigh. "I was up half the night. I just don't feel right about where I left him. Something wasn't right."

"It's a difficult transition," Eve said. "Why don't you give it a few days."

Grace shook her head. "Right before I left the hospital . . ." She hesitated. "Joseph's mother came . . . she came storming into the hospital and then went into his room and . . ."

"And what?"

"And she wasn't happy he was awake."

Eve opened her mouth to speak. Grace cut her off.

"More than that. She hated it. I could feel her anger. Just absolute rage seeping out of her. Something's not right," she said again. "Joseph needs me now. I can feel it."

Eve knew better than to doubt her.

. . . .

Tailing someone through a city isn't easy. When professionals find themselves tasked with that sort of surveillance, they use four to seven pursuit vehicles, and even then, with aerial surveillance compromised by the height of the buildings and the sheer volume of traffic, the odds of pulling it off are generally less than fifty-fifty.

The guys in the Lexus were doing it just like they saw on TV, poking their noses cautiously around corners, then making up distance in the straightaways. The old Jim Rockford special. Anybody with eyesight and a double-digit IQ would have made them in a block and a half.

The police radio crackled. "Fifty-two sixty in place."

"Roger," Dolan replied.

He put on his turn signal and wheeled left onto Church Street, then leisurely turned right onto Roland Avenue, a narrow cobblestone loop that ran along the back of Hardwick's Hardware and an Evangelical Chinese church. Back when he was in uniform, Roland Avenue had been a fair-weather shooting gallery for the local heroin set and had thus been part of his nightly patrol route.

Dolan gave it some gas and ran the length of the alley. He wheeled the Chevy around the lazy corner, braked to a halt where it couldn't be seen from the mouth of the alley, slammed the car into park, and got out. Hurrying to the rear, he popped the trunk, unzipped the plastic gun case, and pulled out the 12-gauge Mossberg pump shotgun. He fed it half a dozen shells and then slammed one into the breech.

By the time he'd finished, he could hear the Lexus rolling his way, hear the tires popping on the rough stones as it negotiated the alley. He dropped to one knee and peeked around the corner. The Lexus was thirty yards away, coming at a good clip. Just then, a black-and-white police cruiser turned into the mouth of the alley and fired up its light bar.

The Lexus skidded to a halt. Started to back up, then rocked to a halt.

Dolan stepped around the corner of the building and leveled the shotgun at the windshield. "Out of the car," he yelled. "Out of the car."

. . . .

The flowers were fifteen minutes late.

With her hair pushed up under a Red Sox baseball cap and a pair of Italian Riviera sunglasses the size of hubcaps, Grace blended right in with the slice of humanity occupying the hospital waiting area.

The kid who arrived with the flowers was wearing the kind of bike shoes that connected you to the pedals, but made walking problematic. Hard as she tried, Grace couldn't come up with a mental image of how you delivered flowers from a bicycle. Just wouldn't compute. She watched as he clomped over to the information desk.

"Joseph Reeves?" he said.

The old lady behind the desk tapped at her keyboard.

"He's on family visits only," she said. "You can leave the flowers here." She tapped the corner of her desk. "I'll get them sent up."

Three minutes later, a teenybopper slouched up to the information lady.

"Yeah."

The old lady jerked a thumb at the flower arrangement. "Take these up to five seventeen," she said.

Little honey heaved a "this is just soooo lame" sigh and picked up the flowers.

Grace watched as the girl shuffled into the elevator, then she left her seat and headed for the stairs.

. . · . · . · .

"Get out of the car," Dolan bellowed. "Hands on your head."

Neither man moved a millimeter. The guy in the passenger seat kept speaking into a microphone, completely ignoring Dolan's commands. Dolan felt his ears getting red. "Turn off the car. Get out with your hands on top of your head."

Again, neither of them moved. Again the passenger brought the microphone to his lips. Again, it really pissed Dolan off.

Dolan pointed to the uniformed officer leaning on the passenger side of the car.

"You got your baton?" he asked.

The guy was a monster. Some kind of South Sea Islander. Tongan, Samoan, something like that. Neck the size of a trash can. Fingers like bratwurst. His sisters would kick your ass. He pulled an expandable baton from his belt system and snicked it out to its full length.

"Get Chatty Cathy out of there," Dolan directed.

He didn't have to ask twice. There's something about breaking glass hardwired into male genes. The big cop grinned and gave it his best Louisville Slugger two-hander. The side window evaporated in a hail of safety glass and the big cop leaned in, popped the seat belt, and grabbed the passenger by the lapels. One heave from his massive arms extruded microphone man out through the saw-toothed window. Looked real uncomfortable to Dolan.

The driver got the message. He turned the car off and raised his hands.

Ten seconds later, the uniforms had them both on the pavement, handcuffed, feet spread, nose to the asphalt. Dolan returned the shotgun to the trunk of his car, where he unloaded it and slipped it into its case.

By the time he walked back, the uniforms had patted the pair down and found the two nine-millimeter automatics and the pair of wallets now resting on the roof of the car.

"Both of 'em heeled," said the other uniform.

"We got carry permits," the driver whined. "We're licensed private detectives."

"Shut up, Jerry," said the passenger.

Dolan read them their rights.

"Take them to holding," he said to the cops. "Book 'em on Hindering a Police Officer in the Performance of His Duty, Interfering with a Police Officer, Resisting Arrest, and Reckless Driving. Call the garage. Impound the car."

The uniforms hauled the pair to their feet and started stiff-legging them down the alley toward the black-and-white.

"It's a public street," the driver yelled.

"Shut up, Jerry," said the passenger.

The big cop looked back and grinned.

. . . .

Grace lingered in the fifth-floor stairway for the better part of thirty minutes. Joseph was garnering a great deal of attention from the staff today. A veritable parade of doctors and nurses coming and going. Wasn't until the nursing shift changed around 5:00 p.m. that things quieted down sufficiently for Grace to slip into his room.

She'd never seen him without the breathing and feeding tubes. Here and there on his face, tape and tubes had rubbed him raw, but, despite the abraded areas, a healthy glow was beginning to color his cheeks.

The sound of the door hissing pulled his attention in Grace's direction. Grace took the baseball cap off and shook out her hair.

Joseph's dark eyes followed her as she walked to the side of the bed, reached down, and covered his hand with hers. He swallowed twice, licked his lips, and croaked out something unintelligible.

Grace gently squeezed his hand. "You rest," she said in a low voice. Instead, he once again tried to speak. She leaned close to his lips.

"I thought I dreamed you," he whispered on about the fifth try.

She patted his hand. He closed his eyes and went to sleep.

That's when the door opened and his mother walked in. Mid-forties. Even-featured. Wasp-waisted in a burgundy wool coat with brass buttons. For a moment, the sight of Grace immobilized her. She stared disbelievingly, took several steps into the room, and stopped and stared again. The door closed automatically.

"You're her," she finally said.

Grace didn't respond.

"You were in here with Paul when Joseph . . . when he . . ."

Grace gathered her hair, gave it a tight twist, and covered it with her Red Sox cap.

"You had no right," the woman said.

"To what?" Grace asked as she zipped her jacket.

"To . . ." She pointed at the bed. "My son . . . you had no right to . . . whatever you did."

Grace started for the door. "You mean like as opposed to pulling the plug on him?" she asked as she took the doorknob in her hand.

Without warning, the well-turned-out middle-aged woman came completely unglued. A guttural growl rose from her chest as she launched herself at Grace like a SCUD missile, talons extended, fully intending to rip Grace's face off.

Grace feinted one way and then dodged the other, allowing the out-of-control woman to rocket past her. Grace pirouetted and spread her feet for balance. Eighteen months in juvenile detention hadn't been good for much, but had done absolute wonders for her self-defense skills. Turned out it wasn't necessary, however.

The former Mrs. Reeves wobbled on her spike heels, turned an ankle, and went down like a cinder block, clipping the sink with her forehead on her way to the floor. The painful sound of bone meeting porcelain bounced around the room.

As Grace opened the door, the woman struggled to her knees. Her mouth hung open. An ugly bruise was already forming on her forehead. She looked like maybe she'd bitten through her tongue when she clipped the sink. She began to scream, thick-lipped and spittle-laced, but at terrific volume. "Eeeelp me! Eeeelp me!" The effort caused her great pain. She brought both hands to her head and began making a high-pitched keening noise.

Grace shot a quick glance at Joseph. His dark eyes were open.

She stepped into the hall, turned hard right, and ducked back into the stairway. A final glance through the little square window showed a pair of burly security guards sprinting in her direction. Grace turned and ran, taking the stairs two at a time, up four risers to the eighth floor, where she hurried down the corridor to the elevators, rode the nearest car down to the first level of the parking garage, and then began jogging toward the smell of fresh air.

. . . .

As Dr. Edward Burke removed the yellowing pile of newspaper from the seat of the wing chair, several decades of dust rose majestically toward the ceiling.

He looked a bit like Paul Bunyan. Big strapping guy with a full beard and a plaid shirt. No ox, though. Living proof that one of the major perks of the academic life was that you could be beyond the Valley of Eccentric and still function.

Burke gestured toward the chair, which, as nearly as Dolan could tell, may have at one time been a floral print.

"Have a seat, Sergeant . . . er . . . ?"

"Dolan. Michael Dolan," he said as he eased himself onto the seat, making sure that only the seat of his pants touched the maybe-floral chair.

They were in what looked an old Edwardian library. Bookcases wall to wall, floor to ceiling, except the wall the door was on. Rolling ladder broken in two in the back corner of the room. A scene from an old black-and-white movie, except there were no guys in tuxedos, just enough dust for a Saharan storm, and enough litter for an obstacle course. Burke seemed to read his mind.

"This is the old university archives building," he said. "These days, everything has gone digital. Nobody uses the archives anymore. I use it to store the messier parts of my collection." He grinned. "Some of my departmental colleagues took umbrage at the clutter. So I moved it out here. I still keep office hours in Taylor Hall with the rest of them, but as long as it's not too cold, I generally work here."

As Dolan pulled out his notebook, Dr. Burke picked his way through the academic debris covering the floor, and settled himself behind the desk.

"How'd you get my name?" he asked.

"At the Colton Clinic," Dolan said.

"Somebody at Colton recommended me?" He seemed incredulous.

"Not exactly," Dolan hedged.

"What, then?"

"Your name came up as they were throwing me out of the place."

"Ah," he said knowingly. "That makes more sense."

"This doctor named Seacrest seemed to feel I was wasting his time."

"Both the Colton Clinic and Gerard Seacrest are quite traditional." His blue eyes crinkled at the corners. "Hidebound, one might even say."

"Seemed to piss him off that I had the nerve to even ask about it. He looked at me like I was claiming to have been abducted by aliens, then told me I was as crazy as that Burke idiot, over at Forman University."

"It's nice to be remembered," Burke said with a grin.

"Exactly what is it you're a doctor of?" Dolan asked.

"Anthropology," Burke said. "I specialize in urban folklore."

"So what did you ask him about that got you on the idiot list?" Dolan asked.

"The Silver Angel."

Dolan was somewhat taken aback by the sudden candor. His first stop at the Colton Clinic, the city's swankiest head trauma clinic, had been a complete bust. About three seconds after he told Dr. Seacrest what he was there about, Seacrest had asked if he had a warrant and then invited him to leave. No offense to our noble police department, of course, but we don't have time for such foolishness. Don't call us; we'll call you.

"So what do you think?"

"Despite what it says in the Yellow Pages about trauma treatment, the Colton Clinic is in the *money* business, Sergeant Dolan, not the *cure* business. Nine thousand dollars per patient, per month, makes cures counterproductive. As they see it, any alternative therapy, especially something as unscientific and off the wall as a layperson supposedly able to accomplish what they can't . . . that's just not in their best interests."

"And the Silver Angel?"

Burke thought it over. The chair let out an anguished groan as Burke leaned back. His lips pursed in and out several times. Dolan could see the lecture emerging. He groaned inwardly and poised his pen.

"Among the nearly innumerable subtypes of urban folklore, Sergeant," Burke began, "one is what I call *the good story*. It's just what the name implies. The one with the cute punch line. You can find thousands of them on the Internet. 'The Hook' is a good example. Couple parked out on lover's lane hears on the radio that there have been a series of serial murders committed by a guy with a hook on one hand. They hightail it out of there, only to find the hook hanging from one of the door handles when they get home. It's cute campfire material. Everybody claims they read it in the paper, or were there when it happened, or knew the people it happened to, or heard it from somebody who knew them."

"And everybody knows it's a crock of shit, but doesn't say anything," Dolan said.

"Exactly. That's what gives this type of apocryphal lore a life. The unwritten rules. You're obligated to shut up. That allows the storytelling process to continue. You can learn quite a bit about a society by studying what they add to and what they remove from oral tradition stories."

"What's the *other* type?" Dolan pressed.

"The other type isn't a good story. There's no hook. No punch line. Just a persistent rumor, which seems to have a life of its own. Those tend to have at least some basis in reality." He raised a cautionary hand. "Which is not to say they're true, in the strictest sense. What it says is that something about the story is likely grounded in fact."

Burke read the policeman's frown. "Like the story of the ice-skating giraffe."

"Never heard that one," Dolan said.

"Because giraffes don't ice skate."

"So you're saying you think there's something to this Silver Angel stuff?"

Burke shrugged and made a *maybe* face. "I never got a chance to follow up. My Fulbright kicked in and I was off to Bulgaria. But"—he waved a professorial finger— "if you ask me, she probably has, on at least one occasion, somehow managed to extricate somebody from a coma." He spread his hands in resignation. "I mean, look at the alternatives. Either she arranged for it to look that way, and fooled absolutely everyone, *including* the comatose person, or she got lucky and an awakening just happened while she was present. Both of which are, as far as I'm concerned, considerably more far-fetched than the possibility that she *really* did it."

"Because giraffes don't ice skate."

"Exactly," Burke said.

"Then . . ." Dolan frowned and searched for words. "Then whatever she's figured out has to have *some* kind of medical or scientific basis . . . right?"

Burke grinned. "Does this mean you're not open-minded to the possibility of miracles or magic?"

"Oh, mine's *wide* open," Dolan said with a smile. "But you'd have to meet my boss."

. . . .

That photo from Jennifer's thirtieth birthday party was staring him in the face from his phone again.

He answered with, "Dolan here." Real businesslike.

"Mickey."

"Hey," he said.

"How are you doing?"

"You mean like in general? Or how am I doing for a guy whose wife walked out on him for another woman?"

"The second one," she said.

"In that case, I'm hanging in there."

Awkward silence.

"I'm sorry," she said, into the void.

He hated it when she said that. Somehow, it never seemed to cover it. Like getting hit by a speeding bus and saying, "Ouch."

"I'll get over it," Dolan said.

"We didn't have much to get over," she said.

He wanted to argue, but stopped himself. She was right. Something vital had always been missing. Some spark. The fiery thing that makes it worthwhile to put up with the rest of the shit. At best, they'd been comfortable.

"Whatcha need, Jen?" he asked, trying to keep weariness out of his voice.

"Joanna and I wanted to use the cabin next weekend. Just wanted to make sure you didn't have any plans."

The cabin was just that. A log cabin right smack in the middle of the Spellman Wilderness Area, hard by the rocky banks of Bluewater Creek. Her great-great-grandfather had homesteaded the place back in the 1830s. Before it became a national park. They hadn't liquidated it with the rest of the community property because the terms of the original deed stated that should the title no longer be held by a direct descendant of the original landowner, the title would automatically revert to the federal government, which made it impossible to sell.

Besides which, if he and Jen ever had a place that could be considered "theirs," it was the cabin. It was where they'd always gone when things got tough. Whenever one or both of them slowed down enough to be reminded that something just wasn't right, they'd head up to the cabin for the weekend, hoping that somehow the peace and serenity of the place would rub off on them, and they'd be able to embrace that ever-elusive *something* that didn't seem to have a name.

"I've got no plans," he said.

An awkward silence followed. The phone company was right, you *could* hear a pin drop. Dolan was busy picturing exactly which of the vast cornucopia of lesbian sexual acts Jennifer and Joanne would be perpetrating upon one another when Jen caught his negative vibe and blithely segued. "What are you working on?" she asked.

"Domestic violence thing. Missing family."

"Missing how?"

He told her. About the family and their sealed records. About the suspicions regarding the Women's Transitional Center. The rumors about Grace. All of it, except the names of the players. Jen was a good listener.

"I'll ask a few people I know. Women's movement people."

"That what it's about, Jen?" he asked. "The movement?"

"It's about having somebody I can talk to."

Click.

. ˙ . ˙ . ˙ .

Grace jogged up the concrete ramp and out onto the sidewalk. It was still light, but the streetlights were on. The nearby buildings were beginning to empty, as people headed home for the evening. She could smell rain in the air.

Before she could fully assess her situation, a voice boomed, "You there. Stop."

Another rent-a-cop had come trotting out the front door of the hospital, and was hurrying in her direction. Heavy-set white guy, bald head, pointing at her as he huffed along the sidewalk, his equipment belt flopping as he ran.

Grace bolted into the street, dodged a couple of taxis and a UPS truck, then sprinted hard for the south side of Harmon Road.

A quick glance over her shoulder showed a wave of traffic engulfing Harmon Road like the Red Sea closing behind the Israelites. The guard was nowhere in sight.

A flash of yellow in her peripheral vision pulled her eyes to a cab running along the curb. She hailed it, got in, and gave the turbaned driver an address.

As they pulled away from the curb, the rent-a-cop came into view. Red-faced and gasping for air, he staggered across the last lane and threw himself up onto the sidewalk.

Grace waved goodbye through the back window.

"You sure you wanna go over there to Coaltown, Missy?" the taxi driver asked. "We're not supposed to bring people down there. That's a bad place. Nothin' down there for a nice young lady like you."

She passed another twenty over the seat. "I'm sure," Grace told him.

He turned off the meter.

. . . .

"Their lawyer made bail before they'd cleared booking," Marcus Nilsson growled. "They tell me he threatened to sue us over the broken car window."

"I showed my badge and ordered them out of the car a half a dozen times," Dolan said defensively.

Nilsson waved him off. "The black-and-white had the dash cam on. I've seen the tape. The uniforms back your story a hundred percent. Those two in the car got what they were asking for." He raised a bushy eyebrow. "The shotgun may have been a bit over the top, but the rest of it was by the book, as far as I'm concerned."

"DA gonna charge 'em?"

Nilsson made a *no way* face and shook his big head. "Not enough meat on the bone for those guys. Budget being what it is, they've got bigger fish to fry than hampering and hindering charges."

"I don't suppose they coughed up why it was they were following me?"

"Not a peep."

"We know who they work for?" Dolan asked.

Nilsson reached out and shuffled the pile of papers on his desk. Handed one to Dolan.

"Richard Coffee and Gerald Robbins. Employees of Western Security," Dolan read. "For All Your Security and Information Needs."

"I feel safer and better informed already," the C of D sneered.

"On the Royster family front . . ." Dolan began. "Family Court's got the Royster family's records sealed up tighter than a bullfrog's ass. I already called the DA's office; they say there's not a damn thing they or anybody else can do about it."

"What *have* you got?"

"No action on any of Cassie Royster's credit cards."

"Phones?"

"The mother's got a cell, of course, and the girls split one of their own. Nothing out of either of them." He tapped his notes. "Last ping from the girls' cell phone is estimated to have come from . . ." He read the coordinates.

The C of D got to his feet and moved over to the huge map of the city on the west wall of the office. He found the intersection of the coordinates with his finger.

"That's the middle of the damn river," Nilsson said.

"Her car is in the garage at the Royster house. There's no record of them taking any kind of public transportation, no large withdrawals from any of the family accounts." Dolan raised a hand. "Most of which the Missus doesn't have access to anyway." He flipped a page in his notebook. "The girls weren't signed out of school or registered somewhere new. They're not registered in any hotel or motel within a hundred-mile radius."

Nilsson was packing his briefcase for the night. "Which tells us what?" he growled.

"It tells us that a bipolar woman with a six- and an eight-year-old girl managed to put all of this together on one day's notice." Dolan counted on his fingers. "More cash in her pocket than she actually has access to. New paperwork for all three of them. Safe transport to someplace that doesn't keep records. Yadda yadda."

Nilsson snapped his briefcase closed.

"I can't *prove* the Women's Transitional Center helped the Royster family disappear," Dolan said, "but, as far as I'm concerned, they look like the smart money bet."

"And the crystal-gazer daughter?"

"Jury's still out on that one."

Nilsson shot him a look that would have wilted lettuce.

"Just saying," Dolan said.

. · . · . · . .

Grace handed the turbaned taxi driver another twenty and told him to keep the change.

He hesitated, surveying the surrounding area with great trepidation.

"Ain't nothin' here, Missy," he said. "You sure you wanna get out here?"

"I'll be fine." She pressed the bill into his hand.

He took the money and managed a crooked smile. Crow Street had been built before the automobile ruled the world, back when carts and horses had moved the freight. Dark and dank and dirty, it looked like something out of a Dickens novel. For as long as anyone could remember, the neighborhood had been called Coaltown. The name seemed to fit.

Across the street, a series of low arches defined the narrow lane. What had once been wagon-loading docks had long since been sealed up, leaving a patchwork of mismatched brickwork running as far as the eye could see. A shadow moved across one of the dirty patches of light. And then another.

She stepped out of the cab and stood on the sidewalk. The air smelled of salt and rotting garbage. The cab driver popped his door and stepped out beside her. "Lemme take you someplace else, Missy," he pleaded. "This ain't no place—"

And then they were there, by his elbows. Two of them. The one with the big bump on his nose reached up and pulled the turban from the driver's head, and slammed it hard into his chest. The driver reflexively grabbed it with both hands. His long gray hair came loose and hung down over one ear.

The one with the bad teeth put his face right up to the driver's. Nose to nose.

"Get back in the car," he said, "and get the fuck out of here."

The driver shot Grace a terrified look.

She nodded, as if to say it was all right. "Go," she said softly.

He was a good man. Truly concerned for her safety. But she didn't have to ask him twice. He slid back into the cab, flipped his turban over onto the passenger seat, dropped the cab into gear and went skittering up Crow Street like a cat with its tail on fire.

Grace stood on the sidewalk and watched the cab bounce over the cobblestones. She could see the driver's frightened eyes in the mirror as he gunned it up the street. She waited until he was gone and then looked around. She was alone.

She pulled off her cap and shook out her long white hair. She'd always found it ironic that this remnant neighborhood, this little puddle of puke left over from another century, was the only place where she could truly be herself. That a neighborhood where her fellow citizens wouldn't even stop at traffic lights, for fear of being dragged from their cars and killed, was her refuge. Said something about her life, she figured.

She stuffed the cap into her jacket pocket and walked slowly up Crow Street.

The rain was gone, but the dampness remained. Centuries of sweat had permeated the stones beneath her feet; she could smell it as she walked along. She could feel shadows moving in the surrounding darkness, too, and hear the faint shuffle of feet, but took little notice. They were there for her.

When she reached the T at the end of Crow Street, she turned left onto what was known simply as "the ramp." An inclined brick plane leading up to an ancient metal door that looked like it hadn't been opened in a couple of centuries. The door slid open just far enough for Grace to slip through. She stepped inside. The door closed.

Directly in front of her, the yawning mouth of a freight elevator beckoned. She walked over and closed the door; the car began to rise. One floor, two, and then on to the fourth, where her mother was sitting in her wheelchair reading a book.

She looked up when Grace stepped into the room.

"How'd it go?" she asked.

"About as bad as it could have," Grace answered.

. . . .

Clouds were swallowing the city, from the top down. When the call came, Mickey Dolan was motoring down Front Street, heading for home.

He thumbed the green "Answer" button on his cell phone.

"Detective Dolan," he said.

"This is Officer Fenene."

"How can I help you, Officer?" Dolan asked, but groaned inwardly. Last thing on earth he needed was some cop trying to sell him raffle tickets.

"You remember me?" the voice asked. "From earlier today. Those two skells that was following you."

Light bulb. It was the bruiser cop from the alley. The one with the baton.

"Damn right I remember," Dolan said. "I haven't seen a swing that good since Mickey Mantle. What's up?"

"Me and Denny—that's my partner—we took a call about an hour ago. Down at the hospital. Lady says this other lady assaulted her."

"Okay," Dolan said tentatively.

"So I'm doing my report and I type the assailant's name into the system and what I get are a whole bunch of 'contact Sergeant Michael Dolan' notices. So that's what I'm doing."

"What's the name?"

"Grace Pressman," he said.

Dolan checked the mirror. He had the street to himself, so he cut hard right, pulled to the curb, and stopped.

"Where are you now?" he asked.

"Still at the hospital."

"Stick around," Dolan said. "I'll be there in ten minutes."

. . . .

Grace made herself a BLT and then sat down at the kitchen table to eat. Across the river, the tops of the buildings were shrouded in fog. Looked like the world was upside down. Which, it occurred to her, was pretty close to how she felt.

She was most of the way through the sandwich when Eve said, "It probably wasn't such a good idea to have gone back there so soon."

Like that was news or something.

"What I can't get my head around," Grace said, "is how any mother could be unhappy that her son woke up from a coma. I just can't get it to compute. He's been lying there in that bed breathing through a machine, and suddenly he's back in the land of the living, and she's angry about it. I mean . . . what's with that?"

"Imagine having to tell your son that you'd given up on him and wanted to pull the plug," Eve said.

"Awkward . . . sure. But compared to what? Compared to having him conscious and back in your life."

"People are strange creatures," Eve offered.

"Not that strange," Grace said. "Something's not right."

They settled into an uneasy silence.

"I called Mr. K," Eve said, finally.

"And?" Grace snapped, angry that her mother had changed the subject.

"And we're going to move the Royster family tomorrow."

"Where to?"

"A new safe house. Something more permanent."

"What time?"

"Between ten and eleven. He's sending cars."

Grace said nothing.

"I can count on you, right?" Eve prodded.

"I'll be ready," Grace said.

. . . .

When Mickey Dolan stepped off the elevator, both uniformed officers were leaning on the nurses' station counter, trying to make time with the duty nurse.

First thing Dolan noticed was the smell. Something about recycled air set his nose to twitching. He rubbed his nose with the back of his hand as he strode down the hall.

Denny, the partner, was the first to notice who was coming their way. He ran a stiff hand through his wavy hair and cleared his throat. Officer Fenene straightened up and tried to look professional. Fenene looked even bigger indoors than he had in that alley. Like being in a phone booth with a freezer.

Dolan motioned with his head. He led them down the hall, away from prying ears. They marched, single file, down the gleaming corridor, into the waiting room, where half a dozen people had spread themselves among the dog-eared magazines and sagging plastic furniture. Looked like Edward Hopper at the hospital.

Dolan took the uniforms to the far corner. Pulled out his notebook.

"Who's the victim?" he asked.

"Roberta Reeves," Fenene said.

"Wants to be called Roberta Green," Denny, the partner, said, "but I looked her up. Her legal name is still Reeves."

"Divorce has a way of doing that to you," Dolan said, and then immediately wished he hadn't. Both officers shuffled their feet and looked away.

"What's she say happened?" Dolan said quickly.

"She's got a knot the size of a softball on her head," Fenene said.

Denny checked his notes. "She says she went in to see her son Joseph and there was another woman in the room. Says the other woman attacked her."

"She say why the woman attacked her?" Dolan asked.

"'Cause she wasn't supposed to be there, I guess," Fenene said.

"Joseph's on family-only visits," Denny threw in.

"What's he in here for?"

The two cops looked at each other. "He's been in a coma," Denny said.

"How long?"

"Better part of a year."

Dolan felt his skin grow cold. He was almost afraid to ask.

"And now?"

"This is where it gets weird," Fenene offered. "The kid's awake now. Seems this Pressman woman somehow woke him up."

"Who says?"

"Everybody," Fenene said. "SWAT had a call earlier today . . ." He told Dolan the story of how Joseph's father had barricaded them in, and about the SWAT team showing up and then how Mr. Reeves surrendered, without incident, and that this pure white woman was in there with him, and everybody's amazement when she came out and announced that the boy was awake and breathing on his own. About how pissed off Roberta Reeves had been by the whole thing, which nobody could figure out, and how the hospital wasn't pressing charges because the father was the legal guardian. And finally about Mrs. Reeves filing an assault complaint and hospital security chasing the white-haired woman out into the street, and losing her to a passing cab.

"How'd you know it was Grace Pressman?" Dolan asked.

Denny shrugged. "I fed the description into the system," he said. "You know—it's not exactly full of six-foot albino women with felony convictions."

Dolan reached over and tapped Fenene's notebook. "Find the security guys who chased her. See if they've got anything else they can tell us. Check the security tapes, inside and out. See if there's anything there that'll help us find her. See if you can get the medallion number for the cab."

While they scribbled in their notebooks, Dolan asked, "Any of the nurses on duty tonight the same ones who were here when all this happened?"

"Just about all of them," Fenene said.

"Start with security," Dolan said as they finished writing.

He stood, leaning in the corner of the waiting room, and watched as the uniformed officers hurried down the corridor and disappeared into the elevator, then bounced himself off the wall and started after them.

He pulled out his ID and badge and set them on the counter. The only nurse in sight was a young African American woman, sporting a frown and a serious set of dreadlocks. The blue name tag read: Rishanna. She wandered over.

"Can I help you?" she asked.

"Were you working earlier today, when the woman was assaulted?"

"Just came on," she said, with a disinterested shake of the head. She picked up a metal clipboard and started to walk away.

"Can you please get me someone who was?" Dolan said evenly.

Her baleful expression said she didn't like being told anything, that she had more important things to do than run errands for a cracker cop.

"It's police business," he added.

She suppressed a sneer and said, "If you'll wait here"—she threw a glance down at Dolan's ID—"*Sergeant*, I'll get my supervisor for you."

Dolan rubbed his nose and looked around. Could have been a hospital anywhere. They all looked the same, as far as he was concerned. Squeaky clean and yet the place you were most likely to contract an infection that would kill you. Something ironic about that, he'd always figured.

Took about five minutes before another nurse came out from behind the counter and walked over to Mickey Dolan. Good-looking. A slim, trim thirty-something, with even features and a head full of red hair that didn't match her swarthy complexion. She picked up Dolan's police ID and studied it. When she'd finished, she handed it back to Mickey and stuck out her hand. Mickey took it. Her hand was soft and dry.

"Pamela Prentiss," she said. "I'm the first-shift nursing supervisor for this floor."

Dolan handed her a business card. She gave it the once-over and stuffed it into her pocket. "How can I help you, Sergeant?" she asked.

"Were you working earlier today when all the excitement took place?" he asked, as he slipped his badge and police ID back into his jacket pockets.

"Yes," she said, with an amused shake of the head. "Quite a circus."

"Tell me about it," Dolan said.

"Which part?"

"Let's start with the part where the boy's father barricaded himself in his son's room, and then it turned out that the boy had awakened from a coma."

She blushed and brought a hand to her throat. "I don't quite know what to say about that," she said. "It was totally beyond my experience."

"How so?"

She sighed and thought about it. "I've been tending to Joseph Reeves the whole time he's been with us," she began. "And he's been in an anoxic brain injury coma for the entire time."

"Injury from what?" Mickey asked.

"An accident. As I understand it, he drowned in the family swimming pool."

"Which did exactly what to his brain?"

"Presumably . . ." She drew the word out, as if to say they'd presumed wrong. "Presumably the lack of oxygen killed part of his brain, leaving him in a vegetative state."

"And?"

"The longer a person stays in that sort of coma, the more their body functions begin to shut down, and the more artificial assistance is required to keep them alive."

"Where was Joseph in this process?"

"At the end. Joseph was being kept alive totally by machines. None of his systems functioned independently anymore."

"So—what happened?" Dolan asked.

She took a deep breath. Checked the hall. "A miracle," she said, with a shrug. "I can't think of any other way to describe it."

"The albino woman."

She nodded. "Don't ask me how, but yes, somehow she brought him back."

"How is that possible?"

She shook her head. "If I had an answer to that, I'd bottle it and sell it."

"I mean . . . how can it be that modern medical science says this kid is never going to regain consciousness and then, some . . . some amateur waltzes in out of the blue and wakes him up? It just doesn't make any sense."

"Supposedly, it's happened before with her," Pamela said.

"The Silver Angel thing?"

She nodded. "That story's been floating around for years."

"You believe it?"

"I believe what I see."

"Which was?"

"Which was . . . that when she walked in there, Joseph was in a vegetative state and in all probability about to die, and when she walked out, he was conscious and breathing without mechanical assistance for the first time in years."

Dolan cocked an eyebrow. "A miracle?"

She made her face as bland as a cabbage. "If you've got an alternative explanation, Sergeant, I'm listening."

"And nobody else—like a third party—was in the room when this happened?"

"Just Blondie and Joseph," she said. "Mr. Reeves was busy holding the police at bay."

"The whole SWAT team thing?"

"Just like the movies."

"I hear the mother was none too pleased to find her son awake."

"Strangest thing. She's normally quite reserved and ladylike. I'd never seen her act like that before."

"Any idea what her problem was?"

"Perhaps . . . you know, the shock was too much for her." Her tone of voice said she didn't believe a word of it.

"What did it look like to you?" Dolan tried.

"Looked like she was furious."

Dolan thought it over. "Can I see Joseph?" he asked after a moment.

"You're the cops. You can see whoever you want."

"Shall we?"

She slid out from behind the counter and led Dolan down the hall to a set of double swinging doors. She backed through the right-hand door and held it open for Mickey, who stepped into the corridor. Construction debris was everywhere in this wing. Plastic sheeting was taped over everything, except the first door on the right, which looked to be an island of tranquility in a sea of chaos.

"We were about to move Joseph upstairs," she said in a low voice. "That's what started the whole thing. That's when Mr. Reeves locked them in." She leaned closer. "Now we're afraid to move him at all," she whispered, as she opened the door.

Dolan stepped over the threshold, into the room. He turned his head back and spoke to the nurse. "Could we . . . maybe . . . just him and I?"

"Sure," she said. "If you need anything, I'll be . . ." She pointed down the hall.

He nodded. "Thanks," he mouthed.

Dolan took another step forward; the door closed behind him.

The kid's brown eyes were wide open and tracking him like radar as Dolan crossed the room to the bedside. Wasn't really a kid anymore either. Dolan wondered how spending one's adolescence in a coma would affect him down the road. All things considered, could well prove to be an improvement, he mused.

He pulled a guest chair up close and sat down.

"I'm Detective Sergeant Michael Dolan."

Joseph said nothing.

He was nice-looking. Even-featured. Slight but sturdy-looking, with a thick head of curly brown hair that could have used a trim. Somebody had given him a bad shave. Looked like he still had a few rough spots from all the wires and tubes that used to be connected to him.

"You want to see my badge?" Mickey asked.

Joseph smiled and shook his head.

"Were you awake when your mother—your mother and the other woman—?"

Joseph nodded slightly. Looked to be quite an effort.

"They had a fight?" Dolan prompted.

"No," Joseph said. His voice was raspy and full of phlegm.

"They didn't have a fight?"

"No," he croaked.

"What *did* happen?"

Joseph swallowed several times. "My mother . . ." He cleared his throat, but that just seemed to make speaking more difficult. Sounded like he was gargling.

He pointed at the sink on Dolan's left.

"The sink?" Dolan tried.

Joseph nodded.

Dolan got to his feet and walked over to the sink. The bowl was clean and dry. The fixtures polished. Dolan dropped to one knee and peered up under the rim. A rust- colored stain ran along the center of the lower edge. Dolan knew dried blood when he saw it. He stood up. "Your mother hit herself on the sink?" he asked Joseph.

The young man nodded.

"Did the other lady—"

"The silver lady," Joseph whispered.

"Did she push your mother?"

Joseph shook his head again. Adamantly, this time.

Dolan ran through the possibles. "Your mother made some sort of move on the silver lady . . . missed and hit her head on the sink. Is that it?"

Joseph smiled and nodded.

Interesting, Dolan thought to himself. Given a choice of backing up either his mother or the Pressman woman, he'd chosen the latter. Not what Dolan would have expected. Boys and their mommies and all that.

"You remember your accident?" Dolan asked after a quiet moment.

Joseph shook his head. Something about his demeanor, though, gave Dolan pause to wonder if he was telling the truth.

"Well, thanks for the help," Dolan said. "You get well now."

Joseph Reeves closed his eyes. Dolan started for the door, stopped in midstride and turned back toward the young man.

"Can I ask you one last thing?" Dolan asked.

The eyes opened.

"The silver lady . . ." He searched for the right words. "When you were . . ." He ran a hand over his face. "Wherever you were before . . ." he started.

Joseph said something unintelligible. Dolan leaned over. "What?"

Joseph closed his eyes. Dolan thought he'd lost him, but suddenly the young man spoke again. "She came to me," Joseph whispered.

"Came to you where?" Mickey asked.

Dolan could feel the boy's great fatigue. Joseph closed his eyes and began to snore softly. Dolan waited and then pushed himself to his feet and started across the room. He was reaching for the door handle when Joseph said something that stopped him in his tracks. Joseph said the word "paradise." That's all. Just "paradise."

The snoring got louder as Mickey pulled open the door and stepped into the hall.

No way he was telling Nilsson what the kid said. No friggin way.

. . . .

"The book was gone," Grace said. "That's what was missing. That damn book." She turned away from the window and began moving quickly toward her mother.

Eve looked up from her reading. "I don't understand," she said.

"The diary thing Joseph's father gave me. I left it on the nightstand by his bed, but this afternoon it was gone."

Eve dropped her book into her lap and slipped off her glasses. "Didn't you say it was all burned up?"

Grace nodded. "Partially."

Eve shrugged. "The nurses probably cleaned it up. Doesn't sound like the kind of thing they'd want lying around a hospital room."

"Something about it was very important to Joseph. Nobody was taking that book away, if he had anything to say about it."

"You're *that* certain?"

"Absolutely," Grace said.

Eve thought it over. "Do you remember any of it?" she asked, after a moment.

Grace shook her head. "All I could read was a word here and part of a sentence there." She cut the air with the side of her hand. "The rest was all black and warped and stuck together like it had gotten soaked and then dried out."

"Doesn't sound like something you'd purposefully do to a book."

"No. It doesn't."

"And you're convinced it had some sort of deep meaning for Joseph."

"No doubt about it," Grace said. "The minute I started reading from it, he began to emerge. That book was what brought him back. I could feel it."

. . . .

The afternoon fog had rolled in like gauze. The rows of cars loomed like half-erased pencil drawings as Dolan carefully worked his way across the hospital's north parking lot. He kept his eyes glued to the ground, watching his feet as he picked his way over dividers and curbs and parking stalls, in damn near zero visibility. Way things had been going lately, if he busted a leg, he figured they'd probably just get a gun and put him down.

Dolan was in a full grouse when he finally looked up and saw the outlines in the fog. Denny and Fenene standing by the side of his unmarked Chevy.

"Something?" he asked testily, pulling out the key fob.

"Couple," Fenene said. "Thought you might want this," he said, proffering a DVD in a white paper sleeve. "CC camera footage from when the Pressman woman managed to ditch hospital security. Got a real good image of the cab medallion."

"Get it enhanced a lot sooner if you take it in instead of us," Denny added.

He was right. Anything submitted to the lab by a couple of uniforms was going directly to the rear of the line. Best if Dolan brought it in on his way home from the hospital. That way he could put the C of D's name on it and get immediate results.

"Thanks," Dolan said as he unlocked the car.

"And this," Denny said, pulling something out from behind his back.

Denny held the bag out away from himself, as if whatever was inside had teeth. He raised the plastic bag to eye level.

Dolan leaned in close. In the limited visibility, Dolan at first imagined it to be a piece of partially burnt tree bark. Then Denny began to rotate the bag.

About halfway around, Dolan could make out the ends of pages, wavy and wrinkled from getting wet.

"What's it wet from?" Dolan asked.

"Hospital maintenance found it stopping up a toilet in the first floor women's room," Fenene said. "Cover's the only page that'll move. Joseph Reeves's name's on the inside."

Dolan reached out and took the plastic bag from the officer.

"We'll let the science geeks have a look at this while they're working on the cab medallion," he said.

The officers turned to leave. Dolan set the bag on the roof of the car and pulled out his notebook. "Hey," he said.

They stopped and turned back his way. "Nice job," Dolan said. "I'll make note of it in my report to the C of D. Let me have your badge numbers."

Dolan took down the numbers and made sure he had their names spelled right. He could hear them chortling to one another as they disappeared into the fog.

Most popular I've been for quite some time, he thought to himself as he retrieved the bag from the roof, pulled open the car door, and slid into the driver's seat.

2

"Mama's got that loopy look," Tessa said.

"She stopped taking her medicine," Maddy said with a sigh.

"We should tell Gus."

"He already knows," Maddy said as she tried, once again, to zip her suitcase, and once again got stuck halfway around. "Help me, will you?"

Tessa didn't move. Just stood there frowning.

Both Royster girls were tall for their age, just as both had the kind of dirty blonde hair that would undoubtedly, in adolescence, morph into a light brown.

"You're going to get wrinkles if you keep doing that with your face," her big sister gently chided. "Come on. Sit on this silly thing."

Tessa walked over and plopped down on the suitcase. Maddy used both hands to pull the zipper around the first corner.

"I want to go to school with you," Tessa said.

"Gus says we've got to go to different schools for a while, so . . ." She dropped her eyes to the zipper and stopped talking. Tessa was a worrier. When she got that way, it didn't matter what you said, she just got worse, so Maddy didn't say anything at all.

"So Pappa won't find us, huh?" Tessa said, after a moment.

Their eyes met. "Yeah," Maddy said.

Tessa got white and stiff like an icicle and then started to cry. Maddy walked over and gave her a hug. They stood in the middle of the room, their arms locked around one another, for the longest time.

. ˙ . ˙ . ˙ . ˙ .

Teddy already knew the answer, but he asked anyway.

"Problem?"

They shrugged in unison. Looked like a friggin conga line doin' the coochie coochie with their shoulders.

Harvin spoke up first. "We got company again," he said.

"Where?"

"Far side of both bridges," Hal said.

Teddy frowned. "I thought they gave up doing that shit."

Manny piped up. "Same as before. Two guys in each car. Just sittin' there, not doin' a friggin thing."

Teddy checked his watch. He was about to speak when a blast of frigid air raked the back of his neck. He turned in time to see Gus Bradley step into the room, wearing his trademark black serge suit, size sixty-four humongous. Either he owned half a dozen identical suits, or he'd been wearing the same one for the past twenty years. Teddy had never been quite sure and wasn't about to ask, either.

Gus was a bruiser, a bare-knuckled leg-breaker of great local renown, whose duties were generally confined to past-due collections and other nonlethal muscle work. Mr. K liked to say Gus was the company's Remorse Manager.

Not lately, though. Lately, Gus was more like a nanny. For reasons known only to little girls, the Royster sisters fell in love with him the first time he'd lumbered into the room. Even stranger, Gus seemed to revel in it. Spent half his time helping with their homework and rolling around the floor with them. Go figure.

And . . . you know . . . as far as Teddy was concerned, if the girls wanted to use Gus as their personal set of monkey bars, so be it. Especially with the mom being such a loose cannon and all. Only thing that woman was missing was a fuse hangin' out of her ass and somebody with a match. Anything that helped keep the situation under control was fine with Teddy.

"We've got forty minutes," Teddy said. "The Yale Street car gotta be gone in under forty minutes."

Everybody nodded like bobblehead dolls.

"Same assholes as before?" Teddy asked disgustedly.

Hal nodded. "The usual rent-a-cop outfit. Western Security."

Ever since Mr. K'd agreed to take care of the Royster family thing for that Pressman broad, Coaltown had been getting a lot of unwanted attention from these Western Security hummers. Teddy guessed that when their high-tech methods for finding the Royster family had drawn a complete blank, they'd focused on the only part of town where their little electronic eyes and ears couldn't reach. Coaltown. No cameras in Coaltown.

Coaltown was, in fact, a delta island. Four hundred ninety acres of glacial silt surrounded by a rusted-over city, accessible only by a pair of rolling lift bridges at the north and south ends. Couple of centuries back, most of the city's industrial infrastructure had been located out on Coaltown. Foundries, fabricators, fish-packing plants, a paper mill. You name it. Anything loud, dirty, or smelly had been relegated to the island, where the river winds were pretty much guaranteed to blow the clatter and the stink out into Barnholder Bay.

A declining economy had, over the past couple of decades, rendered Coaltown not much good for anything. Built to the scale of a previous century, its crumbling brick facades and narrow cobblestone lanes did not easily lend themselves to the oversized, containerized nature of twenty-first century commerce.

The only way to make Coaltown viable again would have been to raze it and start from scratch. That's what the preservationists had wanted, to turn the island into a big ol' city park, with trails and gardens and a big kiddie pool. Eventually, they collected enough signatures to get the matter on the ballot.

Problem was, not even the most Pollyanna optimist could pretend that the city had that kind of dough, or that bike trails and kiddie pools were high on the city's overflowing priority list for infrastructure repairs. So, suffice it to say, the city fathers had been overjoyed when Biosystems offered to take a ninety-nine year lease on the property.

Not only did the privatization of Coaltown save the city the cost of both upkeep and services, but, as promised, Biosystems proceeded to build the largest and most sophisticated waste recycling facility in this part of the country. That which they couldn't recycle, incinerate, or repurpose, they loaded onto barges, towed ten miles offshore, and dropped in the drink. All at no cost to the city.

And then there was the part that didn't get talked about. At least not out loud. The part about who it was actually owned Biosystems. Who it was had the kind of money and political influence required to actually get something like that done.

Those fervid souls who insisted on having their questions answered found themselves wading through dozens of dummy corporations, limited partnerships, and offshore holding companies, until they eventually ran aground on something that smelled a whole lot like Vince Keenan. The smart ones let it go at that. The others eventually wished they had.

Since city government wasn't about to admit to knowingly being in bed with a former crime magnate, they'd just cabbage-faced it. Who? Keenan? Vince Keenan? To my knowledge, Mr. Keenan has never been convicted of anything. Yadda yadda.

Any doubt as to the players was erased when, using the politically correct guise of offering a "Second Chance" to those who had previously strayed from society's path, Biosystems had proceeded to hire every degenerate slimeball felon within a fifty-mile radius to work the recycling plant. Birds of a feather soon joined the migration. Every bucket of blood bar, small-time grifter, bail jumper, welfare cheat, parole violator—you name it, they all picked up and moved over to Coaltown.

And why wouldn't they? It was like a get-outta-jail-free card. Long as they confined whatever it was they did to the island, the cops were prepared to turn a blind eye, allowing Coaltown to become a virtual city within a city—a city where the penalty for shitting in your own nest was getting your dead ass floated out with the garbage. At last count, there were seventeen titty bars and no churches on the island. It was one of those symbiotic relationships where things worked out for all concerned.

Teddy looped an arm around Harvin's shoulders and guided him to the far side of the room. He leaned in close enough to smell fried onions and lowered his voice.

"When I say they gotta go," Teddy whispered, "I'm not talkin' cuttin' the tires, or kicking their ass. Nothing like that. Those assholes probably got a satellite link or some such shit," he whispered. "Those fuckers gotta *not* be there. Period. You understand what I'm sayin'? Tell 'em to do what they gotta do."

Apparently, Harvin did. He raised an eyebrow. The look said, "You sure?" The timeline was bad. They didn't have enough time for anything cute. Worse yet, this was off-island work. They didn't do this kind of work anymore.

"Cops don't like private dicks, either," Teddy assured him.

Harvin turned his face away.

Teddy read his mind. "There's no fucking this up," he said. "You know how he feels about this. Something goes wrong, it's our ass on the line here."

Apparently Harvin agreed. His face was stone as he brought the phone to his ear.

Teddy turned away and walked back across the room. He spoke to Gus.

"Mom and the kids gonna be ready to go on time?" he asked.

Gus nodded. "Mom's off her meds," he grumbled. "The move's got her big-time squirrely. She's not sure she can handle it behind her meds, so she stopped taking them a couple days ago." Sensing an impending admonition, Gus held up a restraining hand the size of a waffle iron. "We'll be ready," he promised as he moved toward the door.

. · . · . · . .

"Did they tell you where we're taking them?" Grace asked.

Her mother's wheelchair was located directly behind the driver's seat, locked onto the lift platform so she wouldn't go rolling all over the place.

"Hardwig. That's all they told me," Eve said. "A duplex, someplace over by the Garden County line, so we can put the girls in separate school districts. Gus is staying in the other unit, until we're sure everything's okay."

Grace frowned. "Hardwig. What's that—twenty miles from here?"

"Closer to thirty, I think."

"Not very far."

"Better than here," Eve said with conviction. "Coaltown's no place for kids."

"Coaltown's no place for anybody, but at least it's safe," Grace said.

"We're working on getting something permanent together for them, but Indra says it could be a couple of months. In the meantime, the kids can go back to school, so they won't get behind. Cassie says the little one . . ."

"Tessa," Grace filled in.

"I understand she has . . ." Eve hesitated, searching for the correct phrase.

Grace saved her the trouble. "Maddy covers for her," she said. "That's why Cassie's so worried about splitting them up."

"We leave them together, they'll be easier for Royster's people to find. You've got to figure they're running computer searches for every school district in the area, trying to find a pair of sisters who registered recently." Eve reached down into her wheelchair, pulled up a thick blue folder, and held it up so Grace could see it in the rearview mirror. "We've got all new paperwork for them. Absolutely bona fide. School records. Everything. All they've got to do is remember their new names."

Grace made a wry face. "Gus has had them practicing," she said. "Maddy's fine. Tessa . . ." Grace pulled a hand from the steering wheel and waggled it. "Tessa needs a little work."

"Indra says you've got a very serious inquiry on the website."

"She told me," Grace said.

"No interest?"

A long silence ensued, before Grace said, "You know Mom, I'm starting to wonder about this so-called gift of mine."

"It's a gift from God," Eve said.

Grace barked out a short, dry laugh. "Don't start the God stuff with me, Mom. You're about as religious as Scotch Tape."

"Think about it though, honey. If it weren't for your gift, you and I wouldn't be riding along having this conversation."

"Wish it were that simple," Grace said. "But, unfortunately, it turns out to be way more complicated than that. These people emerge into a whole new universe. The people they left behind have gone on with their lives. Found new lovers. Learned to cope without them. It never occurred to me that bringing someone back to this world could be every bit as painful and upsetting as losing them had been in the first place. I probably should have thought of it, but I didn't."

Another silence. Eve watched the ancient buildings slide by the van window. She recognized the street. They were very nearly at their destination.

"Indra says the family is offering a cool million bucks," Eve said. "We can help a lot of women with that kind of money."

Ah—the money. It always came back to the money, didn't it? Grace hated that. It made even "doing the right thing" somehow feel shoddy. They'd been naive when they'd first started, imagining an endless supply of concerned women clamoring to help save other women from violence. The line, however, was yet to form. Turned out that shielding the innocent from the inadequacies of the court system didn't come cheap. Even with Mr. K's patronage, it wouldn't be possible without a substantial internal cash flow, which, as far as Eve was concerned, was where Grace came into it. Nothing like a little motherly guilt to grease the skids either.

Grace wheeled the van into a narrow courtyard that, according to the peeling red and green sign, had once served as the loading dock for Fields and Sons Foundry.

She set the parking brake, got out and walked around to the sliding door. When she pushed the green button, the hydraulics seemed to shake themselves from sleep, as they slid the wheelchair out through the opening and then slowly lowered the platform to the ground.

Eve rolled herself out onto the uneven bricks. "I'll go talk to Teddy," she said. "Why don't you go see how the girls are doing?"

. · . · . · .

"This blows goats," Jerry Robbins said.

His partner Richie squirmed in the driver's seat but didn't reply. Way Richie figured it, they were damn lucky they hadn't gotten fired. Getting spotted by the subject, arrested by the cops, and then needing to be bailed out by the legal department was just about as bad as you could screw up in the security business, so if still having a job meant doing shit work—well then, he'd do shit work for a while.

They had a straight shot down the alley, looking right at the east end of the Yale Street Bridge. Trucks, trucks, and more trucks, most of them hauling garbage. For the past five hours, they'd dutifully written down every plate and truck ID number.

The steel wool skies and a crazy, gusting wind made him glad they were inside the car. An icy northern weather system had blown in overnight. The alley swirled with airborne litter, bits of which ticked against the car windows like intermittent static.

Could have been worse, he supposed. Could have been working on foot, freezing their asses off someplace, so if the brass wanted to teach them a lesson about being sloppy, he was more than willing to put up with it.

Jerry leaned back and closed his eyes. Richie thought about mentioning that they were supposed to be doing surveillance, which worked way better if you had your eyes open, but decided to keep quiet. At least, if he was sleeping, he wasn't bitching. Small blessings, Richie figured.

So, a couple of minutes later, when Richie spoke, it was more to himself than to Jerry. "I thought they didn't wear those outfits anymore," he said.

Jerry cracked an eye. The sight of a pair of old-fashioned nuns flapping up the alley in their direction brought him up straight in the seat. *Stop slouching, Mr. Robbins.*

God doesn't like slouchers rang in his ears, as if the words had been trapped in some corner of his skull since childhood, waiting for the right moment to escape. Old habits died hard, he guessed. Old habits . . . ha ha . . . nun joke, he chortled as he straightened his tie.

. · . · . · .

With Cassie Royster, you never had to wonder. On good days, silence was her only enemy, as if some cosmic station manager had tasked her with making sure there was no dead air in the universe. If she ran out of things to say, she'd say things she'd just said about five minutes earlier, and then haul off and say them again five minutes after that, as if, if she didn't maintain control of the conversation, she'd be stripped of her right to participate and thus be out of the loop for eternity.

Other days . . . other days, not so much. On those days, she always reminded Grace of that horrible Vietnam-era photograph of the little girl running naked down the middle of the road, screaming in agony. That's how she seemed. Like she couldn't wash off whatever fiery demons were, moment to moment, incinerating her soul.

Grace knocked tentatively on the bathroom door. Nothing. The vans were loaded. The girls were on board and ready to go. All they were waiting for was word from Teddy that the Yale Street Bridge was cleared. That and collecting Cassie Royster. Grace knocked again. Same result.

From forty yards away, Cassie Royster looked like a million other middle-aged women. When you got up close, though, a couple of things immediately caught the eye. First off, it didn't take much imagination to see what a stunner she once had been. The big blue eyes and the good cheekbones. Even with a bit of middle-aged spread, she was nicely shaped and still rather attractive.

Second thing you picked up on was that *she* didn't think so. That this was a person who wasn't sure about much of anything, least of all about herself. A person who spent a lot of time worrying about what other people thought of her and whether or not she was going to prove capable of handling whatever came next in her life. Must be a terrible way to live, Grace had thought on several occasions.

Grace knocked again, then tried the door. The door swung inward.

The bathroom was empty. Grace called out, "Cassie?" No response, just the brittle echo of her voice against the tile. Grace peeked under the stall. Nobody home.

She could feel the cold stab of fear rising in her chest as she hurried back out into the main room and looked around. No Cassie Royster. She called again. Nothing. She raced around, checking the bedrooms and the kitchen, peering under beds and into closets. Nothing. She was gone.

Both *apartments*, as they called them, were built inside much larger buildings. The apartment where Grace and Eve lived was at the extreme southern end of the island, looking out over Strander Avenue from the Coaltown side of the river, housed in the same refurbished complex as the Biosystems corporate offices, although even a careful perusal of the building's blueprints gave no hint of its presence.

This apartment had been custom built for the Women's Transitional Center to use as a safe house for displaced families. All very chic and suburban, an oasis of good bedding, stainless steel, and granite, built inside a condemned hundred-year-old building. The whole thing welded directly to the freestanding elevator shaft. Completely self-contained and invisible from the street. The entire building could have collapsed around it without so much as rattling a knickknack. The only way in or out was by means of the freight elevator directly across from the apartment's front door.

Grace's heart rose to her throat as she imagined Cassie Royster stumbling around the dilapidated section of the building. She'd only seen it once. Back when Teddy had shown them the apartment for the first time. Looked like something out of a dreary Victorian novel. Parts of the exterior walls missing altogether, collapsed ceilings, four-story deadfalls where the floors had rotted away, an ankle-breaking collection of rusting machine parts and broken glass underfoot, the crunching of which was punctuated by the scrabbling scratch of unseen claws. Grace shuddered at the memory.

Grace pushed the elevator button. Then pushed it again. The ancient mechanism groaned piteously. The car began to rise. Seemed like it took an hour to get to her and another to get her back to ground level.

She hurried out to the courtyard. Gus was behind the wheel of the van. Her mother was in back with the girls. Gus picked it up right away. The big boy was positively prescient that way. Real sensitive as to what was going on around him.

He got out of the van, closing the door behind himself. Walked over close to Grace, so they wouldn't have to shout. "Problem?"

"Cassie's missing," Grace said.

"Missing how?"

"She's not in the apartment."

Grace could practically see the wheels turning inside his head. He looked back toward the van. Grace read his mind. "Mom can handle the girls," she said.

Gus turned away and began to whisper into his phone.

. . . .

The nuns used their voluminous sleeves to protect their faces from the swirling airborne debris that filled the alley. They look like Muslim women, Jerry thought. Nothin' showin' but their eyes.

Jerry and Richie watched in amused wonder as the nuns split up, one of them heading for each side of the car. Richie pushed the button. The window began to descend. He forced a smile and leaned his head out.

He was about to speak to the approaching sister when a sudden flat sound hijacked his attention. Sounded like Jerry farted. He looked toward the passenger seat in stunned disbelief. We got a pair of serious-ass nuns walkin' up to the car and this moron's cuttin' the cheese?

Took Richie's central nervous system an extra couple of seconds to process the blossoming red flower spreading over the side of Jerry's head. He watched in open-mouthed horror as his partner's limp body began to slump in his direction.

Wasn't till Jerry was heeled over as far as the seatbelt would permit that Richie noticed the neat little hole in the passenger-side window.

The breath caught in his throat as he watched the flower's petals begin to drop on the center console—rich, red droplets spreading over the leather like brain syrup.

He turned his head slowly back the other way. Seemingly in no hurry, almost as if some innate survival sense knew exactly where this exit led and wasn't in any hurry to make the trip. He drew in an enormous breath, as if to shout, perhaps, or scream, or beg for his life. He still hadn't decided which, when the bullet took out his front teeth and began banging around inside his skull. He fell forward onto the steering wheel. The horn began to blow. A tattooed hand reached in the window and pushed him over sideways. The horn stopped blaring. Except for the spreading red puddle, Richie and Jerry looked for all the world to be locked in a passionate embrace. Before walking off, the sister on the passenger side bowed her head slightly and made the sign of the cross.

· · · · · · · ·

Grace stayed close to the wall, trying to avoid the dark, rotting patches at the center of the floor. She called out "Cassie" as she moved deeper into the room. Occasionally she thought she heard other voices, on other floors, calling Cassie's name. Gus had mustered a full-scale search party in under ten minutes. Everybody'd been assigned a floor to search and the hunt had begun.

She kept inching forward, moving past the last set of windows. Past the final shaft of dirty light throwing its likeness along the floor. Back toward the shadows where the light never ventured. "Cassie," she called.

The room was immense. Some kind of long-ago heavy manufacturing plant. Overhead, a rusted set of rails ran the length of the space, supported at intervals by crossbeams resting on rough stone columns. What appeared to be a set of boxcar wheels were rusted in place at the near end. Here and there, loops of heavy chain drooped toward the floor like iron vines. Everything designed to support great weight. Grace imagined she could feel the tonnage pressing down on her as she moved along.

"Cassie," she called again. The idea of Cassie Royster negotiating a landscape such as this filled Grace with terror. At best, the woman was inattentive. At worst, completely oblivious to her surroundings. Prone to fits of mindless fancy. Likely to dispense with the look and get right to the leap. Grace trembled as she slid forward.

The sound of movement pulled her attention to the back corner of the room. Down low. Red eyes—maybe a dozen of them—looking right at her. Her skin began to crawl as she inched closer. She stamped her foot and shouted. They held their ground.

She shuffled forward again. One of them got up on its hind legs and hissed at her. She shouted again. Nothing. She could see them now. Rodents the size of schnauzers, none of them the least bit impressed with Grace's feeble attempts at intimidation.

She brought her foot down hard—onto thin air. She teetered for a long moment, scratching at the wall, seeking purchase—any purchase—but finding none.

. · . · . · . ·.

Mickey Dolan caught the call on his way to the station house. Eight forty-five in the a.m., he was driving with one hand, using a matchbook cover to pry a piece of breakfast sausage out from between his teeth, when the radio snapped, crackled, and popped. "One eighty-seven. Two. I repeat, two. Fourteen hundred block of Wentworth. Emergency services en route." Pregnant pause and then the message started over. "One eighty-seven . . ."

Homicides. A double. Over by the riverfront. Normally, when they got a double, it was some kind of domestic beef. Usually a Mom and Pop.

A shoot-the-wife-and-then-blow-your-own-brains-out-thus-eliminating-that-pesky-"go-to-prison" kind of thing. But not in that neighborhood. That neighborhood was wall-to-wall industrial. Nobody lived within twenty blocks of that end of Wentworth. Too dark and dank. No stores. No gas stations. No nothing. But, above all, way too close to Coaltown for anybody's comfort.

Mickey zoomed over into the right-hand lane, hung a hard right onto Pulaski Street and put his foot into it. His hand instinctively reached for the siren, but he stopped himself. You never knew. The perps might still be around.

Took him four tire-squealing minutes to reach the scene. By that time, half a dozen police cruisers were strewn haphazardly about Wentworth Street, blocking the way. Pulsing red and white lights bounced around the bricks. The static crackle of unattended radios scratched at the morning air as Dolan stepped out of the car.

Down here, by the river, the air was cold and angry, seemingly blowing in all directions at once. Mickey turned up his collar and started hoofing it down the street.

A small army of uniforms was huddled around a black Lexus coupe, peering in the car windows like it was full of naked cheerleaders. As Dolan approached, one of the uniforms caught a glimpse of him and quickly started his way.

Mickey took out his gold shield and hung it around his neck. The long gold chain had belonged to his father. The uniform stopped walking. "Waiting for the lab, Sergeant . . ." he said defensively as Mickey approached. Mickey didn't recognize the guy. "Dolan," Mickey filled in. "Sergeant Michael Dolan. Set a two-block perimeter around the scene. No one in. No one out. Call dispatch and get as many units as it takes, but seal this damn place off."

The uniform was writing in his notebook now. Dolan kept talking. "Get those cruisers out of the street so Emergency Services can get down here and then have these guys canvass the neighborhood, see if we can turn up anybody who saw or heard anything." Dolan turned toward the east and pointed upward. "I can see two CC cameras from here," he said. "Find out how many cover the immediate area, who they belong to, and roust out whoever it is can show us what's on the tape."

The uniform's jotting had reached full mouth-breather status. Off in the distance a pair of sirens was howling in two-part harmony.

Dolan stepped around the scribbling officer and hustled toward the assembled multitude of cops. "Gents," he shouted. All heads turned his way. "Move the cruisers so the medics can get down here. Let's go. Hustle."

They broke into a group trot. Dolan pointed at the cop with the notebook.

"See Officer . . ."

"Oh . . . Yablonski," the guy said.

"See Officer Yablonski for assignments."

Dolan waited as the sound of slapping soles got fainter and then walked over to the Lexus. Two guys dead in the front seat. Both with their seatbelts on. Blood and brain matter splattered all over the damn place.

Dolan moved toward the right. The driver's window was down. He made it a point not to touch anything as he bent to look in the window. Looked like the driver had been shot in the mouth. The passenger just above the right ear. Both small-caliber, low-velocity holes. Something that would bounce around inside the skull like a Ping-Pong ball. Looked like they were hugging.

He reached into the car and put two fingers on the driver's carotid artery.

Not only was there no sign of a pulse, but the skin had begun to cool. He had no doubt. These two wouldn't be home for lunch.

As he began to pull back he noticed that the driver's suit jacket had been folded back by contact with the center console. A dark shadow caught Dolan's eye. He found a pen in his inside pocket, leaned into the car as far as gravity would permit, and pulled the dead man's coat back a couple of inches.

Chrome-plated automatic in a shoulder holster. He was betting the other guy was packing too. Dolan frowned and surveyed the scene again. The Lexus sat tight to the curb, right about in the middle of Wentworth Street, pointed straight at this end of the Yale Street Bridge. It was a good forty yards from the car to either end of the street, so, short of SEAL Team 6 rappelling down and landing on the roof of the car, the perps had somehow managed to walk up to a couple of armed men without raising the slightest suspicion in either of them. Neither guy had popped his seatbelt. Neither had pulled his piece. They had just sat there in their car, calm as could be, while a couple of hitters walked up and shot them in the head. Didn't make any sense.

Before Mickey could ponder the matter at any length, the first of three aid cars skidded to a stop. Dolan stepped aside and let the medics do their work. Wasn't till they pulled the stiffs out of the car and Dolan got a good look at the passenger's face that he knew where he'd seen these two hummers before.

The realization sent him reaching for his phone.

. . . .

For a couple of terror-filled seconds, Grace teetered on the edge, her mind's eye picturing herself rocketing downward through the jagged hole in the floor, kicking and screaming as she tumbled into the blackness, in the seconds before being impaled on whatever hundred-year-old, disease-laden debris awaited at the bottom. She saw the rats, too. Gnawing at her mangled, punctured body, even before the final breath had left her.

Her fingernails raked the edge of a steel I beam. She pressed her back into the wall, as if she were trying to push herself out the other side. She was motionless but panting like a miler. Took her a moment to muster the courage to step one foot back over the other, pirouetting on tiptoe as she made the turn and pressed her chest into the wall for all she was worth.

She stood there vibrating, her lips pressed to the peeling metal like it was a long-lost lover, while her body struggled to regain some measure of pulmonary composure.

Wasn't till the blood had stopped pounding in her ears that she heard the horn.

The car horn. Somebody was blowing a horn.

She took several deep breaths and began to sidestep back the way she'd come.

Took her several minutes to make it back to the door where she'd entered. Her knees were like spaghetti as she hurried toward the elevator. The horn was louder now.

Cassie was wearing her sugarplum fairy dress, all pink and puffy. Something you'd wear to a five-year-old's birthday party on a warm Saturday afternoon in July, assuming, of course, that you'd been hired as the entertainment. Standing amid the grimy post-industrial rubble, she looked like she'd been dropped out of a spaceship.

Gus walked out to meet Grace.

"Nicky found her," Gus whispered. "Down by the river. Collecting stones. She says the fairy outfit's supposed to make the girls feel better," he said with an icy stare. He cast his eyes in Cassie's direction. "Scary when you think she's the best option we got for those girls."

"If you knew what their father did to them . . . what he made them do . . ."

"Tessa told me," Gus said. He looked away.

Grace winced as she watched Cassie climb into the back of the van. Watched through the window as she buckled her safety belt and settled back into the seat. A foot and a half of pink fabric dangled from the bottom of the door like Barbie's signal flag.

"We've got to get her back on those meds," Grace said. "We can't be dealing with Tinker Bell day in, day out. Somebody's gonna get hurt."

"She tries," Gus said. "Way too damn hard, but she really tries."

Grace heaved a sigh. "Let's go, while the getting's good," she said.

· · · · · · ·

Apparently, Marcus Nilsson was not feeling festive. His driver Robbie threw Mickey Dolan a "watch your ass motherfucker" look as he hustled around to get the door for the Chief of Detectives.

"This better be damn good," the C of D growled as he stepped out of the car into the blustery street and started toward Mickey. "I'm supposed to be at a Planning Council meeting."

Mickey inclined his head toward a pair of wallets laid out on the hood of the Lexus. "As I'm sure you've already heard sir, we've got two gunshot victims. Both shot in the head at point blank range. Both heeled. Both still buckled up. Couple of private dicks. Richard Coffee and Gerald Robbins."

Nilsson frowned as he ran the names through his brain circuits. "The assholes from yesterday?"

"Yep. Same two guys."

"What the hell were they doing out here?"

"There was a notebook wedged down next to the driver's seat. Looks like they were taking notes about who came and went from Coaltown."

Nilsson's face wrinkled. "Why would they be doing that?" he wondered out loud.

"No idea."

The C of D looked around. "So they were sitting there in their car counting garbage trucks."

"So it seems."

"And somebody—probably more than one somebody—just walks up and shoots both of them in the head. In broad fucking daylight."

"That's what it looks like sir," Mickey said.

Nilsson thought it over. "ME give you any idea about time of death?"

"Thought they'd been down less than an hour."

"Why would they let somebody walk right up on them like that?" Nilsson asked. "You know . . . unless it was a kid or an old lady or something." He stopped talking. Mickey could practically see the light bulb appear above the C of D's head.

"Or a cop," Mickey added with a crooked grin. "One they recognized."

Nilsson raised a thick eyebrow. "And you were . . . ?"

"Packing away breakfast over at Shorty's," Dolan said. "Half a dozen people will put me there. Couple of them from the East Precinct."

Nilsson stared him down. "Good," he said finally. "'Cause, once they put it together, Internal Affairs is gonna be all over you like ugly on an ape."

"I was thinkin' . . ." Dolan said.

"Yeah."

"Well—yesterday these two were following me around trying to get a lead on the whereabouts of the Royster family."

"Uh huh."

"What if they were still working on the Royster thing?"

Nilsson looked around. "Here? Why here?"

"Now I'm just saying . . ." Mickey began, " . . . what if for some reason or other, they think the family is out on the island somewhere?"

"In Coaltown?"

"I mean—you know, with all the databases at our disposal these days, unless you're going to pull a Ted Kaczynski—you know, there's pretty much nowhere to run. You so much as break wind and we're going to find you. Hell, they found Ted way out in the middle of East Jesus, Montana someplace. Yet I can't seem to get a line on any of these damn people. Not the Roysters. Not the Pressman women either. It's like they don't exist, or they live in another dimension or something. So I started asking myself—"

Nilsson cut him off. "A woman and a pair of kids wouldn't last five minutes in Coaltown." The C of D waved a dismissive hand. "Hell, *I* wouldn't go out there without a vest and a full SWAT team." He waved the idea off. "Just not possible."

"Just a thought," Mickey said, defensively.

An insistent beeping pulled their eyes toward the north end of the street, where a city tow truck was backing in their direction. They stepped aside and watched in silence as the driver hooked up the Western Security Lexus. As he began to roll off down the street with the car on his hook, Nilsson said, "Tell you what, Mickey. Royster's all over the mayor—calls him three, four times a day. First thing His Honor does after Royster hangs up is to get on the blower and ream my ass. Sooooooo, just in case there's a tie-in somewhere that we're missing here—something that links these two yahoos to the Royster family . . ."

"Yes sir?"

"Why don't you roll on over to Western Security, give them the bad news. Find out what they were doing out here, other than counting garbage trucks."

"Yes sir."

A woman stepped around the corner. She began moving in their direction, walking fast, pulling a notebook from her coat pocket as she hustled along.

The walk that told the tale. Natalie Mendonhal moved like one of those Olympic walkers. Million miles an hour, all ass-wiggles and flying elbows.

Nilsson groaned. "Oh Christ, it's Mendonhal," he said under his breath.

Natalie Mendonhal had been handling the crime beat for the *Morning Standard* since the ice receded from this part of the continent.

This was a woman who never let a complete lack of information get between her and a story. She could do five columns on how nothing was new today. And often did.

Back when the TV cabinet was bigger than the screen, Natalie had started out in television. Did the morning news for the local NBC affiliate, back when newswomen looked like Betty Friedan and sportscasters were always four-hundred-pound guys wearing plaid sports jackets.

When the network replaced her with a cutesy talking head half her age, she'd gone all indignant and sued the station for age discrimination. Made quite a splash. And lost. Bye-bye TV. Hello *Morning Standard*.

Marcus Nilsson whistled. His driver quickly hopped into the car and started the engine. "Let me know what you find out from Western," Nilsson said as he headed for the car at warp speed. As he rounded the trunk he looked back at Mickey. "Give Natalie my regards," he said with a wicked grin.

Mickey watched as the C of D's car rolled up Wentworth, cut between two furniture warehouses, and disappeared from view. When he turned back, Natalie Mendonhal was creeping up on the Lexus, peering in the driver's window, scribbling in her notebook.

"That's an ongoing crime scene, Miz Mendonhal," Mickey Dolan said, as he started her way. "I'm going to have to ask you to step back, please."

"Who got whacked?" she asked.

"Nobody said anybody got whacked," Mickey reminded her.

"Radio did. Two of them." She pointed at the Lexus. "All that damn blood. You gonna try to tell me that was a shaving accident?"

"I'm going to try to tell you absolutely nothing," Mickey said with a grin.

He used his arm to gently move her away from the car.

"You touched me," she complained. She bobbed her eyebrows and leered at Mickey. "I'll give you half an hour to stop," she said.

Mercifully, salvation was at hand. At the north end of the street, a uniformed officer suddenly stepped into view. "Hey," Mickey shouted.

The guy turned toward the sound. Mickey gestured for him to come.

"Little birdy told me Marcus has got you bird-doggin' the missing Royster family. That true?" Natalie asked as they moved along. "They say the mayor's sick of Royster bracing him about it. He's thinking about starting his own task force."

Mickey stonefaced it. Kept her moving. "Even if that were true, that'd be an ongoing investigation, and as you know . . ."

The cop arrived. Mickey said, "Officer, would you please escort Miz Mendonhal back outside the yellow tape? She seems to have lost her way."

"Got lots of knowledgeable people saying Royster's missus got a raw deal in court. Saying the custody thing should have gone the other way . . ."

Mickey turned and walked away. "Nice seeing you Natalie," he said.

· · · · · · · ·

Despite all the anxiety, registering the girls at their respective schools had turned out to be a piece of cake. Both girls kept their new names straight. The paperwork passed muster. Cassie had managed to avoid flitting about the room, and other than eliciting a few sideways glances regarding her tooth fairy ensemble, she'd performed rather admirably. She'd signed on the dotted line and then walked each of them to take a peek at her new classroom, with Gus trailing along behind like a doting Uncle Fester.

On the way to their new apartment in Hardwig, they'd stopped at Burger King for lunch, so as far as the girls were concerned, everything was at least temporarily right with the world.

Grace watched through the doorway as Cassie and Eve helped the girls unpack. Maddy had magnanimously agreed to let her little sister have the larger of the two bedrooms. Tessa smiled for the first time in a week.

"So far so good," Gus rumbled.

"Went a whole lot better than I thought," Grace admitted.

"How long you been doin' this?" Gus asked.

"Doing what?"

"Helping out families."

Grace thought about it. "I guess I was sort of born into it."

"It's a good thing you do," Gus declared. "Anybody who'd abuse his own kids . . ."

"Hopefully, not anymore," Grace said, crossing her fingers.

"I had a little girl once," Gus said out of the blue. "Me and my wife Hannah."

"I didn't know you were married."

"No more," he said. "Losing Beth kinda tore us apart."

Grace wanted to inquire, but didn't want to intrude. Turned out, Gus had a story to tell, and he was going to tell it.

"She was four," he said. "Prettiest thing you ever saw. Looked just like her mama." He pointed at his own face. "Which was a good thing."

Grace laughed.

"Rode her tricycle out into the street. Got hit by a beer truck."

"I'm sorry," didn't seem to cover it.

"Tore me and Hannah apart," Gus said. "Just too much strain. It was like all of a sudden we didn't have nothing to say to one another. Like somehow we'd been talking to each other through Beth and when, all of a sudden she wasn't there . . ." He let it trail off.

"Like all the good stuff that had ever happened to us suddenly went away, and there wasn't anything left but the bad stuff, and both of us wishing it had been one of us under that truck instead of her, and feelin' guilty as hell that we were still alive."

Eve came rolling out of Maddy's bedroom, checking her watch. "We probably better be going," she said.

Grace threw an arm around Gus's massive shoulders and planted a kiss on his cheek. "Take good care of them," she said.

"Ain't nothing bad gonna happen to them as long as I'm standing up."

. . . .

Western Security occupied what had, at one time, been an old laundry and dye works on South Fulton Street. Dolan threw the Police sign on the dashboard, parked in front of a fire hydrant and got out. Here, away from the river, the breeze was little more than a whisper. Must have been ten degrees warmer too. Dolan started across the street.

He took his time. Having to break bad news was his least favorite part of the job. Always left him feeling as if he were at least partly responsible. Like an after-the-fact accessory to misery or something.

As Mickey mounted the curb, his phone began to ring. He winced slightly at the sight of Jen's face on the screen. On several occasions, he'd thought about deleting her picture. Even started to do it a couple of times, but somehow, he never could bring himself to push that final button. "Hey," he said.

"I did some asking around about the Roysters."

"And?"

"Rumor has it he's got a judge in his pocket."

"Nalbandian. Family Court."

"My source says she lives way beyond her means."

"Don't we all."

"My source also says that Royster's children testified in closed court that they'd been sexually abused by their father. Went into graphic detail, from what I'm told. So graphic the court stenographer had to be excused. Everybody figured it was a slam-dunk for the mother. But the judge said she thought they'd been coached and awarded custody back to the father."

"Probably explains why the files are permanently sealed," Mickey said.

"From what I hear, it was a very unpopular decision. Legally sketchy, at best. Caused a big ripple in the local legal community."

"Not enough to fix it," Mickey groused.

"The Women's Law Center appealed the decision."

"And?"

"The judge gave them a court date a year and a half down the line."

"Meanwhile the two girls . . ." Mickey let it trail off. Something about sexual abuse turned his blood to ice water.

"Yeah," Jen said.

"Thanks for the tip," Mickey said.

"I find out anything else, I'll give you a jingle."

"Yeah . . . thanks."

Mickey thumbed the ringer to "Off" before returning the phone to his pocket. This was going to be hard enough without being interrupted.

The young woman at the reception desk was round in all the right places. She looked up from her nails and smiled as Dolan stepped inside. "Welcome to Western Security," she said through perfect teeth.

The place looked like the bridge of the Starship Enterprise. All computer screens and colored, blinking lights. Dolan wondered if any of it was functional.

Mickey pulled out his police credential and flopped it open. "Detective Sergeant Michael Dolan," he said. "I need to speak with whoever's in charge."

"Why don't you let me see if perhaps I can—" she began.

Dolan cut her off. "What you can do is get me whoever's in charge. I'm here on police business."

She checked her watch. "Mr. Hellman's in a meeting, he'll be available at—"

Dolan cut her off again. "Mr. Hellman's first name is Charlie?"

"Well . . . yes . . . Charles," she stammered.

"You tell Charlie that Mickey Dolan is outside and needs to see him right now."

Charlie Hellman was a retired cop. Not a particularly good cop, but one with enough sense to know when it was time to hit the bricks. About the time the mayor appointed a civilian review board to investigate police corruption, Hellman pensioned out and segued into the private security business. One of those glossy firms whose primary function was to keep the poor from eating the rich. Did quite well for himself, from what Mickey had been told. Big house out on the lake. Boats. Kids back east in good schools. All the shit that didn't come with a cop's salary.

Mickey watched the syncopated sway as the receptionist put one foot directly in front of the other on her way to the door at the end of the hall. One of the shapely feet came off the floor as she leaned into the room and whispered something.

Charlie Hellman emerged from the doorway as if he'd been shot out of a cannon. He'd gained about thirty pounds since the last time Dolan saw him, but the extra cargo didn't seem to have slowed him down a bit.

"Mickey," he called. "Mickey . . . Mickey . . ." he chanted as he hustled in Dolan's direction. "You finally piss off the powers that be and get your ass canned?" he asked half jokingly. "'Cause we could use a guy like you around here. I've always got a place for a guy like you."

"Naw . . . I'm still pounding the pavement," Mickey said.

The receptionist had returned to her desk and was doing her best to appear busy. She was so bad at it that Mickey knew right away that Hellman must be banging her on the side. With those nails, she sure as hell didn't type.

Dolan leaned around Charlie Hellman. Spoke directly to the girl.

"Could you give us a few minutes?" he asked.

She didn't move, except to pout. Charlie Hellman cleared his throat.

"Why don't you take a little break Maggie," he wheedled. "Maybe get yourself one of those sweet rolls over at the deli."

"You know I can't be eating that crap," she whined. "I'm pre-diabetic."

She took her sweet-ass time leaving. Mickey waited till she'd sashayed out the door and closed it behind her.

"You better hope your old lady don't find out about her," Dolan said when she was gone. "Be a damn shame you have to give up half of all this."

"What . . . about what? Her? Oh . . . I . . . we don't . . ." He stopped talking. His eyes ran over Mickey's face like ants at a picnic. "Is it that fucking obvious?"

"Only to the sighted."

He started to say something, but Mickey cut him off.

"I'm here about the two guys you had watching the Yale Street Bridge."

Looked like he thought about playing dumb, but had a sudden spasm of lucidity.

"What'd you do, pinch them again?" he joked.

"No."

Suddenly, Hellman was cagey. Something about Mickey's demeanor put him on his guard. "What about them?" he asked.

"I've got some bad news for you."

"Such as?"

"Such as I regret to inform you that they're both deceased."

Hellman opened his mouth to speak, but nothing came out.

"This some kind of a joke?" he said finally.

"If there's any humor in there, I must be missing it."

Mickey watched as Hellman's florid face turned the color of oatmeal.

"Dead? No . . . you . . ."

"Somebody shot them in the head, Charlie. Right in the middle of Wentworth Street," Mickey said. "They were pronounced dead at the scene. The bodies are down at the ME's office. Next of kin can probably pick them up sometime late tomorrow. The car will be with the lab boys a while."

"You're shittin' me."

"Wish I were."

Hellman ran a hand over his suddenly sweaty head. "I've got to make some calls," he said after a moment. "I've got . . ."

Mickey reached out and put a hand on his arm. "First," he said, "I've got some questions I need answered."

"We never lost anybody," Hellman said. "I mean accidents . . . but . . ."

"What were they doing out there?"

Even in the face of disaster, Charlie wasn't giving anything away for free.

"I'm sure you understand," he started. "Most of what we do is strictly—"

Mickey headed him off at Confidentiality Pass: "I'm sure *you* understand, Charlie. There's no privilege for private dicks. You know that as well as I do."

Hellman shrugged and turned his head.

"This isn't going away, Charlie. You're not going to be able to take a dump around here until we know what was going on. Might as well tell me now, and then you can get on with what you need to get on with."

A young guy burst out into the hallway. His narrow, unlined face was a mask of concern. "Mr. Hellman?"

Charlie looked his way but didn't answer.

"I just got a call from—"

Hellman waved him off. "Robert," he said. "Get the Operations Team together in the conference room. I'll be right along."

"Is it true? Both of them?"

Hellman nodded. Robert began a wobbly backpedal. Half a minute passed before the corridor came to life. The sounds of tears and whispers, of clacking keyboards and shuffling feet suddenly became the background music.

"So?" Mickey said. "What were they doing out there?"

Hellman huffed a couple of big breaths. "First off—I guess you could say it was kind of a punishment detail. You know, for getting themselves busted yesterday."

"And?"

Hellman was inclined to get cagey again, but thought better of it.

"And—you know—we're on retainer. We need to be able to document our expenses. Our clients expect weekly reports."

Mickey barely contained a sneer. "Billable hours," he said. "You were creating some billable hours for the firm. Something you could charge Royster for."

"It's how the game is played," Charlie Hellman said with a semi-repentant shrug. "Surveillance pays ninety bucks an hour, per man."

"Why there? Why Wentworth Street?"

"The Pressman women," he said. "It's not just the Royster family investigation. This isn't the first time we've been retained to get a line on those Pressman women. Usually the daughter. She's supposed to have—"

"The whole Silver Angel thing," Dolan interrupted. "People wanting her to wake loved ones from comas."

He seemed surprised that Dolan knew. "Yeah," he mumbled. "The one in the wheelchair—"

"Eve."

"She's down there at that women's joint making trouble every day."

"So?"

"So, nobody ever sees her come or go. All of a sudden, in the morning, she's just there. Same with the blondie daughter. She appears someplace in the city and then just disappears." He snapped his fingers, as if to add "just like that."

"So you think they stay out on the island?"

"Possibly," was as far as Charlie was willing to go. "I mean, Mickey, we've put some serious man-hours into finding those two honeys. I don't want to brag but—you know, with the resources available to us, if you're out there, we're generally gonna find you pretty damn quick."

"If it's any consolation," Mickey said. "I can't find 'em either."

Hellman looked Mickey in the eye. "We were trying to get a line on the traffic pattern on and off the island. Hoping maybe we could get some idea how they get back and forth."

"Any luck?"

Hellman shook his head. "Garbage trucks, trade vehicles, delivery vans—damn near no private traffic. We've got bubkes." He made a pained face. "And Edwin Royster's not a patient guy, if you know what I mean."

"Nilsson thinks it's impossible. Says they wouldn't last five minutes."

Hellman shrugged again. "Unless Vince Keenan wanted 'em to."

"Why would Keenan give a shit about a fucked-up family and a couple of bigmouth women's libbers?"

"Got no idea," Hellman said.

Over his shoulder, Robert made his second appearance. "Sir," was all he said.

Hellman straightened his shoulders. "I gotta go," he said to Mickey.

"I think of anything else, I'll be back," Mickey said.

. · . · . · . ·

"I think we need to get something permanent for Cassie and the girls as soon as possible," Grace said as she slid the van into the right-hand lane. "That woman is a disaster waiting to happen. Given enough time, she could screw up just about anything."

"This one's hard," Eve said. "Edwin Royster's got so many connections and so much money, we can't do it the way we usually do." She waved an angry hand in the air. "It's a much more complex relocation than anything we've done before. Usually we provide a safe respite. These people need a whole new life."

Grace put on her signal and took the Terry Street exit.

"You know what Gus asked me?" Grace said, as she wheeled around the cloverleaf and rolled toward a line of cars at the stop sign at the bottom of the hill. A motorcycle cop had dismounted and was blocking the intersection. He held up a black-gloved hand. Grace braked to a halt.

"What did Gus ask?" Eve said.

"He asked me how long I'd been doing this."

"What did you say?"

"I said I felt like I was born doing it."

"In a way, you were."

"What way is that?"

"You were born into a male-dominated world. A world where domestic violence is the rule, rather than the exception."

Eve looked up and checked her daughter's eyes in the rearview mirror. Lately she didn't like what she saw. Grace had run aground on the shoals of doubt. Eve could feel it. Her voice rose. "Look at me," she said. "All the years I've been sitting in this damn chair because some idiot thought he had the right to hurt me anytime he wanted to, just because we were married."

When Grace didn't say anything, Eve went on. "If I can help it, this"—she gestured down at the wheelchair— "this kind of tragedy isn't going to happen to other women, just because some idiot thinks he owns them, and can do whatever he wants."

Three police motorcycles came inching past the intersection. Riding in formation, lights ablaze, sirens groaning. Then a couple of shiny black flower cars, filled to the brim with blossoms of remembrance. Then the hearse, all stolid and solemn. Then two long black limos, probably the immediate family. More motorcycles zipping in and out, riding shotgun alongside the procession. Half a dozen smaller, rented

Caddies, before the first of the regular cars began to cross in front of the windshield. The procession seemed to go on forever.

"We're fighting the good fight here, Grace," Eve tried.

"You're sure of that, are you?"

"As a matter of fact, I am."

"I mean—who died and left all this to us? How'd all this *good work* end up being *our* job?"

Eve heaved a sigh. "That's the same question the new cop asked me yesterday."

"Maybe because it's a damn good question."

"Maybe," was as far as Eve was willing to go.

"I mean, what happened to you—to *us*—was a tragedy, and somehow it turned into a career." She pointed out through the windshield. "You suppose that's how *he* got so many friends?"

"Who?"

"The dead guy." She waved an angry arm at the funeral parade. "I mean—look at this. There's hundreds of people following this guy's dead body down the road. It's like some remnant pagan ritual. All that's missing are the torches."

The cop got back on his motorcycle and started the engine.

"You figure the dearly departed is such a popular guy because he spent his life doing the right thing? Fighting the good fight?"

"What kind of a question is that?"

"You think—you know, when it's our turn—you think this many people are going to show up to send us off?"

"I have my doubts."

"Me too," Grace said.

"Sometimes there's a price to pay."

"So why is it that *we* always have to pick up the check?"

"The legal system is broken," Eve snapped. "The minute it involves lawyers, it's the old golden rule—whoever's got the most gold, rules."

"It works for some of the people, some of the time."

"That's not good enough for me, and I certainly hope it's still not good enough for you either."

Must have been over fifty cars altogether. Seemed like half an hour before the final pair of motorcycle cops brought up the rear. Their cop roared away from the intersection in hot pursuit of the procession. Grace sighed and dropped the van into drive.

"You don't seem quite yourself," Eve commented as they pulled out onto Terry Street, leaving the grief and the flashing lights behind them.

"Who else would I be?" Grace asked bitterly.

· · · · · · · ·

"I keep telling you Sergeant. We don't take people out there. Not ever. Last guy drove a fare onto the island got his head busted and his ride stolen. Also got his ass fired. It's against company policy to take fares to Coaltown."

His name was Ben Thayer. He was the general manager of The Sunshine Cab Company. Hadn't seen either his belt buckle or his hairline in a couple of years, but still looked like he could maybe go three rounds in a pinch.

Unlike the futuristic Western Security office, the place was The Wreck of the Hesperus. Cleaning lady must have died. Looked like it hadn't been so much as straightened up in the past twenty years or so.

Dolan again looked down at the photo on his cell phone screen. The blowup of the cab medallion had arrived in his inbox, along with a brief note saying they were going to have to stabilize the paper in the diary, whatever the hell that meant, before they could pull the pages apart. Be at least several days, they figured.

Sunshine Cab Company. Number 76354. Dolan turned the phone in Thayer's direction. "About seven thirty last night. Four hundred block of Harmon Road. Directly across the street from Memorial Hospital."

Thayer began to poke a thick finger at his computer. "Friggin' thing takes forever," he groused as the screen came to life.

"Remember when computers were supposed to save us time?" Mickey joked.

"Yeah—what happened to that shit, huh?" The computer screen blinked and rolled. "76354 was out with Barry last night."

Dolan pulled out his notebook. "Barry who?"

Thayer was shaking his head. "That's just what *we* call him. He's an Indian guy—you know, like a Bombay-type Indian. Real name's"— he squinted at the screen—"Bharat Agnihotri." He spelled it. Dolan wrote it down.

Thayer pointed at something on the screen. "Signed out for dinner, between seven thirty and eight."

"Where's he now?" Mickey asked.

"Drivers' meeting."

"Let's get him in here."

Thayer scowled. "Hey man," he said. "I don't want to make any trouble for the guy. He's a solid citizen. Wife and kids. Never misses a shift. Never short with the money. I should have six more like him."

"I'll be gentle," Mickey promised with a malicious grin.

Thayer looked grim as he pushed himself to his feet and disappeared out the office door. Three minutes later, he was back. Barry, as they called him, was a short, stocky Indian guy in his midforties, sporting a handlebar mustache and an orange turban.

He took a seat at the table, directly opposite Dolan.

Dolan slid the photograph across the table. "You seen this woman?" he asked.

Bharat Agnihotri studied the image like there was going to be a test. Mickey could tell right away: this was a guy with an eye for the ladies.

"Very beautiful," the cabbie said.

"Yeah," Mickey agreed. "Seen her before?"

G.M. Ford

"No," Mr. Agnihotri said. "Very exotic-looking. I surely would remember her."

"You're certain?" Mickey pressed.

Thayer was leaning against the corner of the room with his hairy arms folded over his chest. The look on his face said, "I told you so."

"Oh, I'm quite certain," Agnihotri said. "That's not a face a man could forget."

Dolan slid his phone over in front of the man. "Seven thirty-three last night. Harmon Road. By the hospital. That's your cab, isn't it?"

He looked over at Thayer. "What does my log say?" he asked.

"Log says you were signed out for dinner," Thayer said.

"They must have gotten the date wrong," Bharat Agnihotri suggested.

Dolan kept his mouth shut. Wanted to see what effect the silence had.

Bharat Agnihotri showed the ceiling his upturned palms. "I wish I could help you sir," he said. "But, as Mr. Thayer said . . ."

Mickey looked over at Thayer. "You suppose I could have a few minutes alone with Mr. Agnihotri?" he asked.

"He's on shift in ten minutes."

"We can do this here in your sandbox, or downtown in mine," Dolan said.

Thayer held his ground for a couple of beats and then grudgingly levered himself off the wall. "Okay, okay," he grumbled on his way out the door.

Mickey put his elbows on the table, and leaned toward Bharat Agnihotri.

"This is just between us," Mickey said in a low voice. "No reason why anybody but the two of us has to know what goes on here."

Bharat Agnihotri opened his mouth to protest, but Mickey didn't give him the chance. "Hard to say no to a good-looking woman," Mickey said.

"I don't understand," Agnihotri said. "I told you sir, I was—"

Mickey kept talking. "I know what you told me. And I know it was bullshit."

He held up a stiff, restraining hand. "I know you've got a family. I understand that you need to make a living. But if you want to keep this just between us, I'm going to need you to stop feeding me that line of crap."

Couldn't have been much over fifty degrees in the room, but Bharat Agnihotri was beginning to sweat. "Please sir . . ." he stammered.

"Where did you take her?"

"She gave me sixty dollars," he said. "I told her this was no place for a lady. I told her—"

"Where?" Mickey repeated, louder this time.

"She insisted."

"Last time I'm going to ask you," Mickey promised.

Bharat Agnihotri released a great breath of air. "Crow Street," he said. "The lady wanted to go to Crow Street."

. . . .

Indra brought the paperwork up close to her face and began to read aloud: "Diana Lee

Thurmond. Twenty-seven years old. Attacked in the street in West Hollywood, California, a little over a year ago, on her way home from church. Police listed it as a mugging."

"That's a long time to be gone," Grace said.

"You've had way longer," Indra said.

It was true. Sierra Abrams had been in a vegetative state for nearly four years when her aunt had contacted Grace. As was usually the case, the longer the patient had been non-responsive, the slower the recovery. People didn't just sit up in bed and ask for a cheeseburger. In most cases, they had to relearn how to do just about everything. Took years.

In Sierra's case, another two years before she was able to go home. Sometimes it didn't happen at all. Others initially made great strides and then gradually slipped back into unresponsiveness. Brain trauma care was, in the final offing, really little more than highly educated guesswork, a fact that the medical community was, not surprisingly, loathe to admit.

"Where's she on the Glasgow Scale?" Grace asked.

"Depends on who you ask," Indra said, shuffling through the pile of paperwork on the desk.

The Glasgow Coma Scale was a measurement device by which the severity of the head trauma and likelihood of recovery could be numerically represented. It measured the patient's eye-opening response, verbal response, and motor responses on a scale from one to six. Patients scoring between three and eight were more or less goners. Something like ninety percent of them either remained in a vegetative state or died. At the other end of the spectrum, those scoring between eleven and fifteen could generally be expected to at least partially recover some of their functions.

"When she was first tested in the ER, right after the injury," Indra began, "she tested nine."

"And then?"

"Apparently, she was never tested again."

"Maybe the original nine was optimistic," Grace suggested.

Indra shrugged. "People like to hope," she said.

Hope was the mind killer when it came to head trauma. Over the years Grace had been asked to help any number of poor souls whose physiological damage was so great as to preclude any hope of recovery whatsoever. People who'd left half their brains splattered on barroom floors or bridge abutments. But somebody loved them, so somebody held out hope. These days they could keep somebody artificially alive until they grew moss on their north side. Grace had long ago decided that her definition of being alive didn't include machines.

"Her vital signs and MRIs are good," Indra offered. She slid the data across the table to Grace. "No swelling. No visible trauma." She pulled another page out of the pile and pushed it over to Grace. "Her doctors expected her to come out of it before this."

It was true. Her original prognosis was a consensus expectation that she would regain consciousness and at least some of her functions. Hadn't happened though.

"I don't know," Grace said. "She's been away quite a while."

"Her husband offered—"

Grace cut her off. "I know. The money."

"We could do a great deal of—"

"You and my mother sound like a tape loop."

"The woman is in town," Indra said.

Grace frowned. "I thought she lived in Southern California."

"She does—she did. Her husband—"

"I didn't agree to anything," Grace said.

"I couldn't stop him. We talked once and then he calls and says she's in town. What was I supposed to do?"

"Even if I had agreed to try to help his wife . . ." Grace waved an angry hand.

Indra cleared her throat. "Your mother . . ."

"My mother what?"

"Your mother told Mr. Thurmond you'd meet with him tonight."

"You're kidding me."

As if on cue, Eve rolled herself into the room. Grace was about to light into her, but her anger was quickly dampened by the look on her mother's face. The face said something was seriously amiss.

"What?" she demanded.

"The TV," Eve stammered. "Joseph . . . You better come and see."

. . . .

Dolan's desk looked like one of Vince Keenan's garbage trucks had backed up to it and dumped its load. Dolan smirked at the unruly sight. Usually took him at least a week to trash his desk. This was a new record.

Nilsson's secretary Joan must have read his mind. "IT dropped all that stuff off this morning," she said. "Said it was per your request."

Mickey reached out to grab the top folder, but instead knocked the whole pile over. The folders fanned out over the desktop like oversized playing cards. Nearest one was labeled Merla Fritchey. Mickey remembered the name. One of the people Grace Pressman supposedly awakened from a coma. They all were. Jesus, Dolan thought. How do you collect this much information on this many people in less than forty-eight hours? Amazing.

He was still standing there contemplating the death of privacy when Joan put a hand on his shoulder. "His nibs wants a word with you," she said.

Dolan raised his eyes toward the C of D's office, but the blinds were closed.

"A word to the wise . . ." Joan made it a question.

"Sure."

"Mr. Royster's already called twice," Joan said, with a concerned grimace. "The mayor's been in touch also."

Mickey thanked her for the heads-up, took a long minute, pretending to organize the pile of files, and then started across the room.

He knocked. "Yeah," rumbled out from under the door. Mickey stepped inside.

The C of D got to his feet at the sight of Mickey. "Hope you got something," he said. "That son-of-a bitch Royster's been dogging my ass all day."

"Well . . ." Mickey began. "I know what the two vics were doing out there on Wentworth Street."

"Enlighten me."

Mickey did. Nilsson was shaking his head disgustedly halfway through.

"What a way to earn a living," he grumbled when Mickey finished talking. "Hundred eighty an hour to count garbage trucks."

"Times two," Mickey amended. "They had two more guys in a car watching the other bridge."

Nilsson let out a disgusted grunt. He pinned Mickey with a feral glare. "That it?" he asked. "'Cause I need some damn progress I can show to the mayor. Royster's got the mayor questioning your fitness for this investigation. Hizzonor thinks maybe I threw you into the fire a little too soon after your personal leave. We don't make some tangible progress here, they're talking about setting up a task force with the DA's office and Family Services and going looking for the family themselves."

"I've got one more thing," Mickey said.

Mickey told him about the purported altercation between Grace Pressman and Roberta Reeves at the hospital the previous afternoon. Told him how Joseph Reeves said it didn't go down the way his mother said it did. How Mickey thought it a bit odd that the kid sided with a relative stranger. "The hospital's outdoor CC cameras got a good image of the cab that picked up the Pressman woman," he added.

"And?"

"I spoke with the cab driver. He says he took her to Crow Street."

"Bullshit."

Mickey gave him a thumbnail sketch of his interview with Bharat Agnihotri.

"He was being straight with me Chief," Mickey said as he finished up. "I had him by the short hairs. He was in no position to lie."

Nilsson opened his mouth just as his phone began to buzz. "Probably the fucking mayor again," he grumbled as he picked it up. He listened briefly and then held the receiver out to Mickey Dolan. Mickey took it. The C of D pushed a button on the phone and sat down heavily in his chair.

"Dolan," he said into the mouthpiece.

"Sergeant Dolan?" A woman's voice, vaguely familiar and obviously distraught.

"Yes ma'am."

"This is Pamela Prentiss—from Memorial Hospital."

The name straightened Dolan's spine. The unflappable nurse sounded most definitely flapped. "You gave me your card," she added.

"I remember," Mickey said.

She was welling up; Mickey could hear it in her voice.

"This afternoon . . ." She swallowed and gathered herself. "Joseph Reeves took his own life," she blurted.

The news hit Mickey Dolan like a shovel to the head. "I'm sorry to hear that," he mumbled, after a moment.

"Hung himself in the shower. Used the cord from his bathrobe."

"Is the body still there?" Mickey asked.

"Yes. Funeral home's going to pick him up in an hour or so. They're burying him this afternoon, out at Holyrood."

"Isn't that kind of quick?" he asked. Dolan came from one of those Irish families where they liked to get hammered for a week or so before actually sticking anybody in the ground.

"Mrs. Reeves insisted. They had quite a scene about it."

"Well—thanks for the info," Dolan said.

"Pity," was her final word.

. · . · . · .

If, as tradition dictates, the dead deserve to be shown great respect, then somebody should have made sure the weatherman got the memo, because it was raining buckets as they slid Joseph Reeves's body down into the sodden ground. Another thirty minutes it would have qualified as a burial at sea.

The pounding rain was beginning to seep through the shoulders of Mickey's raincoat as he watched the proceedings. One too many trips through the washer, he figured. He was hunkered down about thirty yards from the hole in the ground, keeping a life-sized statue of Our Lady of Fatima between himself and the other mourners.

Despite the distance and the shimmering sheets of windblown rain, it would have been difficult to miss the cleft in those paying their respects.

To the left of the grave was the Paul Reeves contingent. Twelve, fifteen of them, men, women, and children, all looking devastated as they watched the last mortal remains of Joseph Reeves being lowered into the sloppy ground.

Behind the family, half a dozen young men and women, probably Joseph's classmates, stood sullen sentinel in the ever-worsening downpour.

On the other side of the grave, Roberta Reeves stood alone, her hands strangling a small black purse, her face impassive as she watched her only son disappear into the cold, cold ground. Behind her, out on the road, the limo driver who'd brought her to the cemetery had opted to watch the proceedings from the front seat. The flip-flop of the windshield wipers beat staccato rhythm to the service.

The preacher was offering his final blessing when Dolan first caught a flash of white up among the fir trees. He smiled to himself. God I love being right, he thought.

Mickey began to back up slowly, keeping the statue between himself and the hillside as he stepped out into the narrow road and disappeared into the thick shrubbery on the far side.

Unbelievably, the rain picked up a bit. Twenty-three soaking minutes seemed more like a month. Once the service had ended, everybody said hurried goodbyes, and then slogged en masse for the protection of their cars. Mrs. Reeves dispensed with the formalities altogether and headed directly over to the limo and got in. The big black car began to roll the moment she closed the door.

Took another twenty-five minutes for the cemetery workers to fill in the hole and then load the backhoe onto the truck. And then finally, after they drove off, all that remained was the wind in the trees and snare drum hissing of the rain.

She had quite a stride for a woman. Her long legs covered a lot of ground, without appearing to hurry. By the time the sound of the cemetery truck had been swallowed by the rush of water, she was standing alone by the graveside.

Dolan gave her a couple of minutes to pay her respects, and then stepped out of the shrubbery and began to walk slowly in her direction. The deluge absorbed the sounds of his movement. He was no more than ten feet from her when her senses picked up on his approach. She whirled around. Her eyes seemed to have no color.

Dolan stopped and held up his badge. "I've been looking for you," he said, closing the distance between them.

She didn't say anything. Just took him in with those big colorless eyes.

"Joseph's mother say I attacked her?" she asked finally.

Dolan nodded. "Yep," he said. "She sure did."

"I didn't."

"I know," Mickey said. "Joseph told me what happened."

Her eyes bypassed Mickey's face. Focused back over his shoulder. Dolan turned his head. Two men had seemingly appeared out of nowhere. They were standing hip to hip on the road, maybe twenty feet from him, their hands folded in front of themselves. The silver rain danced around their boots and dripped from the brims of their hats.

Dolan showed them his badge. "Detective Sergeant Michael Dolan," he announced. Neither of them exactly came down with the vapors.

"It's okay," Grace said to them. "I'll be along in a few minutes."

She began to slosh her way slowly around the grave, pulling Dolan along behind like a wagon. Mickey was transfixed, following along in her wake, without having willed himself to do so.

She was nearly translucent. Whiter than white. Paler than pale. She moved with an economy of motion that made her almost seem to float. Despite the brace of bruisers lurking behind him, Dolan couldn't pry his eyes from her. When he finally managed to check back over his shoulder, the muscle brothers were gone, melted into the mud, as if they'd never been there at all.

"He seemed like a nice young man," Dolan said, above the roar of the rain.

She looked directly at Mickey now, anger flooding her gin-colored eyes. "Joseph was scared to death is what he was." She clamped her mouth shut. The muscles along her jawline rippled.

She had her jeans tucked into a pair of green Hunter boots and was pretty much impervious to the muck. Dolan, on the other hand, was wearing dress shoes, and was sliding around in the slop like a drunken hockey player. He held his arms out for balance. Looked like he was playing airplane.

"Scared of what?" Mickey asked.

"I should have left him where he was. He was happy there."

"Where was that?"

"A place where everything is connected to everything else. Where it's all one piece and has no edges."

"I don't understand," Mickey said.

"No," she assured him, "you don't."

Mercifully, she stopped moving when she reached the head of the grave. Stood still and looked over at Dolan. "How'd you know I'd be here?"

"I'm a detective," Mickey said. Dolan inclined his head in the direction where the muscle brothers had been standing. She picked up on the implied question.

"My accounting firm," she said.

"Ah," Mickey said. "That's what I figured."

"So, if you're not here to arrest me, how come you're standing around in the pouring rain?"

He shrugged. "You're a hard person to find, Miss Pressman. What with the big rush to get the kid into the ground and all, I figured—you know, since it was the only chance anybody was going to get to say their good-byes to Joseph Reeves, it made sense that you might show up here."

She turned away. Dolan skated over closer to her. From the side it was difficult to tell whether the rain had found her face or if she was crying.

"Can you . . . ?" Dolan started.

She turned her liquid eyes his way.

"Can you—you know, the whole Silver Angel thing," Dolan said. "Can you really wake people from comas?"

"You wouldn't understand."

"Try me."

She thought it over and said, "Sometimes."

"Sometimes you can?"

"Yes," she said, and then looked down at the grave. An air of profound sadness settled around her shoulders like a shawl. "But . . ." she began and then stopped.

"But what?" Mickey pressed. "But you're beginning to have doubts about whether it's such a good idea?"

Her eyes lingered on him this time. Taking him in from head to toe.

"This isn't going away," Mickey said. "They're going to keep pressing on this Royster family thing until something cracks."

"I'm going now," she announced.

"You got any idea what's going on with Joseph's mother?" Mickey tried.

She pinned him with a glare. "Do you?" she demanded.

Dolan said he didn't have a clue.

She turned and walked away, short stepping it down the embankment, out onto level ground, headed for the dark stand of trees at the south end of the graveyard.

Dolan began to follow. Or, at least, that was the plan. The second his feet hit the incline, however, they went shooting out from beneath him. He landed flat on his back in the mud and then slowly slid to the bottom of the hill. As he collected his wits, he heard the sound of laughter.

He rolled over and pushed himself up to one knee. He looked down at the sodden mess he'd become. "Shit," he said out loud.

Halfway to his feet, he slipped again and went down heavily onto his chest.

By the time he'd steadied himself on his hands and knees, wiped the big glob of mud from his chin and crawled over to solid ground, Grace Pressman was little more than a shimmering shadow in the distance.

. . . .

"I met the new cop today," Grace said.

Eve looked up from her seat at the dining room table, genuinely surprised. "You're kidding. Where?"

"At Joseph's funeral."

"He came to the funeral?"

"Sort of," Grace hedged. "Actually, he was looking for me."

"Regarding the confrontation with Joseph's mother?"

Grace shook her head. "No," she said. "He'd already talked to Joseph. He knew what really happened."

"What did he want then?"

"He wanted to know if I could really wake people from comas."

"And you said?"

"I said I could do it sometimes."

"That all?"

Grace thought about it. "He also wanted to know how come Mrs. Reeves didn't seem glad to have her son back."

"What did you tell him?"

"I told him I didn't have a clue."

A quiet moment passed. Eve went back to pecking at her laptop. Grace wandered over to the window. Across the river, traffic was at a standstill. Taillights blinked on and off as a solid line of cars wound along the rain-slicked streets in super slow-mo.

"He's looking for Cassie and the kids."

"So he informed me," Eve said. "With Gus to watch over them, they should be alright, for the time being."

Grace pressed her nose against the glass. The warmth of her breath fogged up the area in front of her face. "Indra was right," she said after a minute.

"About what?" Eve asked, without looking up from the screen.

"He's very handsome," Grace said.

"And very dangerous," Eve added quickly. "Think of how many people have tried to find you over the past several years." She paused for effect. "Took him all of a day and a half." Eve sat back in her chair and wagged a stiff finger in Grace's direction. "We're going to have to be careful with Sergeant . . ."

"Dolan," Grace prompted. "Sergeant Michael Dolan."

"This isn't Officer Quinton. This is a whole different kettle of fish," Eve warned.

"Yes," Grace whispered. "It certainly is."

"You know who he used to be married to?" Eve asked.

"Who?"

"Jennifer McCade."

"From the marriage equality TV ads?"

"That's the one. She left him for Joanna Bloom."

"No kidding."

"Woman leaves you for another woman, must put one hell of a crimp in your . . ." Eve smiled like a wolf and let it go at that.

Grace made a dubious face. "He felt kind of lost, to me," she said.

· · · · · · · ·

Joan hid a grin behind a hand. "I'm not going to ask," she said.

"Thanks," Mickey said.

Every head in the building had turned as Mickey made his way upstairs to the C of D's office. Looked like he'd been dragged behind a tractor. His clothes, front and back, were completely coated with mud, but it was his shoes that had taken the worst of it. He'd done what he could to knock off the mud, but his feet were still little more than round globs of compacted soil.

"You got a bag?" Dolan asked Joan.

"What kind of bag?" she asked.

"You know, like a shopping bag." He held his mud-crusted hands a couple of feet apart. "Big enough for all this crap on my desk."

She rummaged around in her desk for a moment before producing a white plastic Macy's bag about two feet square. "That'd be great," Dolan said.

She passed it over, using only the very tips of her fingers.

She watched from a distance as Mickey swept all the files IT had put together on Grace Pressman's awakenings into the bag. All that remained was a purple Post-it note stuck to his desk lamp. "A Miss Prentiss from over at Memorial Hospital called asking about where to send that young man's effects."

Dolan thanked her and pocketed the Post-it.

"Just as well you get that stuff out of here," Joan said. "The painters are coming to paint the office tomorrow."

Mickey Dolan heaved a big sigh and threw it all into the Macy's bag with the rest of the stuff. "I'm going home to clean up a little," he deadpanned.

Joan laughed out loud. "You look like a breaded veal cutlet."

"Mickey," boomed from the far side of the room.

Marcus Nilsson was standing in his office doorway. He beckoned with his head. Mickey gathered up the Macy's bag and walked in that direction. The Chief disappeared inside. By the time Mickey closed the door behind himself, Nilsson was seated behind his desk with a silver remote control in his hand.

"No need to sit," he said with a smirk. "Thing's pretty short, anyway." He thumbed the remote. The wall-mounted TV rolled into a view of Wentworth Street. The gray Lexus was right where it had been earlier in the day.

"Watch this," Nilsson said.

The view was from the front of the car. Way up high. You could tell it was windy. Bits of paper and other trash swirled around like a swarm of bees, occasionally ticking against the closed-circuit camera's lens.

That's when the pair of black-clad figures entered the frame from the bottom. Nuns. Dominicans. Two of them. What with all the airborne crap floating around, it didn't seem the least bit unreasonable that they were protecting their faces with their sleeves.

Once they split up and headed for opposite sides of the car, things got hairy in a hurry. The driver rolled down his window at just about the same instant the other sister pushed a black long-barreled revolver out of the sleeve of her robe.

Sister Silencer shot the passenger through the window about two seconds before the other nun stuck her gun inside the car and took out the driver.

Nilsson stopped the tape. "Watch this," he said. "Passenger side." And then thumbed it on again. Dolan watched as the nun made the sign of the cross.

"Those are the best images we've got," Nilsson said. "We're sure not getting any kind of an ID out of that crap."

"Could be anybody," Dolan agreed.

"Didn't that—what's his name? The guy lost his front teeth down there on Tremont Street. Didn't he—"

"Yeah," Mickey said. "That Donnely Kimble character. Told me it was a couple of nuns who kicked his ass."

"Probably the Smith & Wesson sisters right there," Nilsson said.

"So why?" Mickey asked. "Why whack a couple of private peepers?"

"Maybe they saw something they shouldn't have."

"Like what?"

"Like maybe they were moving something on or off the island, and they didn't want those guys to see it go down."

"Could be," Mickey allowed.

Nilsson's eyes narrowed. "Like the Royster family, you're thinking."

"Social Services is stone convinced, Chief. As far as they're concerned, the Pressmans are running their own private little underground railroad."

"And *you* still think they're doing it from Coaltown."

"Sure would explain why nobody can ever put the finger on them. They hide them out on the island someplace. Then truck 'em off to wherever they're gonna go."

Nilsson shook his big head. "Couldn't any of that happen without Vince Keenan's approval," he said. "I know he's gone mostly legit, but legit or no legit, you go sneaking around on Vince Keenan's turf without his say-so and they'll find your ass floating out in the bay."

"And don't forget the cab driver," Mickey said. "He told me he left her on Crow Street. Says she just got out and walked off down the street."

Marcus Nilsson leaned back in his chair and laced his fingers over his vest. "Okay. Just for the sake of argument, let's assume you're right and they're using the island. What's in it for Vince? Charity's never been big with the Keenan family. If Vince's letting this go on, there must be something in it for him."

"No idea," Mickey Dolan said. "Howsabout maybe I ask him?"

Nilsson made a skeptical face. "And why would Vince Keenan talk to you?" he wanted to know.

"We went to grammar school together."

"And he's gonna spill his guts 'cause you two were locker buddies?"

"We weren't exactly tight, and he sure as hell isn't going to cough up anything incriminating, but we did *know* each other. He was on my Little League team when I was twelve. After that they sent him back East to private school—you know, but I saw him once in a while on vacations and stuff like that."

"And you think he'd be willing to have a chat with you."

"Can't hurt to try," Mickey said.

Marcus Nilsson thought it over. "Real polite," he cautioned. "Real polite." He waggled a finger. "Anything goes wrong, we'll both be flipping burgers."

"The very soul of discretion," Mickey assured him.

The C of D was working up to a full sneer when the phone rang. Nilsson raised his eyes. Joan was holding the receiver tight against her chest and frowning.

"It's the damn Mayor," Nilsson said.

. . · . · . .

"I can't do this," Grace said. "Not with everything that's happened."

"Mr. Thurmond came a long way to see you," Eve said.

"It's too soon," Grace said. "My mind hasn't made any sense of Joseph yet. You had no right to tell this Thurmond guy to come here."

"I was just trying to—"

"You were just trying to drum up a million bucks."

"The work we do—"

"We don't do the work! The work does us! Don't you get it? Look at us, for pity sake. A pair of biddies living on a godforsaken island with a bunch of criminals. Can't go anywhere without protection." She waved a disgusted hand in the air. "We don't have a life. All we have is the goddamn work. I feel like I've turned into an idea."

Eve opened her mouth to protest, but Grace raised her voice and kept talking. "There's got to be more to life than this. If this is all there is—"

Eve's phone began to blink. "Your ride is here," she said.

Grace swept her coffee cup from the counter. The cup seemed to hover in the air for a moment and then shattered all over the tile floor, sending pottery shards and coffee dregs fanning out over the stony surface.

"I'm not sure about any of this anymore Mom," she said. "I'm starting to feel like maybe—like maybe I'm doing more harm than good. I'm—" She stopped herself. "I'll go speak with Mr. Thurmond, but I'm not promising anybody anything."

Grace stepped over the mess on the floor and walked quickly from the room.

. . . .

The house was a light blue, mid-century modern and about the size of your average junior high school. Not a neighbor in sight. Maybe ten acres of lakefront for a yard. Mickey ran his hand through his hair and then rang the bell.

Strangest of strange: Vince's mother answered the door. He remembered her from Parents' Night at Saint Ignatius. She always showed up. Her old man Sean, the gangster, not so much.

She looked Mickey over like a lunch menu. "You're Emma Dolan's boy," she announced.

"Yes ma'am," he said.

"I understand you turned out to be a cop like your old man."

"Yes ma'am."

"What can we do for you?"

"I called Vince's office at Biosystems. They said he was working from home today. I'd like to have a word with him, if that's possible."

This was a woman who, back in the day, got a lot of practice dealing with cops. Mickey could feel it. Most people started to dissolve when pressured by serious authority figures. Not her. She just got harder and more likely to tell you to stick it.

"Is this an official visit?" she asked.

"No," Mickey said. "Just wanted to have a chat."

Her faced softened. "Michael, isn't it?"

"Yes ma'am."

She pulled the door open. "Well, come in Michael. I'll see what Vincent is doing."

She left Mickey Dolan standing on the polished marble floor and disappeared around the corner to the right. When the click of her stubby heels had faded to silence, Mickey looked around. "Open concept" was what they called it these days. Most of the house one big room, so everybody could stay connected during galas. Sort of the opposite of the way Mickey was raised, in those little houses, with those little, self-contained rooms—places for the women to go after dinner and talk about what assholes the men were, and down in the basement with the cigar guys, bending elbows and breaking wind.

Looked like the whole back wall of the house was a single sheet of tempered glass, looking out over the windswept lake, over toward the arched eyebrow of trees lining the far shore. Surveying the domain, Mickey mused.

And then Vince Keenan was standing beside him. Looking just like he'd always looked, except richer. Shirt and tie. No jacket. Nary a wrinkle in sight. He stuck out a hand. Mickey took it.

"Mickey," Vince said with a mini-grin. "Been a while."

"Too long," Mickey said.

"What brings you out to our humble abode?" he asked.

Mickey couldn't help himself. He laughed out loud.

"I remember when we both lived on Wallace Street," Mickey said, evoking images of their childhood roots among the littered streets south of downtown.

Vince laughed at the memory and took Mickey by the elbow.

"Come on back to my office," he said.

Mickey followed him down the long hall. Best word for Vince Keenan was *compact*. Tight and springy, but not very big. Didn't play sports or anything. The kind of kid who normally would have been a target for bullies back in school. Except he wasn't. Even the kids who didn't speak English knew who Sean Keenan was. Didn't want their parents finding them nailed to a garage door in Coaltown. No. Nobody fucked with Vince Keenan. Ever. Life was too precious for that.

The office was a space Mickey could relate to. Tucked in the middle of the house, with no view of the lake. Coffin-dark, with the kind of furniture you could put your feet up on. Just like home. Vince beckoned for him to sit wherever he wanted, and then stationed himself behind the big wooden desk.

"So?" he said.

"I got a problem I was hoping you could help me with."

"For old times' sake?"

"That's as good as anything, I suppose."

"What's your problem?"

"Edwin Royster."

Vince showed him the courtesy of not pretending he didn't know what Mickey was talking about. "Not sure I can help you there," he said with an unrepentant shrug. "That ship's already sailed."

Mickey ran it by him. Who was yelling at who, and why. Took a full five minutes. Vince listened politely. "Royster's a child-molesting piece of shit," he said when Mickey finished. "Only reason he's still on the street is because he owns a superior court judge."

"Nalbandian," Mickey offered.

Vince nodded. He leaned back in his chair. "You know, Mickey. Back when my old man was alive . . ." Mickey watched as Vince considered not speaking ill of the dead, but decided to make an exception in Sean Keenan's case. "If my old man so much as reached up to take off his hat, my mother would cover her head and hurry out of the room."

Mickey understood. Back in the day, a man had the right to rule his castle with an iron fist.

"He had big hands," Vince continued. "Liked to use them, too." He gave it a minute to sink in. Then finished with, "Nobody should have to live with that shit."

"No. They shouldn't," Mickey said.

"Those girls of his—the Royster girls . . ."

Mickey nodded.

"He makes them shower with him," Vince said.

Mickey nearly groaned out loud. "Don't tell me that shit, man," he muttered.

"You want to hear what he likes to do with his fingers?"

Mickey showed his hands in surrender.

"It's one of those places in life where if you *can* do something about it, you *do*."

Vince sat forward and placed his hands flat on the desk. Nice little visual metaphor for *I'm going to level with you*. "I've got nothing to hide, Mickey."

"So how come so many of your old man's leg-breakers are still around?"

"They're family, Mickey. What am I going to do? Put them out with the trash?" He made a face. "They keep things in order out on the island. Handle other odd jobs for me." He smiled. "Leg-breaking for my old man didn't come with a 401k plan."

"We've got a couple of dead PIs down at the morgue," Mickey said.

Vince spread his hands. "Shit happens," he said. "I'm guessing they were in the wrong place at the wrong time."

"Just the price of doing business?"

"I hear you're not married anymore," Vince said, before Mickey could pose another question.

"That's something of an understatement," Mickey replied.

"She was a nice girl," Vince reminisced.

"Too nice for me."

"Found her another nice girl."

Suddenly desperate to change the subject, Mickey asked, "So you—you never . . ."

"Got married?"

"Yeah."

"I'm gay." Vince said it like he was sharing the time of day.

"No shit" probably wasn't the PC response, but it fell out of Mickey's mouth anyway. He threw a furtive glance back at the office door. "Your mama . . ."

"Mama's always known," Vince said.

Mickey adopted his best conspiratorial tone. "But not your old man."

Vince chuckled. "I'm still here, aren't I?"

Mickey nodded. "Yeah—he was probably a bit old-school," he allowed.

"How you dealing with your wife leaving you for another woman?" Vince asked.

By this time, Mickey had worked up a thousand off-the-rack answers to the question, but for reasons unknown blurted out, "It's made a pretty good dent in me."

"Imagine it would," Vince said.

"Funny how some things sometimes turn out to be a lot more complicated than you ever imagined."

"How so?"

"Well," Mickey said, "you know, way back when, I was one of those schmucks who thought sex was really simple. You know—flange A seemed to fit nicely into grommet B, and, far as I was concerned, that's all there was to it. And now it turns out things aren't that simple at all—that some people *identify* as—as—something other than what their plumbing parts say they are. Or something like that." He had Vince's undivided attention. "Whole thing confuses the shit out of me, to tell you the truth," he admitted.

"Me too," Vince said.

Mickey suddenly felt like he was breathing mud. Like if he didn't get some fresh air he was going pass out. Vince picked up on it from across the room.

"Is there anything else?" he asked. "I've got some calls to make."

Mickey took the hint and got to his feet. "No," he said. "Thanks for your time. Nice seeing you again. It really was."

Vince agreed and then hopped to his feet. "Come on," he said. "I'll show you out."

Vince walked Mickey out onto the porch, then reached into his pants pocket and pulled out a business card. A phone number was handwritten on the back of the card. "That's my private number," he said. "You come up with something to keep those girls away from that asshole father of theirs—you know, something where I might be able to help—you be sure to let me know."

Mickey said he would.

"You'll say goodbye to your mom for me?" Mickey said.

"You bet."

. . . .

Harold Thurmond was a lot younger than Grace had expected. And Mexican. Grace's alarm bell began to clang. About the time they started talking a million bucks cash, you had to figure it was going to have to be somebody old enough to have come up with that much money. This was a scruffy fellow, hadn't seen thirty yet. His clothes, his shoes—none of it said he could come up with change for a twenty.

He was sitting at the round table over by the window, drinking a latte. His hair looked like he hadn't quite settled on an adult cut yet and was still getting by with the standard part-on-the-side grammar school special. He started to push himself to his feet when Grace walked in the door, but stopped midstoop when Grace shook her head and motioned him back down.

Instead of joining him at the table, Grace walked over to the service counter, took her time getting herself a glass of ice water, and then wandered over. She pulled out the other chair and sat down. He had big watery eyes like a cocker spaniel.

"Thanks for coming," he said.

"I need to be honest with you, Mr. Thurmond," Grace began.

His face sank. "Please," he said anyway.

"I'm sorry my mother brought you all the way here, but this isn't a good time for me." She looked around the inside of the coffee shop and then took a sip of her water. "I just lost somebody."

"Lost?" He looked confused. "You mean . . . you didn't . . . to . . ."

"He killed himself," crossed her lips before it ever crossed her mind.

"Oh . . . sorry."

Grace didn't say anything. Half a dozen high school kids burst through the doors, shattering the silence in a hormonal wave of shoves and shouts. Grace and Mr. Thurmond watched as the kids acted like kids, ordering coffee and pastries, bantering, permeating the place with their youthful energy. They were still roughhousing when they finally migrated back outside, leaving strained silence bobbing in their wake.

"Thurmond's not your name, is it?" Grace said.

He looked down at the table and shook his head. When he looked back up, he was beginning to get teary. "Please," he said in a low voice. "You got to help me. I got no place else to go. My wife . . . she's . . ."

"What's your name?" Grace asked.

"Roberto," he said.

"Roberto what?"

"Roberto Salazar."

"Was that your wife's medical chart that you sent?"

"Oh yeah," he said. "I just changed the name."

Grace spread her hands. "So why all the subterfuge?"

"The what?"

"Why all the lies and shit?"

"I thought . . . you know . . . if you saw a name like mine . . . you know . . . you'd think I was just was some LA beaner or something. I figured . . . you know . . ."

"I know," Grace said. "Money talks."

He got to his feet. "I'll go . . . I'm sorry I . . ."

"Sit down," Grace said. "I didn't say I wouldn't help you."

Roberto eased back into his chair.

"I just need you to understand something."

He ran a sleeve across his nose.

"Most people come into a situation like this thinking it's either black or white. That either I can help them or I can't. But that's not how it is. That's one of the things that I've learned over the past few years. Helping someone back to this world has a number of outcomes that I never envisioned when I started."

"Like what?"

"Like not everybody wants to come back."

This was the hard part for most people. This was the place where they were forced to come to grips with the fact that the stories they'd been telling themselves—stories about their own lives and how it was they'd come to find themselves at this juncture—that those precious, oft-told tales could well bear little or no resemblance to reality.

So she gave it a couple of seconds to sink in and then, out of kindness, took the edge off it for him. "Most people leave this plane of consciousness during periods of great stress and chaos. That's the last thing they remember. Being here with us . . . they associate it with pain and suffering, and would rather stay where they are. From what I've observed, and from what my mother's told me, it's a hard place to leave."

"But . . . you *can* bring them back."

She shook her head. "Actually . . . they bring themselves back. They make a decision that what they had before is better than what they have now, and decide to return."

"I'm sure my Sophia would like to return."

"Everyone always is," Grace said. "Everyone's sure their loved one is just itching to get back to this reality." She pinned his eyes with hers. Leaned forward. "Lots of the time . . . it's not true. They'd prefer to stay where they are. Turns out we don't know the people in our lives *nearly* as well as we'd like to think we do."

Roberto didn't say anything for a moment. "So what you're telling me is . . ."

"What I'm telling you is that it works both ways. Some people want to stay where they are. Others really want to return. They have things they feel they need to finish. Love affairs they want to play out. Children they want to see grow up. But mostly, they have things they feel they've left undone. Things they regret. Things they'd like to do over. Finding one of those is the key. Everybody has things they wish had turned out differently. If you can find one of those, they'll generally come with you."

"How can I . . ." he stammered.

"You can't," Grace snapped. "That's the rub. The world they come back to is not the one they remember." He had that "deer in the headlights" look, so Grace kept talking. "You know," she said. "Like when you have a long-term goal and you picture what it's going to be like when you get there . . . and you use that picture to keep you going, and then when you finally get there, it doesn't look a bit like you imagined it was going to."

He nodded. "Sophia was . . ."

"I've read her file," Grace said quickly. "There's not much there."

Grace looked out over his head. It had started to rain again. Shards of windblown water began to tick against the front window. "The young man who killed himself . . ." she began. "Joseph hadn't really made up his mind. I can feel that now. Part of him wanted to stay and part of him wanted to come back to us." She folded her arms across her chest.

"Things were messy. I had to hurry." Grace didn't like the sound of what she was saying, so she clamped her jaw shut and just sat there.

"I shouldn't have done that," she said finally. "I should have left him where he was, until he decided for himself."

"Can you help me?" Roberto asked.

"I can't promise that," Grace said. "Every case is different. On paper, your wife probably ought to have come around by now." Grace shrugged. "She hasn't. We have no idea why that's so, but it is."

"But you will try?"

Grace thought it over. She had every reason to turn him down, but, for some reason, felt her resolve beginning to wane. It was the money thing. Every time she thought about refusing, she saw her mother's face. Saw Eve sitting in her chair with that self-satisfied smirk. Heard her say it was money that made the world go round.

"I'll need to spend a couple hours alone with your wife. Uninterrupted hours. I'll know more after that."

He sat up straight in the seat. "Tell me what to do."

"Where is she now?" Grace asked.

He hesitated. "She's in private care," he said finally.

"Where?" Grace pressed.

"Here," he said. "In the city."

He looked down, and suddenly Grace was sure. She could feel it. He was scared of something. Or maybe someone. Whatever it was had put the fear of God in him. This was a man tiptoeing along the edge of terror. "Okay," she said.

He looked up. "So you'll . . . you'll still . . ."

"I'll try," she said.

"Thank you," he said, getting to his feet. "For my wife too. She'd want me to . . ."

Grace tapped the table. "Right here. Tomorrow night. Nine p.m."

. . : . : . .

Mickey Dolan stepped out into the living area and looked around. The place was a mess.

Somebody ought to clean this joint up, he thought, and laughed.

Over on the couch, the Macy's bag he'd gotten from Joan lay propped up against a pillow. His heart sank at the sight of that much paperwork. He immediately decided he was therefore entitled to consolation, so he padded into the kitchen, where he rummaged around until he found a clean glass in the cupboard, and poured himself four fingers of Bushmills Malt.

His old man had been strictly a Jameson's man, and never would have approved of dropping better than a C-note for a bottle of booze, but the way Mickey figured it, this was America; every generation had a right to do a little better than the generation before.

He swirled the dark liquid in the glass as he walked back over to the couch and sat down beside the Macy's bag. He could smell the twenty-one years the whiskey had spent lounging in bourbon barrels and sherry casks.

He poured some of the elixir into his mouth. Took his time swallowing, milking every bit of its smooth, old malt flavor, before letting it trickle slowly down his throat.

He turned on the lamp, set the whiskey glass on the end table, then pulled one of the files out of the bag and flipped it open.

The label said: Linda Karston. Several yellowing newspaper articles tumbled out onto the couch. Mickey picked up the nearest one. "It's a

Miracle!" read the headline. Seems a local woman, who'd been in a semi-vegetative state for the better part of a year and a half as a result of a New Year's Eve car accident, had suddenly and inexplicably awakened from her trauma-induced stupor.

Medical authorities, it seemed, were as surprised as everyone else. No one, regardless of medical specialty, could provide a plausible explanation for her sudden awakening, other than noting that sometimes, in cases such as this, miracles happened. Quite naturally, her family was overjoyed, and thanking any number of deities for their loved one's seemingly miraculous return.

Mickey went through the rest of the file, one page at a time. Birth certificate, high school diploma, the whole ball of wax. No mention of Grace Pressman or Silver Angels. Linda Karston had been thirty-one years old at the time of the accident. She'd worked at her family's dry cleaning establishment and been a member of the local Presbyterian church choir. The last thing in the file was a copy of her death certificate. According to the Macon County, Georgia, Coroner's Office, Linda died of ovarian cancer four years and four months after her miraculous awakening.

Mickey made a mental note to check for death certificates before taking on the rest of the folder. Way he figured it, the dead were likely to be of less assistance to his inquiry than were the living. No offense intended, of course.

Another sip. Another life. No death certificate. Andrew Wright suffered a massive stroke three days after his fiftieth birthday, and slipped into what his doctor described as an unresponsive state, where he remained for the next seventeen months.

And so on and so on. It was nearly 1:30 a.m. Mickey worked his way through five more files. All five people were still alive and leading presumably productive lives in various and sundry locations around the country. No mention whatsoever of Grace Pressman, or angels of any kind.

Until, of course, he came upon Eve Pressman's file. Five and a half years ago this month. The one that started it all. Mickey sorted through the collection of articles, laying them out on the coffee table in chronological order.

They'd gotten a lot of national press. The story had a certain Hollywood quality about it, so naturally the network vultures had gnawed the carcass right down to the bone . . . and then some.

Rehashed a lot of ancient history, way back to Eve's husband throwing her down a flight of concrete stairs. How she'd severed her spine on the way down and how her seventeen-year-old daughter Grace, enraged at the sight of her mother's broken body lying on the landing below, had hauled off and crushed hubby's head with an aluminum softball bat. Hit him six or eight times, according to the county medical examiner. Beat his head to mush, Mickey thought, if you read between the lines.

Then on to the triple tragedy of the Pressman family, with the stepfather dead, the mother lying paralyzed and comatose in a local hospital, and the beautiful young albino daughter convicted of aggravated assault and sentenced to eighteen months in the state juvenile facility in Farmington. A cautionary tale of a family torn apart by violence.

Fast forward . . . twenty-one months later. The stepfather's still dead. Mom's still comatose. The daughter has paid her debt to society and now spends her days sitting dutifully by her mother's bedside. Cue the violins . . . because, you see, the poor girl has no place else to go. The house has been repossessed by this time, and being a convicted felon has made getting a job nearly impossible, so the young Grace divides her time between foraging university libraries for medical books and sitting by her mother's bedside.

According to hospital staff, Grace sat there for better than six months reading to her comatose mother. Reading the newspaper. Reading every known medical text on the subject of head trauma. Telling family stories when her eyes got too tired to read. Often falling asleep in the chair, but never giving up.

And then, one rainy afternoon in April, the miracle happened. Eve Pressman opened her eyes, and Act III began. Eve recovers from the shoulders up. Donations start rolling in. Questioned by a *Denver Post* reporter, Eve swears she could hear what everybody in the room around her was saying the whole time she was in a coma, but was unable to respond in any meaningful way.

Eve claims that the physical sensation was akin to lying in a pool of warm oil, except that after a time, she began to experience the sensation of becoming diffuse, of "spreading out toward the edges." Of being everywhere at once, as it were. According to Eve, she eventually came to exist only as a series of waves that rolled gently though the warm oil, while still completely aware of what was going on and being said in the room.

Grace's responses to media questions regarding her part in the arousal were, from the outset, considerably more guarded. She simply described the process of arousing her mother as helping her mother "reestablish her boundaries."

But that was enough.

Eve and Grace were immediately inundated with hundreds of requests for help. Families from all over the country showed up on the Pressmans' doorstep, often with an ambulance in tow. Finding the attention disconcerting, they went underground.

Mickey padded back into the kitchen and poured himself another couple of fingers of whiskey. He thought about going to bed, but decided to go through another file or two before packing it in for the night.

Wasn't till he got to Shirley Bossier that things got interesting. All the newspaper articles celebrating Shirley's unexpected return to the land of the living were from the *Bergen Evening Record*, a paper, as Mickey recalled, native to Northern New Jersey.

All except one. That one came from something called *The Call*. That was it. Just *The Call*. No other information available. The article was entitled "Return from the Edge."

Whereas the *Bergen Evening Record*'s clippings had been pretty much the usual "we don't know how this happened, but we're extremely joyful about it" stuff, *The Call* took a different line of inquiry altogether.

There was no byline. Just an interview with Shirley's sister Adelle, who claimed that Shirley's sudden awakening had been neither a medical nor a religious miracle, but instead had been precipitated by a young woman whom she claimed to have found on the Internet. A young woman with what she called "unusual psychic gifts." According to Adelle, this woman, who by solemn agreement was to remain nameless, had singlehandedly coaxed her sister back to consciousness. In the last paragraph of the article, she referred to this woman as the Silver Angel.

Mickey Dolan was still pondering the turn of phrase when the phone began to ring. He checked the clock. One forty-seven in the morning. Calls this late were never good news. He couldn't remember the last time he'd gotten a call this late. Probably the last time somebody in the family had died. Mickey pushed the "Home" button on the phone. BLOCKED. He sighed as he thumbed the green button.

"Dolan," Mickey said into the phone.

"Mickey . . . it's Charlie Hellman. Hope it's not too late."

"Naw," Mickey lied. "What can I do for you, Charlie?"

"So I'm notifying next of kin, dealing with some very distraught people today—some of whom, I'd like to mention, are talking lawsuits—and, right in the middle of all this, who do you think gives me a jingle?"

"I'm too tired for guessing, Charlie," Mickey said.

"Edwin Royster." He gave it a second to sink in. "Calling to express his condolences. Right? I mean those poor guys *were* looking for his missing family, when this tragedy came down. That'd be the decent thing to do. Right?" Hellman didn't wait for an answer this time. "Fuck no! That son of a bitch tells me we're fired. Can you believe it? The nerve of that bastard. We been doing his dirty work for something like fifteen years. From back when he was just an ambulance chaser. We got two dead boys laying on slabs and that asshole's screaming at me and telling me how incompetent we are and that he's canning us, as of right now."

Mickey stood up and stretched. Hellman was big-time worked up over this. Sounded like he might rage all night, so Mickey tried to ease the conversation out the door. "I'm sorry about your guys, Charlie," he said. "Lives thrown away that young . . . those are really tough."

"You guys get anything?" he asked.

"You know I can't discuss the case with you, Charlie."

Pin-drop silence, and then, "What I called you for . . ." he began.

"Yeah?"

"So . . . you know, after Royster gets through giving us the boot, he tells me that the only way he's going to settle up for the account is if we hand over all of our files. Says he'll send somebody over to pick up the stuff later in the day."

"So?"

"So . . . about three o'clock these two gorillas show up asking for the Royster material. Wasn't such a damn sad day, I'd have laughed in their friggin' faces. You know, buzz-cuts and aviator shades, fatigue pants tucked into big shiny boots. The whole black ops starter kit. Like something off TV. I make them sign for the files. Just so there won't be any bullshit about it later."

Dolan failed to stifle a yawn. "Sorry," he said. "It's been a long day."

"Worst of my life," Hellman admitted.

"I'm still pounding on some paperwork," Mickey said finally. "Thanks for the . . ."

"They signed for the stuff as employees of Relentless Technology."

Mickey sat down hard in his chair. "Why would Royster hire those guys?" he asked, as much to himself as to Charlie. Relentless provided security services for the rich and famous. Drivers, bodyguards, armed courier escorts, that sort of thing. Serious muscle work. Sort of like a private secret service. Very expensive, very hush-hush.

On at least two occasions that Mickey knew of, their agents had been involved in shootouts, in the course of which people had been killed. The interesting thing was that, on both occasions, after highly publicized court cases, and much to the chagrin of local law enforcement officials, the Relentless agents had walked away scot-free. Hiring Relentless was akin to having your own private army.

"Thought you'd like to know," Charlie Hellman said. "Body bags seem to follow those guys around."

"Thanks Charlie," Mickey said, before breaking the connection. He took a short pull on the Bushmills and picked up the files. Wasn't till he put the files in chronological order that the obvious emerged. Eve was first. That much he was sure of. Who was second was a question not so easily answered. By the time he figured it out, the answer was staring him in the face.

Turned out that the second person Grace Pressman had supposedly brought around was a young woman named Mary Rose Ross from Denver, Colorado. Like Eve, she had been a victim of an act of domestic violence. Blunt force trauma. She'd lain in a coma for just over a year, until that fateful day when she'd suddenly opened her eyes.

Apparently, she'd staged a complete recovery. As of this year, she was remarried, the mother of two girls, and teaching the fifth grade in Golden, Colorado. What got Mickey's attention was a Boulder County, Colorado, "Missing Persons" report stapled to the back of the file.

The MP's name was Daniel Wayne Ross. Twenty-six years old at the time of his disappearance. Mary Rose's abusive husband. Out on bail. Charged with everything from felonious assault to attempted murder. He'd walked out of the Denver County Courthouse just before noon on April thirteenth, and had never been seen again.

At the bottom of the clippings file, somebody named Carla Henderson had written a follow-up article, several months after Daniel's disappearance. A "how the family was coping" kind of thing. Daniel's father Ruben had some questions regarding who had put up Daniel's bail. His family claimed it wasn't any of them, 'cause even if they'd wanted to, which they didn't, they could never have come up with the two hundred thou in cash it took to spring young Daniel. The bail bonding agent was no help. He'd received the bail order along with a cashier's check drawn on a bank in rural Montana. The check was good, which was as far as his interest extended. No help there.

Mickey thumbed through the missing persons information. For some reason they'd included a copy of the Rosses' marriage license. Daniel Wayne Ross had been joined in holy matrimony to . . . Mickey laughed out loud.

3

"Come on girls, we don't want to be late on our first day, do we?" Cassie Royster trilled.

Maddy appeared in her bedroom doorway, looking a bit short of thrilled. "I'm ready," she said, as she threw her backpack over her right shoulder and stared resignedly out the window.

"Tessa," Cassie crooned into the hall. No answer.

The front door opened and Gus came into the room. "Morning," he said.

"Good morning Gus," Cassie sang.

Gus kept his face together, trying not to let on how much he hated it when she got all singsongy like that. It was like spending the day with Mary Poppins. He kept expecting a talking umbrella or some such crap.

"'It's a beautiful day in the neighborhood,'" she sang, slightly off-key.

Gus figured somewhere in the universe, Fred Rogers had to be contemplating suicide. "We ready?" he asked, with as much faux glow as he could muster.

"I'm going to take the girls to school by myself this morning," Cassie announced.

"I don't know . . ." Gus began. "Maybe we should . . ."

"You're not always going to be here, Gus. Sooner or later, I'm going to have to get used to doing it by myself, and now is as good a time as any."

Gus kept his mouth shut. When she got like this, nothing short of sedating her was going to make any difference. If he pushed it, they'd end up having a dustup folks could hear out on the sidewalk.

"Tessa," she called again. Again nothing.

Gus stepped around Cassie and walked down the short hall to Tessa's room. He knocked softly on the door, and then, not getting an answer, eased it open.

Tessa was sitting on the edge of her bed, looking as if the end of the world was surely nigh. She looked up at Gus.

"I don't want to go to that school," she said with all the conviction she could muster.

Gus went down to one knee. He put a big hand on her shoulder. "It'll be alright," he said softly. "It's just for a little while. Next thing you know, you'll have a new life going on and you won't remember any of this stuff at all." He nudged her with his elbow. "I'm betting there's a boyfriend in your future," he said.

She almost smiled. "You think?" she asked.

"You'll be beating 'em off with a stick," he assured her.

He picked up her backpack. "Come on," he coaxed. "School menu says they got whole-grain muffins and milk for breakfast." He held out his hand. Tessa took it, and together they walked out into the living room.

"Ready to go," Gus announced.

Cassie held out her hand. Gus dropped the rental car keys into her palm.

"Careful," he said.

"Of course," Cassie chirped.

Gus followed them out the front door. He watched as Cassie got everybody strapped into the rental car. Tessa waved at him through the window. He waved back, with a great deal more enthusiasm than he felt.

· · · · · · ·

"You look like death warmed over," Marcus Nilsson growled.

Mickey started to speak, but found himself unable to stifle a massive yawn. He held up an apologetic finger as he unsuccessfully tried to gain control of his quivering lower jaw. "Up late," he eventually chattered out.

Since he'd gone back to batching it, Mickey had become quite the nine-to-fiver. Mr. Salaryman. Up at the same time every day. Dead-ass asleep by ten thirty every night. He hadn't fallen asleep until sometime after 2:00 a.m. last evening. Felt like he hadn't slept in a week, and, if Nilsson was to be believed, he looked it.

"Tell me you came up with something," the Chief said. "The mayor's so far up my ass I can smell Vitalis."

Mickey shrugged. "I've got a pretty good idea why we can't find any of the people we're looking for. Problem is, it's not gonna do us one damn bit of good."

"Try me."

Mickey laid several documents on Nilsson's desk, then stepped aside and watched him scan the paperwork. Outside in the office area, the city painters had arrived and were in the process of draping everything with canvas. He watched as Joan waved them this way and that. Not there! Over there.

"No shit," Nilsson said after a few minutes. "The Ross woman is Vince Keenan's little sister."

"And apparently, Grace Pressman woke her up from a coma."

Nilsson shot Mickey a disgusted look.

Mickey shrugged. "It's the only explanation, sir. Either she woke the girl up or she managed to convince Keenan and his unconscious sister that she did, when she really didn't. And I don't about you Chief, but to me that first one sounds a whole lot more likely than the second."

Nilsson frowned but didn't say anything, so Mickey kept talking. "By the time she woke up Mary Ross, the heat was already on. Social Services and DA's investigators from about five different jurisdictions were looking hard at the Women's Transitional Center. I don't have the exact figures, but by that time they were suspected of having intervened in about half a dozen civil custody cases. Hospitals had restraining orders taken out against Grace.

"At the same time, every grieving relative of a comatose patient was after Grace to perform a miracle. Collectively, they were under a hell of a lot of pressure. They needed someplace they could operate without being harassed. So . . . about the time Vince Keenan is saying thank you for bringing back his little sister, he has a magnanimous moment and asks if there's anything he can do to help the cause. They tell him their problems, and he offers the island as a sanctuary."

"And you're telling me this honey can do what medical science can't?"

Mickey waggled a hand. "Sometimes. From what I've read, she gets a pretty wide range of results. Everything from complete recoveries to people who wake up for a few days and then die, because their systems have so atrophied that they won't function on their own. It's not magic or anything like that. She spent six months reading to her mother . . . every available piece of information about comas. She knows enough about it to know what kind of head trauma offers some hope of waking up and which don't. They're pretty good at picking the ones they might be able to help."

"I don't see how this gets us any closer to finding the Royster family."

"Unless you want to get a warrant to go looking for them," Mickey pointed out.

Nilsson snorted. "Fat chance. Christ. Even if we had probable cause . . . which we don't . . ." He threw a hand in the air. "Even if they were shooting at us from the rooftops. You're talking about our county's largest employer. Biggest taxpayer. Biggest charitable donor. Whole bunch of shit nobody's gonna want to lay a glove on. Short of catching them building nuclear weapons, nobody's kicking in that door anytime soon."

Nilsson sat back in his chair. The air in the office was suddenly thick and heavy. The Chief sighed, and set his palms on the desk. "I think we better keep this to ourselves for the time being, Mickey. Social Services gets wind of this, they're gonna want me to send an armored division out there, and I don't want to even think about the fallout from that."

"Charlie Hellman called me last night. Says Royster fired Western Security and hired Relentless Technology as his new goon squad."

"Yeah . . . I was wondering about that. I got an email from the DA. Relentless had their lawyers down at the DA's office first thing this morning. Courtesy call, they said. Just letting us know they were in town."

"Nice of them."

"I was touched," Nilsson sneered.

. · . · . · .

Maddy unbuckled her seat belt and leaned toward her mother. "I'm okay," she said.

"I don't need you to walk me in." She kissed Cassie on the cheek, popped the door and got out. Maddy waved good-bye to her sister. Tessa just frowned.

"Have a good day," Cassie trilled, as the door swung shut.

Cassie looked back over her shoulder at her youngest daughter. "Why don't you ride up front with me?" she suggested cheerily.

Tessa shook her head.

"Come on sweetie," Cassie said. "It's going to be okay."

"No it's not," the little girl said. "It's not going to be alright at all."

Cassie started the car. As they pulled away from the curb, she said, "We'll go to Burger King on the way home. How's that?"

"I don't want to go to Burger King," Tessa said. "I want to go to school with Maddy."

"Oh honey . . ."

Tessa began to cry.

Cassie pulled over and stopped the car. "Don't cry, honey," she said. Tessa sniffled and turned her face away.

"Be a big girl now," Cassie gently chided.

Cassie felt the familiar tide of defeat begin to rise in her chest. Something that went all the way back to her beginnings. Maybe even before that, like it was part of the box she came in. In rare moments of clarity, Cassie recognized that moments such as this were the places where things always fell apart for her. That the choices made at this particular intersection had shaped her life in ways she was unable to acknowledge.

When things went wrong, as they always did, she told herself that they happened because she was too nice to people, and just a bit too pure inside for a malevolent planet such as this one.

Occasionally, the truth flitted by like an arrow in the night, and she saw, for the briefest instant, that what she really was was scared. That all the disasters in her life were a result of her terror of conflict. That she made the same mistakes over and over because, as far as she was concerned, anything was better than the grating of souls.

Cassie heaved a massive sigh, and for the umpteenth time in her life, stepped off into the void. "Okay," she said. "You're right, honey. A girl ought to be able to go to school with her sister. We'll march in there and tell them there's been a change of plans."

. . . .

Travis . . . that's all it said. Little white patch on his black Relentless Technology shirt. First name . . . last name . . . who knew? Just Travis.

"We'd need a court order," Travis said. "And the only way that can happen is if everyone involved is appointed an officer of the court."

Royster didn't want to hear it. "We ought to be able to claim exigent circumstances," he countered. "Who knows what kind of danger my daughters might be in? That woman's a danger to herself and others. If that's not exigent circumstances, I don't know what is."

Travis was shaking his head. "Without a gun pointed directly at somebody's head, exigent just doesn't float with the courts. The fact that you think there *might* be danger isn't sufficient reason. Legal precedent is quite clear on that matter."

"Don't tell me what you can't do," Royster bellowed. He banged the desk with his hand. "I want action. I want my daughters returned to me, and I want that woman and anyone who helped her prosecuted to the full extent of the law." He threw an angry hand into the air. "If I wanted excuses I'd still have those other assholes working for me."

"As I said . . . for that sort of an operation, we'd need to be appointed officers of the court. A judge can—"

Royster cut him off. "Any judge?"

"Yes."

"I'll make some calls," Royster said.

"We picked something up from the Women's Transition Center website. Looks like the daughter may have another coma patient on the line." Travis shuffled a few papers.

"Harold Thurmond," he read. "Some kind of Hollywood hotshot, with a twenty-seven-year-old daughter in a vegetative state. Says here he rented an air ambulance and flew her up from Southern California, day before yesterday. Supposedly cost him a cool seventy grand. She's at The Colton Clinic, room thirty-seven. I figure we'll put a team on the father, see if that doesn't give us a line on Grace Pressman. He's staying at the downtown Hyatt. He ought to be easy to pick up there."

Someone rapped three times on the office door.

"Yeah," Royster grunted.

The door eased open. A young man poked his head tentatively into the breach.

"Mr. Travis," he said.

"What is it Mark?" Before he could answer, Travis gestured toward the desk and said, "Mark, this is Mr. Royster. Mr. Royster, this is Mark Loftus, one of our IT specialists."

Edwin Royster didn't bother to look up. The kid began to stammer.

"I . . . um, we got a rather strange flag on our school registration sweep, a little while ago. I'm not sure—"

"Is there some point to this?" Royster demanded.

"Well sir, we've been scanning for two girls, aged six and eight, looking for new registrations. And . . . this morning . . . we got a flag from someplace called Hardwig Elementary School. Had a new girl aged eight register this morning. Teresa Miles. The interesting part is that she'd just registered at Garden City Elementary School, in Garden County, the day before."

"Which means what?" Royster snapped.

"Those two schools are less than a mile apart. Different school districts, different counties, but real close to each other. If you were looking to hide . . ."

Royster stopped fiddling with his Rolodex and looked up.

Travis rose from his chair. "I'll get an intervention team on the way," he said.

. . . .

Quiet day at Memorial Hospital. Mickey Dolan stepped off the elevator to an empty hallway. The sound of his shoes on the polished floor accompanied him down to the nurses' station, where he found Nurse

Prentiss standing over a sink in the far corner of the room, wearing a pair of elbow-high rubber gloves.

"Ah," Pamela Prentiss said, upon catching sight of him, "the long arm of the law hath returned."

"Beware the nurse in rubber gloves," Mickey intoned.

She crooked an eyebrow. "You'd love every minute of it," she promised with an unabashed twinkle in her eye.

Mickey laughed out loud. "I came to get Joseph's things," he said.

"And here I was thinking you just couldn't stay away from me."

"That too," Mickey said.

"Hang on while I clean up a little, and I'll find them for you."

She disappeared, leaving Dolan to settle into the dull underlying hospital hum. The PA system whispered for Dr. Brennan to please call obstetrics, and then went silent.

Prentiss returned swinging an oversized Ziploc bag between her thumb and forefinger. "We wanted to return these," she said. "Turns out we don't have a current address on file for the father, and neither of them is answering the phone numbers we have on them."

"Nasty divorce," Mickey said. "People tend to change everything."

"I remember it well," Prentiss said.

"Yeah . . . me too."

Mickey reached out and took the bag. Looked like the shirt Joseph had been wearing the day Mickey had visited his room. Pair of slippers. Pair of jeans. Socks. Some loose change and a white smartphone nestled down at the bottom.

"The dad's staying over at the Vantage," Mickey said. "I'll take them over."

"What do you do when you're not saving the world?" she asked.

"Not a hell of a lot," Mickey said.

"You ought to stop by some afternoon. I get off at six."

Would have been better if he'd just smiled and thanked her for her offer, but something inside of him was closer to the edge than Mickey had realized.

"I seem to be a little off my feed lately," he blurted. "Lately, I divide the world into two kinds of women. Those to whom I'd be prepared to be an enormous disappointment, and those to whom I wouldn't."

"Like you said, Sergeant, nasty divorces tend to change everything." She reached out and bopped him gently on the arm. "You regain your sanity, you be sure to look me up," she said with a grin, and then turned and strode off down the hall.

"Nurse Prentiss," Mickey called after her.

She turned his way. Put her hands on her hips, and tilted her head.

"Thanks," he said. "I needed that."

. . . .

The Hotel Vantage was a remnant of an earlier age, the age of railroad tycoons, robber barons, and dry goods fortunes. The expansive mahogany-paneled lobby was a hodgepodge of leather settees, ancient Morris chairs, and overgrown potted plants. Looked like Teddy Roosevelt might pop out from behind a palmetto at any moment.

"He was such a happy little kid," Paul Reeves was saying. "Always had a smile on his face. Just like . . . you know . . . like a regular kid."

Grace leaned over the tea table and put a comforting hand on his arm.

"I'm so sorry," she said. "I feel like . . ."

"No, no," Paul Reeves began. "You did everything you could."

"I feel like I should have left him where he was. It was all just so chaotic."

"It wasn't your fault. There was . . ." He seemed to be sorting it out for the first time. "Back when he had his accident . . . right before that . . . something had changed about him." He brought his hands to his head and began to massage his temples. "I know adolescents are . . . you know . . . they're moody. But it was more than that. He just didn't seem to be happy anymore. Always looked uncomfortable. He and Roberta were always at each other's throats. It was . . ." He stopped himself.

"She certainly didn't seem overjoyed to have him back."

The minute it was out of her mouth, she regretted saying something so thoughtless and unkind. Bad enough he'd lost his son without her bringing up that creepy crap.

Mr. Reeves sighed and then rolled his eyes. "Truth is . . . I don't think Roberta was cut out for parenthood. It was always very hard for her. Not something she took to naturally. She always struggled."

Grace knew the feeling. She'd long ago been forced to face the fact that her mother was about as nurturing as a saw blade. For Eve, it was always about the cause. Always the need to recoup what had been lost at the hands of the system. At the hands of men. The single-minded pursuit of her personal version of justice. Or at least that's what she'd say if you pressed her about it. Personally, Grace had always had her doubts.

Always seemed to her something internal drove Eve. Something left undone, rather than something done *to* her. As if she had a wound that was never going to heal, so she figured she might as well pick at the scab for a living.

Paul Reeves hailed an old-fashioned black-tied, white-shirted waiter, who wandered over and refreshed both cups of coffee. When he'd gone, Grace leaned closer to Reeves.

"You know that diary you gave me?"

He nodded as he sipped coffee.

"You know what happened to it?" Grace asked.

He shook his head, swallowed, and set the cup back in the saucer.

"I thought you had it," he said.

"I left it for Joseph. Seemed like it was important to him."

Paul Reeves sat back in the chair. His lips were as thin as a pencil line.

"Guess he won't be needing it now," he said.

. . . .

Cassie was making an effort not to be a total embarrassment. She'd parked the car half a block west of the Hardwig Elementary School, gotten out and waited on the grass for the bell to ring. Hard as she tried, however, it seemed as if some unknown form of gravity kept pulling her, one step at a time, closer to the school's front door.

By the time the dismissal bell split the air, she was very nearly trampled by the wave of children bursting out into the hazy afternoon sunshine.

Maddy and Tessa were near the back of the pack. Tessa was talking excitedly to an Asian girl in a black jumper and red knee socks as they came out the door. Maddy lagged behind, looking serious.

Cassie forced herself to stand still and let the girls come to her, rather than rushing in like a mother hen. That always embarrassed Maddy no end. As the girls approached, she turned and started down the sidewalk toward the car. She held out her hands. Tessa took one. Maddy ignored her.

"How was your day?" she asked Tessa.

"It was fun," Tessa said. "I met a girl named—"

"Mama," Maddy interrupted.

Cassie held out a restraining hand. "What was the girl's name?" she asked Tessa.

"Mama," Maddy said again, tugging on Cassie's dress.

Cassie stopped walking and turned toward Maddy. She took a deep breath and collected her temper. It was bad enough that she was going to have to tell Gus what she'd done. What she didn't need at that moment was Maddy driving her crazy.

"Maddy," she said. "I was talking to your sister."

Maddy pointed to the corner where Fulton Avenue ran into Van Dyke Boulevard.

"Why is that man taking pictures of us?" she asked.

Cassie felt herself go numb. Told herself that no matter what, she shouldn't look in that direction, and then, as she knew she would, did precisely that. A dark blue Mercedes was sitting along the curb with the motor running. The passenger had climbed out of the car and was using the roof to steady his hands as he aimed a big black telephoto lens in their direction. She imagined the machine-gun snapping of the lens and suddenly felt sick to her stomach. Her throat was frozen. Her tongue seemed as big as her shoe. With great difficulty, she swallowed twice and croaked out, "Come on girls . . . hurry."

. · . · . · .

Mickey Dolan flopped his detective's ID onto the Hotel Vantage's registration desk. The clerk was a sexy young woman about twenty-five. Bettie Page clone, poured into a black pencil skirt. Black bangs and lipstick red enough to glow in the dark.

"Would you check and see if Paul Reeves is in for me?" he asked.

The clerk's deep brown eyes went back and forth between the gold shield and Dolan's face a couple of times before she used a long, fiery fingernail to point at something back over Mickey's shoulder.

Mickey craned his neck and swept his eyes slowly over the area. His gaze came to a slot-machine stop on the back of Grace Pressman's head. She was seated at a low table, drinking coffee with a middle-aged man, who, Mickey figured, had to be Paul Reeves.

He quickly turned back to the desk clerk. Held his forefinger up to his lips, in the classic "be quiet" pose. She nodded her deep understanding.

Mickey kept his face averted as he made his way to the far corner of the lobby and found a chair. He had to lean to his right in order to see Grace, which meant she didn't have a direct line of sight to him either. No way she could walk out any of the exits without Dolan seeing.

Some childish remnant in him wanted to make the wiseguy move.

Wanted to amble over and hand Joseph's personal effects to his father, throw Grace's amazed face a curt nod, and then sphinx it out the door, to everyone's full-blown amazement. But no. That wouldn't do.

The *woman nobody could find* was right here in front of him, for the second time in as many days. Last time had been a complete bust. He'd ended up looking like a horse's ass. Not looking for an encore, Mickey grabbed a copy of *Architectural Digest*, slid down into the chair and waited, all hunched and furtive, like a spy in one of those old black-and-white movies.

· · · · · · · ·

The rental car's rear bumper rocked the car behind it hard enough to set off the alarm. Cassie was still arm-wrestling with the transmission lever when the other car's security system began to whoop-whoop, splitting the afternoon air with its urgent electronic whoops, the sound of which scattered Cassie Royster's attention span like wind-blown leaves.

Confused, Cassie threw a quick glance over her left shoulder. Over to the arching row of sycamores where the Mercedes was parked. The windows were tinted so dark she could barely make out their silhouettes. The photographer had gotten back into the car. The whooping alarm poked at her consciousness like an accusing finger. She felt her lip begin to quiver. A sob tried to leap from her throat, but she forced herself to swallow it, then dropped the car into drive and hand-over-handed the steering wheel to the left for all she was worth.

They clipped the copper-colored Honda on the way out of the parking space, but she didn't have time to think about it, because, as they angled out onto North Walnut Street, they were greeted by the screech of sliding tires, followed by the folded metal thump of two modern motor vehicles mashing into one another. Something tinkled to the ground. Two horns began to blow harmony. Cassie put the pedal to the metal. The car roared and leaped forward.

"Mama!" Tessa screeched at a pitch available only to girls her age.

"Hang on," Cassie grunted, as they fishtailed out into the street.

The car roared up Walnut Street. Cassie began to chant, "Oh my God . . . Oh my God," as they rocketed away from the school.

When she threw her eyes up to the mirror, the Mercedes was right behind, not making the slightest attempt to be furtive. She began to sob and claw at her purse.

"Get my phone," Cassie shouted.

Maddy pulled the purse into her lap and began to feel around inside for the phone. The tires screeched as Cassie slid the car around the corner, carrying way too much speed for the car's suspension. Halfway through the turn, the car began to drift, banging up over the curb, onto the manicured grass strip that separated the sidewalk from the street. A rooster tail of topsoil and powdered turf rose into the air like a flora fountain as they peeled through the landscaping at warp speed.

In the second before the car thought about rolling over onto its side, the tires somehow found purchase, sending them drifting back toward the street, banging down over the curb with a sickening crunch. The car wiggled its ass twice, righted itself, and then went roaring off down the street.

"Call Gus," Cassie yelled to Maddy, who was still trying to locate the phone with one hand while white-knuckling the door handle with the other. "Come on, honey," Cassie pleaded.

And then Maddy had the phone in her hand. She pushed the "Home" button, scrolled down to the Gs and aimed her finger at "Gus," in the split second before her mother locked up the brakes to keep from rear-ending a mail truck.

Tessa began to whimper.

. · . · . · .

"I'm going to take some time off," Paul Reeves said. "I've got a bunch of vacation days coming to me. I'm going somewhere warm for a while and see if I can't make some sense of all this."

"Sounds good to me," Grace agreed. "Theoretically, anyway. The sun and I don't get along so well. Five minutes outside and I look like a lobster."

"Joseph's like that," he said. "Really fair. We had to be careful . . ." He let it trickle off into silence. "Was like that," he corrected.

In the front pocket of her jeans, Grace's phone began to buzz against her thigh. Six vibrations and then it stopped. Then started again and buzzed another half a dozen times, before she fished it out and checked the caller ID. UNKNOWN.

She held up the phone and looked over at Paul Reeves. Talking on the phone in front of other people had always seemed rude to her, as if the person you were with just wasn't enough for you. "Do you mind?" she asked.

"No . . . go ahead," he replied.

She brought the phone to her ear.

"Gus . . . Gus . . ." someone was shouting. Grace recognized the voice.

"Maddy?" she said.

"Gus . . . Gus you gotta . . . Mom . . . she . . ."

"Is that you, Maddy? It's Grace. What's wrong?"

"There's men!" she screamed. "Behind us in a car."

Grace turned her back on her companion and made an effort to keep her voice down. "Where's Gus?" she asked, as calmly as she was able.

"Home . . . back home," Maddy said. In the background, Grace could hear the rush of the wind, the roar of the engine, and Tessa's high-pitched keening floating over the top of it all, like the plaintive whine of a steel guitar.

Grace got to her feet. "Get home to Gus," she said. "Can you do that Maddy? Can you get home to Gus?"

"Mama's lost," Maddy said. "We're in some neighborhood."

"Help her," Grace implored. "Use the MapQuest app. Remember?"

"I remember," Maddy said after a moment.

"Help her get back to Gus."

"Okay . . ." took a while.

"Tell your mom I'm on the way. I'll be there as soon as I can. Get home to Gus. Do you hear me, Maddy? Get home to Gus." The connection went dead.

Grace looked down at Paul Reeves. His face was slack with concern.

"Emergency," she said, with an apologetic shrug. "Sorry, but I've got to go."

He held up a "don't worry about it" hand. "Thanks for all your efforts," he said.

Grace pocketed the phone and began to sprint across the hotel lobby toward the front door.

. ˙ . ˙ . ˙ .

"I need this," Edwin Royster said. "Just make it happen, Dorothy."

"You're not listening to me, Edwin," she said. "This isn't something I can do for you. If I could, I would."

"All you're doing is providing the means for your own judicial order to be carried out. That's it. Nothing more."

"Enforcement is outside my purview," she said.

"Well, move it inside. Put it in your front parlor. I really don't care," Edwin Royster said. "I expect this done first thing tomorrow morning."

Three knocks rattled the office door. Royster pushed the phone hard against his chest and frowned. The door opened and Travis came hustling into the room, closing the door behind himself. He was carrying an open laptop.

"What . . . are you blind? I'm on the phone here," Royster growled. He pointed at the door. "Why don't you—"

"You're going to want to see this," Travis insisted as he set the laptop on Royster's desk and pushed two buttons.

Edwin Royster began to nod at the screen, as if he'd expected this all along. He brought the smothered phone back up to his ear. "I've got to go," he said into the mouthpiece. "First thing tomorrow morning," he repeated, before breaking the connection.

"Hardwig?" he asked Travis, without pulling his eyes from the screen.

"Ten minutes ago."

Royster pointed at the slide show on the screen. "Those are my daughters."

The image changed. His face went dark. He pointed again. "That dumb-ass bitch," he spat. "I want that sow arrested."

"Team one has them under surveillance. I've got a backup unit on the way to Hardwig. As soon as they're in place, we'll move in."

. ˙. ˙. ˙. ˙.

As they raced up the street, the neighborhood kaleidoscoped past the car windows, the colors flashing past Maddy's eyes like a ribbon in the wind.

She popped her seatbelt and crawled up onto her knees, so she could see over the top of the seat. The Mercedes was still half a block behind. She peered down at the phone in her hand. Keyed in the address of their new apartment, realized she'd put it in the wrong place, and started over.

"Stop," Maddy said. "Stop the car, Mama."

Cassie Royster was glassy-eyed and breathing like a distance runner. "I don't know where we are," she admitted to nobody in particular.

"Pull over Mama. Please," Maddy said.

Cassie threw her eyes at the mirror. "I can't," she said. "They're back there. If I stop . . ." She banged the steering wheel with her hand, "Oh God . . . what did I do?"

"Just for a second, Mama. Just stop for a second."

Cassie Royster hesitated, and then reluctantly began to slow the car. She licked her lips and checked the mirror again. The Mercedes was still maintaining its distance, so she began to feather the brakes, pulled over to the curb and stopped.

She checked the mirror again. Same deal. They were sitting half a block behind, nestled up against the curb, waiting to see what she did next. Maddy was squinting down into her hand, inputting something into the phone.

"Are they going to take us back to Daddy?" Tessa wanted to know.

"No honey . . . it's going to be alright," Cassie said.

Maddy looked to her right. The number on the nearest house read 2611. She keyed it into the phone. The green street sign up at the corner said they were sitting on Muldowny Road. 2611 Muldowny Road.

She keyed that in too, and then pushed the button. A map appeared on the screen. Maddy turned the map in a circle, trying to orient herself. She looked out through the windshield, then back into her palm again. And then again.

"Go up two blocks," she announced finally, "and then turn left. Teller Street," she said. "Turn left at Teller Street."

. · . · . · .

Mickey Dolan let the FedEx truck pass him. He was four cars behind the white van Grace Pressman was driving and figured the FedEx truck might provide a little bit of highway camouflage.

They were rolling north on 156, doing about five miles an hour over the speed limit, in the right-hand lane. Whatever had been said during that phone call Grace had fielded back at the hotel . . . whatever it was had galvanized her. She hadn't looked back once.

Dolan could feel her impatience from a quarter mile behind. The way she darted in and out of lanes, looking for an angle and then, after a moment, seemed to regain her composure, as the surge of anxiety abated. This was a woman in a big hurry to get where she was going.

He reached for the radio. His inner cop was telling him to call Dispatch. Tell them where he was and what he was doing. That was the protocol. Everybody knew where everybody else was one hundred percent of the time. That's how it worked.

His fingers seemed to have a life of their own, though. They stopped just short of making contact with the microphone. He frowned as he eased his hand back on the steering wheel, telling himself that since he didn't actually know where he was going, maybe he ought to wait. At least, that's what he told himself. Himself didn't believe a word of it, but what the hell?

Five miles later, Grace's turn signal began to blink yellow, announcing her intention to take the Hardwig-Allensville exit, about half a mile up. Dolan lifted his foot from the gas. The car began to slow. The cars behind began to swoop around.

Mickey felt a familiar pang begin to build in his chest. He knew this exit all too well. If you drove west for long enough, past the winter orchards, with their frosty fields and shuttered fruit stands, in one end of Hardwig and out the other, and then kept on going for another fifteen miles or so, the land began to rise around you like dark fingers, until you eventually found yourself in the thick virgin forests of the Spellman Wilderness Area. Right where Jen's great-great-grandfather had built that cabin along the banks of Bluewater Creek. Where . . . He lost the thread on purpose. No point going there.

Dolan hung back. The exit was a long, sweeping arc, with a stop sign at the bottom. No place to hide if he got too close, so he backed off the gas and let the van sweep down onto the plain all by itself. Left to Allensville. Right to Hardwig.

Right toward Hardwig. "Had to be," he groused to himself, as he watched the white van get smaller and smaller as Grace accelerated down the two-lane blacktop.

. . . .

The rental car bumped up into the driveway and lurched to a stop, rocking back and forth on its springs like a hobbyhorse.

Cassie rummaged in her purse, trying to locate the house keys. She cast a furtive glance back the way they'd come. Her breath caught in her throat. A block to the west, the blue Mercedes had settled ominously against the curb. As she watched, the passenger-side window slid halfway down. The long lens appeared. She looked away. Her rummaging became more frenzied.

"Come on, Mama," Maddy pleaded.

"Oh God," Cassie groaned.

And then she had the keys. Holding them in her hand like a trophy. She grabbed the door handle and started to get out of the car, but the seat belt had other ideas, jerking her to a halt, forcing her to reach back across the seat to get at the release button.

As Cassie struggled out onto the driveway and slammed the car door, the girls made a mad dash for the front porch. Maddy was wide-eyed at the blue Mercedes across the street. Tessa was jumping up and down as she waited for her mother to stop fumbling with the keys and get the door open.

Took three tries with the key and twenty seconds before the three of them disappeared inside. Cassie leaned against the inside of the door and threw all the bolts. She looked over at Maddy, who was peeping between the drapes.

"Maddy. Go get Gus," she panted.

Tessa made a beeline for her room and slammed the door. Maddy ran toward the back of the house. That's how they'd practiced it. Going from one duplex to another via the back doors, so nobody could see they knew each other. Gus said it was best that way. Safer for all of them.

Gus had a white towel slung over one shoulder. His face was covered with soap.

Maddy blurted it out. "Mama put Tessa in the same school as me," she said. "There's men in a car. Across the street."

Gus was a quick study. "Go back and look after your mom and sister, Maddy. Tell everybody to pack. I'll be over in a second." He left the door wide open as he turned away and disappeared into the duplex's dark interior.

· · · · · · · ·

Seven miles from Hardwig. Mickey was so focused on Grace, a half mile in front of him, that when a huge Chevy SUV with blackout windows blew past him at better than a hundred miles an hour, he nearly jumped out of the seat. His unmarked cruiser rocked from the buffeting of the air as the Chevy powered by. Even the cattle in the nearby fields seemed vaguely startled by the hullabaloo.

Mickey gave it a little more gas and watched as it took them all of ten seconds to do the same thing to Grace and then disappear over the horizon in a cloud of dust.

And so it was with no small amusement when, five miles later, just as they were coming into the city limits of Hardwig, he saw the blackout Chevy SUV pulled over to the side of the road. Just like Charlie Hellman had described, the GI Joe driver was dressed in fatigues, sporting a butch haircut and aviator sunglasses as he stood by the side of the car, right next to the glowering state trooper. It was all Dolan could do to keep from honking the horn on the way by.

He had barely finished chortling ten minutes later when Grace pulled the white van to the curb, got out, and ran up onto the front porch of what looked to be a duplex on West Collier Street.

Dolan backed the cruiser into an unnamed side street, rolled down the window and waited. Protocol said he should inform local law enforcement that he was conducting an operation within the Hardwig cops' jurisdiction, but he'd decided to wait until he had something more concrete.

. . . .

Gus eyeballed out through a crack in the blinds. The blue Mercedes was right where it had been for the past fifteen minutes. He turned back to the room. Both girls had hurriedly packed their belongings and stood like refugees, awaiting further orders.

After a moment, Cassie staggered out of her bedroom dragging an overflowing suitcase along the floor, with a pair of garment bags thrown heavily over her shoulder. Her face was a mask of defeat. "I'm sorry, Gus," she said for what seemed like the two thousandth time, "I wanted Tessa to . . . I wanted the girls—"

"We'll talk about it later," Gus said, cutting her off.

A loud knocking rattled the front door. Gus brought his hand to his hip and turned to Cassie and the girls. "Leave the bags. Go into the kitchen," he said in a low voice. He took a step and then turned back. "Go!" he mouthed. They went.

Gus had to bend at the waist in order to look out through the peephole in the door.

He looked once, and then again, just to make sure, before flipping the bolts and pulling open the door.

Grace stepped into the room. The girls had been peeking out from the kitchen. They called her name in unison and rushed to her side. She threw a protective arm around each of them. She looked to Gus.

"We got company," he said. He walked over and used his big fingers to part a couple of slats on the venetian blinds. Grace let go of the girls and took a peek.

"The blue Mercedes back at the corner," Gus said. "Followed them from the school this afternoon."

"How'd that happen?" Grace asked.

Gus rolled his eyes, and Grace immediately knew the answer. Had to be Cassie.

"Just trying to please," Gus said disgustedly.

"So what now?" she asked.

"This place is blown," he said. "We gotta go."

"Where?"

He shrugged. "Someplace else. We'll figure it out as we go along."

Grace nodded. "What can I do?" she asked.

He told her. Grace told him she understood.

She followed him to the back door, standing with a hand on either side of the doorway as Gus trotted the length of the yard, nimbly hopped over the neighbor's decorative garden fence, and disappeared from view.

She grabbed both girls' suitcases and carried them over to the door.

"Everybody be ready to move," she said.

. · . · . · . .

Mickey Dolan thought, for a moment, he'd witnessed a murder. His attention was focused on the West Collier Street duplex, when a flash of movement in his peripheral vision pulled his eyes to the left. Took his brain a few seconds to sort it all out.

Enormous guy in a black suit walking up the street. Blue Mercedes parked at the corner. As he approached the car from the rear, Black Suit stepped up onto the grass. Guy looked to be eight feet tall. From the inside pocket of his coat, he pulled the unmistakable silhouette of a revolver. He held it down against the side of his leg as he approached the Mercedes.

Mickey was just reaching for the door handle when a flat report echoed around the neighborhood. Looked like the Hulk maybe shot the guy in the passenger seat. Mickey jumped out of the cruiser and reached for his weapon. But no. The Mercedes was leaning now. The guy had shot out the right front tire, and then kept on walking, like nothing had happened.

Mickey slid his weapon back into the holster and waited. The passenger was out of the car now. Incredulous. Inspecting the damage. He shouted after the big guy, but the Hulk kept on walking. Not about to be ignored, the passenger broke into a run, sprinting over the corner of somebody's lawn, in hot pursuit of the tire shooter.

Might have been better if he hadn't gotten there at all. About the time he put an angry hand on the black suit jacket, the big guy pirouetted, drew back an arm, and punched him full in the face . . . hard enough to stop a train. Two blocks away, Mickey Dolan winced at the sound of meat on meat.

The passenger's feet flew from beneath him. He landed flat on his back and lay there twitching, one arm spastically flailing in the wind, like a signal flag.

The big guy kept walking, out of the grass now, crossing the pavement toward the duplex. As the black suit got closer, Mickey recognized him. That was Gus Bradley. One of Sean Keenan's old-time head busters. A collection specialist, as Mickey recalled. Word on the street said Gus had killed three guys with his bare hands. Last Mickey recalled, Bradley had drawn a double nickel for felonious assault and, as a guy with a sheet as long as his arm, had been invited to spend a decade or so as a guest of the state. Probably explained why Mickey hadn't seen him in so long.

Mickey watched as Gus raised his arm as if to beckon somebody forward. Five seconds passed before the front door of the duplex flew open. Dolan sunk down in the driver's seat. He was peeping over the dashboard when two little girls with backpacks came bursting out of the duplex on the right. Grace Pressman, carrying a pair of suitcases, was a foot and a half behind them as they hustled down the sidewalk and threw everything into the white van.

What had to be Cassie Royster was bringing up the rear. Looked like she was walking in mud as she dragged a distended suitcase and a couple of bags across the asphalt.

The driver was out of the Mercedes now, kneeling in the grass, trying to revive his friend, with little result. Gus grabbed Cassie Royster around the waist and hauled her, suitcases, garment bags and all, over to the van and dropped her unceremoniously inside the sliding door. He slid it shut with a bang and then trotted around to the other side and levered himself into the driver's seat.

. . . .

No telling what the Mercedes driver was thinking. Stress does strange things to people. He still hadn't managed to coax his punched-out partner into the sitting position when Gus Bradley started the van, dropped it into gear, and began rolling up West Collier Street at a stately Sunday afternoon pace.

Must have been frustration rearing its ugly head. All driverman knew was the people he was charged with keeping an eye on were about to drive off up the street and, what with an unconscious partner, and a shot-out front tire, he couldn't do a damn thing about it. Probably explains why he, all of a sudden, came down with such a serious case of the stupids.

What good he thought jumping in front of a moving motor vehicle was going to do was anybody's guess, but as the van closed in, he scrambled to his feet and stepped out into the street. Standing on the white line, waving his arms above his head, X-ing them back and forth as if to signal *Stop*.

Apparently, Gus Bradley hadn't quite mastered the *Stop* semaphore. Mickey had just nosed the cruiser all the way out onto West Collier Street when Gus ran the crazy bastard over like a speed bump. Mickey watched in horror as the driver disappeared beneath the van.

What saved the guy's life was that the van had a lot of clearance under it. That and the fact that Gus hit him dead center, making it so none of the tires rolled directly over his body, thus sparing him a bunch of pulverized bones and several months in traction.

Other than the initial force of the impact, which, from Mickey's vantage point, looked painful as hell, most of the damage to the guy happened when some article of his clothing caught on the undercarriage of the van and he was dragged for half a block.

By the time he disengaged and slid out from under the back bumper, he'd collected a world-class case of road rash.

He was up on his skinned knees, trying to figure out what the hell had just happened, when Mickey swerved the cruiser around him. He'd left most of his forehead somewhere on the asphalt. A welling patch the size of a clutch purse now seeped crimson from the area his furrowed brow had formerly called home.

Mickey was watching the van roll off down the street and weighing his options when the screech of tires hijacked his attention. He looked back over his shoulder. A cloud of tire smoke rose into the air. Apparently, the cavalry had arrived.

The blackout Chevy SUV skidded to a stop next to the Mercedes. Another GI Joe type jumped from the rear passenger seat and double-timed it over to his fallen buddies.

The guy Gus Bradley had coldcocked was still down on the grass. The new hero stopped there first, throwing an arm under the guy's shoulders and sitting him up. He said something. Tried again. To zero avail. The guy was in never-never land. Hero laid his colleague back on the grass and made a dash for the street, where the driver of the Mercedes was still down on his hands and knees dripping blood all over the pavement.

Mickey watched the van pulling away with one eye and the scene in the street with the other. Hero offered a handkerchief. Driver took it. Pressed it to his brow. Hero said something. Got small shake of the head. He pulled a handheld radio out of his pants pocket and brought it up to his face. Whatever message he sent roiling out over the airwaves seemed to have the desired effect, because whoever was driving the SUV immediately lit up the tires, sending another oily cloud of smoke spiraling skyward, as the vehicle fishtailed around the corner and screamed up West Collier in hot pursuit of the van.

Mickey Dolan stayed put, turning his face the other way as the SUV roared by. Then he counted a slow three, dropped the cruiser into gear, and joined the parade.

He sorted through the situation in his mind. First off, he was way out of his jurisdiction, and should have called the locals the minute he got into town. That was going to be a number-one Grade-A pain in the ass. Secondly, assuming the guys in the black SUV worked for Relentless Technology, which seemed like a pretty good bet, then figuring out who had the right to do what, to whom, and how was about to get real confusing.

Cassie Royster was in contempt of court, which, as far as the law was concerned, was a serious game-changer. She was a custodial fugitive, in violation of a court order. Once a legal decision had been reached, and you decided you were going to ignore it, a number of your constitutional rights immediately flew south for the winter. You became one of *them* instead of one of *us*.

Because the cops possessed neither the manpower nor the inclination to chase petty criminals over hill and dale, they outsourced the chore to the private sector. Meaning sleazeball bail agents and sketchy skip-tracers suddenly had the legal right to place you under citizen's arrest, which, Mickey figured, might be about where things stood at the moment. All in all, not a good situation.

The van made a leisurely right turn at Burger King. The black SUV was two blocks back and closing fast. Mickey put his foot in it. The cruiser got up and went.

By the time Mickey made it to the intersection, the SUV had closed the distance on the van. The skin on Mickey Dolan's face began to tighten and tingle, like that electric buzz you feel in the air right before the onset of a thunderstorm.

Looked like Gus was trying to get everybody back to the friendly confines of the city. At least, that's the direction he was rolling in when the SUV swerved over into the oncoming lane, roared past him, and then swerved back over in front of the van.

Mickey held his breath.

And then . . . bang, red lights and a cloud of smoke as the SUV locked up the brakes. Mickey gritted his teeth and waited for the impact. Only the perfect combination of luck and skill could have prevented the van from plowing into the back of the SUV.

But somehow Gus pulled it off. The van dodged left and then, a second later, veered hard to the right, shuddering out onto the shoulder, spewing dust and gravel into the air as it scrambled for traction.

Just as it seemed the van would surely lose control and slide down into the ditch, Gus somehow willed it back onto the pavement, and went screaming off down the road.

Not for long, though. The SUV had lost the element of surprise, and, from the look of it, Gus Bradley was a quick thinker. He knew there was no way he could hope to outrun these guys. Another mile and they'd be out in the cow pastures, where there weren't any witnesses and these guys could get all medieval on them. Whatever was going to happen needed to happen right now.

. · . · . · . · .

The speedometer read eighty-seven. Gus was driving down the middle of the road, not leaving enough room on either side for the Chevy to creep up on him, sweeping back into the right-hand lane only when oncoming eighteen-wheelers threatened to vaporize all of them.

"Okay," Gus said. "This is what we're gonna do."

Dead silence. Cassie and the girls huddled together in the rear seat, looking like they were carved out of stone. Grace was hanging on to the overhead handle for all she was worth, but seemed to be in touch with her faculties, so Gus directed himself to her. "We're comin' up on the mall here in a second. When I pull this thing to a stop, you guys open the slider and run like hell for the mall. Leave all the stuff here and just run. Lose yourselves in the crowd. Lock yourselves in the ladies' room. Do whatever you gotta."

"What are you going to do?" Grace wanted to know.

"I'm gonna buy you a little time," Gus said.

Grace opened her mouth just at the moment when Gus crimped the steering wheel hard right, sending the van into a full drift as it slid toward the entrance to the mall parking lot. The van screeched in a half circle before coming to rest, facing back the way they'd come. Gus grabbed the shift lever and backed the van across the entrance. "Go," he yelled, when they finally bounced to a stop.

. . . .

Mickey Dolan skidded to a stop on the shoulder. A hundred feet ahead, up at the entrance to the mall, Gus had the van wedged between the Northhaven Mall sign and the rough stone pillar intended to give the entrance a touch of baronial splendor. Gus was leaning against the driver's door as the Relentless Technology SUV jerked to a stop.

A pair of GI Joe clones hopped out of the car, the driver pulling a bright yellow Taser from the pocket of his jacket and the other one flicking a telescoping metal baton out to its full length. They spread out to the edges of the pavement and began to inch toward Gus. Apparently, the beat-down that Gus had perpetrated on their colleagues had made quite an impression. These guys were taking no chances.

The driver pointed the Taser at Gus and, without further ado, pulled the trigger. Mickey watched the pair of silver wires float through the air. Watched the darts hit Gus full in the chest. If they'd imagined that a mere fifty thousand volts were going to reduce Gus Bradley to a simpering mass of protoplasm, they must have been sorely disappointed, because all he did was jerk once from the juice, and then pull the barbs out of his chest and hurl them to the ground. From where Mickey sat, it looked like all they'd accomplished was to make him mad.

Just as the two of them started shuffling toward Gus, Mickey's peripheral vision caught a familiar flash of white out in the enormous parking lot . . . Grace . . . Grace and the Royster family, dodging cars, making for the Northhaven Mall's front doors.

A trio of cars had stacked up behind the SUV now. One of the drivers began blowing his horn, and then a second joined in. These folks were ready to do a little retail grazing and didn't much appreciate being kept from it.

Baton rushed forward with his arm raised above his head. Would have been a good move too, except that Gus Bradley was way too quick for him. Gus reached out and grabbed the guy's neck like he was going to embrace him.

Instead, Gus head-butted the guy's nose flatter than a pie plate. GI Joe was still trying to come to grips with a caved-in face when Gus grabbed hold of his wrist. Took Gus about a second and a half to pull the baton out of the guy's hand and rake him across the chops with it a couple of times. That's when things went directly to hell. Cue the sirens.

A pair of local police units, blue light bars ablaze, came roaring past Mickey. Up in the entrance, baton man had both hands cradling his face as he walked in wobbly circles, spitting blood. If body language was any indication, his partner was having serious second thoughts about whether or not this Relentless job paid enough for this crap.

Mickey didn't hang around for the festivities. He dropped the unmarked cruiser into gear and went blasting up the road just as the trio of local cops jumped from their patrol cars and began sprinting toward the fray.

He drove all the way up to the next traffic light, hooked a right, and began driving along the north end of the mall. The driveway was way down the end, even with the front of the building. Mickey banged the unmarked car over a series of bright orange speed bumps, stopping half a dozen times to avoid running over pedestrians before finally coming to a stop directly outside Northhaven Mall's front doors.

He left the car running, got out, and stepped up onto the sidewalk. Grace and the Royster clan were still swimming across the crowded lot toward the doors. Now two rows from him, Grace was moving in fits and starts as she shepherded the girls through the maze of parked cars. Mickey waited.

They were breathing heavy when they popped out from between a pair of Dodge pickup trucks and started for the front doors. Grace took one look at Mickey Dolan, standing there next to his car, and slid to a stop. Her mouth hung open; eyes were like icicles. She held out her arms to hold back the girls. By the time Cassie Royster puffed into view about ten seconds later, an insistent siren had begun to assault the air.

Mickey gestured back over their heads toward the mall entrance and the clamor of pulsing blue lights. Yet another siren was wailing now.

"Cops got Gus by now," Dolan said. "You better get in."

"You're a damn cop," Grace said.

"Not today," Mickey said. "Get in."

. . . .

Mickey swung the Forest Service gate back into place, and snapped on the padlock. From here on, the road was little more than an overgrown track, cut into the earth by wagon wheels better than a century and a half ago.

Mickey climbed back into the driver's seat. Tessa had moved up front and was sitting in Grace's lap. Cassie and Maddy held down the back seat.

"What's this place?" Tessa asked, as Mickey began to drive slowly along in the narrow ruts.

"This is a homestead," Mickey answered. "Only piece of private land in the whole National Forest."

Beneath the car, the overgrown vegetation slapped against the undercarriage as they crept along. "Is there a witch?" Tessa asked.

"No witch," Mickey said. "Just a cabin."

Maddy was up on her knees now, her face between the seats. "It's like Grandma's place," she said. "Huh Mama?"

Cassie hadn't spoken a word since they'd left the mall. All that adrenaline coursing through her veins seemed to have doused her demons a bit. "My mother," she said as she gazed out at the forest. "My dad brought her there when she was seventeen." She sighed. "Going to carve a life out of the wilderness, he was. Ended up living there for the rest of her life."

"Where was that?" Mickey asked.

"Idaho. Banks, Idaho."

"Never heard of Banks."

"Doesn't show on maps," she said. "You want to get mail, you got to go over to the Thomasville store. That's the nearest post office." Cassie coughed out a short bitter laugh. "I'd have done just about anything to get out of there."

"Funny how some people are just destined to live and die in one place," Grace piped in, "and others . . . seems like . . . like they're just born to run."

"Thank you Mr. Springsteen," Mickey joked.

Grace had a rich laugh. Not a giggle or a twitter, but a rich contralto that rattled around her chest for a bit before she spit it out.

Mickey wheeled around the final bend and the cabin appeared in front of them.

Varnished logs. Shake roof. Short and stout. Designed to withstand six feet of snow on the roof and seventy-mile-an-hour winds whipping in over the mountains.

The girls were out of the car and running for Bluewater Creek. "Come see, Mama," Tessa called over her shoulder.

"It's so beautiful," Maddy said, grabbing her mother by the hand and dragging her along the leaf-covered path.

"Help me with the shutters?" Mickey asked.

Grace shrugged and followed him over to the cabin. She watched him unlatch and then fold back the first pair of storm shutters. "Got it," she said and then disappeared around the south side of the cabin.

Five minutes later, they met at the back of the house.

"How'd you come to own a place like this?" Grace asked. "You don't seem like the woodsy type to me."

"I'm not," he assured her. "Far as I'm concerned, the only excuse for camping out is that your house burned down." He pulled open the last pair of shutters. "My ex's great-great-grandfather homesteaded this place back in the 1830s. When we split up, we didn't have a prenup or anything like that, so I ended up with a half interest as community property."

"Why didn't you sell it? Isn't that what people do when they get a divorce?"

"Because other than this ten acres right here, the rest of it got declared a National Forest, back in the 1930s, which means we can't sell it to anybody except the US Forest Service, so we just decided to keep it for as long as we can."

"This is the wife who left you for Joanna Bloom?"

"The very same," Mickey said, dusting off his hands and starting around the corner of the cabin.

"I'm sorry," she said from behind him.

"No need," Mickey said. "It is what it is."

"I sounded like my mother there."

"I've met your mother," Mickey joshed.

"Then you know how scary *that* is."

She reached out and put a hand on his shoulder. He stopped and turned in her direction, and then looked down at her hand. It was almost as if you could see through her skin, down into the inner workings of sinew and bone.

"I didn't mean to be hurtful," she said.

Mickey tried to seem nonchalant. "Comes with the territory," he said. "Your lady leaves you for another lady . . . especially if you're a cop . . . you're going to take some static about it. It's just the way of the world."

Grace wasn't buying it. "I don't know much about the ways of the world," she said. "Sometimes I'm rude when I don't mean to be."

"Love's . . . love's tough sometimes."

"I wouldn't . . ." She stopped herself, but her face kept talking.

"Never been in love?" Mickey asked.

She shrugged. The muscles along her jaw rippled like snakes.

The rustle of wind in the pine trees was swept aside by a sudden high-pitched squeal and the slap of shoes on winter leaves. Maddy and Tessa rounded the corner of the house at a full gallop. "Can we go inside?" they squealed in unison.

"Sure," Mickey said.

The girls took off running. "Come on, Gracie," Maddy shouted.

Grace threw Mickey a smile and then took off running after them.

Mickey had the urge to wax poetic about how quickly kids got over things, but managed to stifle it. He stuffed his hands in his pockets and started around the house.

Out in the front yard, Cassie Royster was pumping the hand pump. A thick stream of water slopped onto the ground below. She looked up. "Just like my mom's house," she said, with a wistful smile. "Couple years after I left for good, they finally got electric power, but they never did get around to indoor plumbing."

"You should feel right at home then," Mickey said.

Whatever transient joy she'd derived from the pump faded in an instant.

"This is all my fault," she said. "If I'd just done what Gus told me."

"Spilt milk at this point," Mickey said. "Hopefully we learn from our mistakes and do better the next time." Apparently, that wasn't what she wanted to hear. She looked even more stricken.

"Come on . . . take a look at the cabin. It's pretty cool," Mickey said.

Grace and the girls waited impatiently on the porch as Mickey found the right key and pulled open the door, then stepped aside and let the girls go inside first. They found the bunk beds on the first try.

Maddy wanted the top bunk, so naturally Tessa did too. Cassie followed them inside, just in case dispute resolution was required.

Mickey walked over to the cupboards and looked inside. "Peanut butter, jelly, and a couple of full boxes of Ritz crackers," he announced. "Fit for a king."

"Queen," Grace corrected.

Mickey laughed, closed the cabinet and walked over to her side.

"I'm going to have to go," he said. "I'm on call."

She nodded.

"Worst-case scenario, I'll be back before noon tomorrow."

"You didn't have to do this," Grace said.

"Yeah," Mickey said. "I did."

"What about Gus?" she asked.

"Gus is a pro," Mickey said. "This isn't his first rodeo. He knows how to handle himself. He'll make his one phone call and be back on the street before noon tomorrow, I guarantee it."

Her eyes swept over his face. "You won't leave us here."

"No way," he said.

She leaned over and kissed him on the cheek.

. . . .

She answered on the first ring. The fact that she couldn't tell who was calling told him she hadn't had the same difficulty deleting his picture that he'd had with hers.

"Jen here," she said.

"I need your help," Mickey said.

"With what?"

"The Roysters."

"What about them?"

"They're at the cabin."

Pregnant pause. "How so?"

He gave her the *Reader's Digest* condensed version of everything that had happened. Everything she needed to know, anyway.

"Where are you?"

"Tellers," Mickey said.

Tellers Oasis was a miniscule gas station-truck stop combination about halfway back to Hardwig from the cabin. It was also the first place you could stop where your cell phone was going to show any bars at all.

"Joanna has a show tonight," she said.

"They'll be alright for a while, but they're going to need food, and company. And someplace to go, while everything gets sorted out."

"Can't you take care of it?"

"I'm on call," he said. "I've got thirty-five messages on my phone, none of which I've answered, and most of which are from my boss."

"I don't know what I can do," she said, as if that was supposed to be the end of it.

"You can put your feminist money where your feminist mouth is," Mickey snapped. "This is the real world here, Jen. The one I live in. This isn't ungendering the toys from McDonald's, or protecting spousal benefits. These are real people. Exactly the kind you're always running your mouth about being exploited by society. What say you, just for the hell of it, actually do something other than talk for a change?"

"I . . . you . . ." she sputtered and then caught herself.

"The cops find them, the kids are going back to daddy, and Cassie's going to meet some interesting new friends down at the county lockup."

A trio of log trucks came roaring by on the road, filling the air with debris as they rumbled toward town in the gathering darkness.

"I'll take care of it," she said. Mickey could picture the look on her face from thirty miles away. The tightness around the eyes and the way anger made her lips all but disappear. For some reason, the prospect of her being angry with him bothered him less than it ever had bothered him before. Go figure.

"I'll check with you later," he said, and broke the connection.

. · . · . · .

Mickey was all the way back to the city, running down Bozeman Avenue, about six blocks from the precinct, when his phone began to jingle. He hadn't answered or returned a call all day long and couldn't think of any reason to start now. Way he figured it, everybody was already as pissed off at him as they were going to get. Then Jen's picture flashed onto the screen and all that crap flew out the window.

"Dolan," he said.

"We've got it covered," she announced. "Short-term, anyway."

No way he was telling her about Vince Keenan. She didn't keep her mouth shut well enough for that. She'd tell you she did, swear up and down, but, as far as Mickey was concerned, it was Dial M for Motormouth.

In all likelihood, Gus Bradley had by now used his one phone call, which meant his homeboys already knew things had gone to shit, and were working on getting him out. Only thing none of them knew was where to find the family, and Grace would take care of that for them.

"When you get there, talk to Grace," he said. "She can put you together with people who can help them out in the long term."

"I don't understand . . ."

"You will," he said. He jerked to a stop behind a bakery truck. "Got to go," he said and hung up.

Took the better part of fifteen minutes to return the unmarked cruiser to the police garage. And then another ten checking in with the Duty Sergeant. It doesn't generally take that long, but when you've got to make up where you've been and what you've been doing for most of a day, it's a little more time-consuming. So it was just after six when Mickey moseyed into the office, figuring he'd have a quick look at his desk and then pack it in for the evening.

The place was deserted. Even Joan had gone. Only light coming from inside Nilsson's office. The door was closed and the shades were drawn, but the muffled clash of angry voices was audible from across the room.

He threw a glance down at his desk. Message light blinking like a prison break. An inch and a half of handwritten notes impaled on the old-fashioned spindle. What caught his eye, however, was a single sheet of copier paper, propped up against the desk lamp. Big magic marker arrow pointing across the room. YOU, was all it said.

Mickey was tempted to turn around, walk out the door, and drive home. Maybe get a pizza on the way home. Turn off the phone and then finish off that bottle of Bushmills. Sounded like a natural, as far as Mickey was concerned. Across the room, an angry adenoidal whine rose above the others.

Mickey sighed. Took his time crossing the office and then knocked on Nilsson's door. "Yeah," came filtering out from inside the room.

Mickey stepped inside. Marcus Nilsson was dug in behind his desk, red-faced and rearing for a fight. Mayor Bagley was, as always, looking composed in the red leather chair. Edwin Royster had dragged the guest chair six feet closer to Nilsson's desk and was hovering over the C of D like a cobra. The air was thick with contention.

It was, however, the two other guys sitting in the wooden chairs along the back wall that got Mickey's attention. One was Gary Warner, the City Attorney. Worked across the street in the City Administration Building and was not seen in this neck of the woods very often. The other was a lieutenant from the East Precinct, Bobby Thomson, like the old Giants infielder. Thomson was Mickey's union rep, and none of the possible reasons for his presence boded well for Mickey Dolan. This was an official *close ranks and cover your ass* crew, if ever a wiz there was.

Mickey checked the upper corners of the room. The cameras were on. Probably the audio recorders too. All of which said there was some serious shit going down here.

Nilsson glowered at Mickey. "Where the hell have you been?" he demanded.

"Keeping the world safe for democracy."

Edwin Royster came out of the seat like a missile. "Don't you dare . . . you son of a bitch . . . don't you . . ." He started waving a finger in Mickey's face. Mickey thought about breaking the thing off and sticking it up his ass. Saner heads prevailed, however.

"Councilman," the mayor intoned. Mickey could feel Nilsson's gaze boring a hole in the side of his head. They had a freeze-tag moment, before everybody settled uneasily back into their seats.

"Did you report to the Duty Sergeant?" Nilsson growled.

Mickey nodded. "About five minutes ago," he said.

Nilsson grabbed the green phone, spun his chair so his back was to Mickey, and pushed a couple of buttons. Waited and then pushed a few more, before swinging his chair back around.

"You get anywhere near Hardwig in your travels today, Sergeant?" Nilsson asked.

"Hardwig?"

Nilsson didn't bother repeating himself.

"Why do you ask?" Mickey countered.

Royster was starting to rise again. The mayor reached over and put a restraining hand on his arm. "Edwin," he said softly.

Mickey turned his attention to the union rep. "Do I need a lawyer?" he asked.

Lieutenant Thomson thought it over. "Might be a good idea," he said.

"On the advice of my union representative, I'm afraid I'm going to have to exercise my right to council before we go any further with this."

"I want him fired," Royster shouted. "Right here. Right now."

"It's a process," the mayor said.

"Fuck the process," Royster snapped. "I want him fired."

"It doesn't work that way," Thomson said.

Mickey had no illusions. If they'd managed to put him in Hardwig this afternoon, and could connect him to the missing family, his ass was grass, union lawyer or no union lawyer, and, worst of all, that greaseball Royster would get his daughters back. That was the part that bothered Mickey the most.

"What's with Hardwig?" Mickey Dolan tried.

Instead of an answer, Marcus Nilsson picked up the remote control from his desk, pointed it at the video player, and thumbed the power button. "Little something the Hardwig PD sent over to us."

Mickey kept his face together, but the rest of him felt like it was about to melt into something the janitor would have to mop up later. The screen blinked to life. Closed-circuit view along the front facade of the Northhaven Mall. Mickey and the unmarked cruiser coming right at the camera, bouncing over speed bumps, stopping to let shoppers pass, just the way he remembered it. Big *oh shit* factor here.

Any hope of deniability went out the window the second Mickey stepped out of the cruiser and stood there waiting for Grace and the girls to show up. That was either Detective Sergeant Michael Dolan or . . . or . . . there was no *or*.

That's when, just for a little icing on the cake, Grace and the Royster family came stumbling into the frame, got in the car, and were last seen riding away in a northerly direction, with Mickey at the wheel.

"You include that incident in your report?" Nilsson asked.

"No sir," Mickey said.

Nilsson pitched a piece of paper across the desk at Mickey. Standard cop stuff. Somebody's phone logs. One of the numbers circled in yellow highlighter.

"Call bounced off a tower seven miles north of Hardwig," the C of D said. "Connected with a city number assigned to The Coalition for Equal Rights."

"Where that dyke wife of yours works," Royster sneered.

"Dyke ex-wife," Mickey corrected.

"Where's my fucking family?" Royster demanded. He began to rise from the chair, but Mickey stepped in close, making it so Royster would have to bump him out of the way in order to stand all the way up.

"Mickey," Nilsson growled.

Royster lowered his ass back into the seat.

Nilsson grabbed the initiative. "Motor pool says the squad car had"—he read a number, thirty-two thousand and something—"and had"—another number—"when you brought it back this afternoon."

Mickey kept his mouth shut.

"Even accounting for a trip to Hardwig, there's an extra forty miles or so in there. You want to enlighten us, Sergeant Dolan?"

"No sir."

"According to the Hardwig PD, they responded to a series of assaults this afternoon. Seems they've got several private security guys and one Augustus Bradley in custody at this time. You know anything about that?"

"No sir."

"You know Gus Bradley, Sergeant?"

"Not personally sir. I know who he is, but I've never met him."

"From what I'm told," Nilsson said, "those rent-a-cops wish they'd never met him either."

Mickey hid a smirk. As far as Nilsson was concerned, a lifetime criminal like Gus Bradley was still to be considered several notches above private security agents on the evolutionary ladder.

"Where's the Royster family?" Nilsson asked.

Mickey didn't say anything.

"Last time, Sergeant Dolan. Where are they?"

Mickey swallowed hard. "On the advice of my union representative, I respectfully decline to answer, without an attorney being present."

Marcus Nilsson rose to his feet and held out his big hand. "Your gun and badge, Sergeant Dolan," he said. "You don't get to make the rules, you just get to enforce them."

Mickey pulled out his service piece, checked the safety, and put it in the Chief's outstretched hand, then found his badge and set it on top of the gun. Nilsson set them on the corner of his desk. He had the speech memorized. "Detective Sergeant Dolan, in accordance with the terms of collective bargaining agreement and in the presence of your union representative, you are hereby suspended from duty, without pay, for an indefinite period, pending possible charges and/or other disciplinary action regarding dereliction of duty." His glare threatened to melt Mickey's forehead. "Do you understand?"

"Yes sir."

"You'll be notified about the hearing."

. . . .

Grace sat on the old handmade sofa and watched the darkness gather around the cabin. To her senses, darkness seemed to close in more quickly out here in the woods. The forest on the far side of the clearing, green and vibrant what seemed like just a minute ago, had suddenly been reduced to a jagged, black silhouette against the darkening sky. She scrunched down into the cushions and stared out into the gloaming.

"It's cold, Mama." Tessa danced in a circle, hugging herself.

That was the first time Grace remembered that they'd left everything behind in the van, and that, like the old song said: *Everything they had was hanging on their backs.*

"You suppose there's any firewood?" Cassie asked nobody in particular.

"There's a woodshed out back," Grace offered. "Lots of wood, too."

Cassie jumped to her feet. "Come on girls, let's make a fire," she said gaily.

The girls followed her out the door and down the porch stairs. Grace pushed herself up from the couch and wandered into the bedroom. She sat on the edge of the bed and watched out the window as Cassie and the girls found some dry wood. Watched as Cassie expertly used the hatchet to split off some kindling. Then had the girls hold out their arms while she loaded them with the fruits of their labors.

They came back inside the cabin, staggering under the weight of the wood, giggling and grunting with exaggerated exertion, as they dumped everything into the wood box next to the stove. Cassie knelt down and opened the wrought-iron door.

"Now girls, when you make a fire in a woodstove, the first thing you've got to do is make sure the flue is wide open, because if it's not, the whole room is going to fill up with smoke." She made an expansive move with her arms. The girls were suitably impressed. More giggles filled the room.

Grace was thinking how nice it was to see Cassie Royster feeling in charge. To see her dispensing wisdom and taking the lead in something. She could tell, the girls liked it too. She went through the whole process with them. Newspaper, then kindling, then skinny sticks and, only when those were fully ablaze, the split firewood.

Took maybe forty minutes for the warmth to reach the far corners of the cabin. By that time, they'd devoured most of the peanut butter and jelly and were about to open the second box of Ritz crackers when the unearthly halogen headlights swept over the cabin like a death ray and everybody's blood froze solid in their veins.

The flickering glow of the kerosene lamps reflected off the logs, making it seem as if the room was lit from everywhere at once.

Grace glanced back over her shoulder. Cassie and the girls were huddled in a corner, wide-eyed with terror. Grace took a deep breath and reached for the door handle.

Expecting a face full of cops, she drew in a great breath and pulled open the door. No cops. Two women holding Safeway shopping bags.

"Oh," escaped her lips.

"Didn't mean to scare you," the nearest woman said with a tentative smile. She was maybe five foot nine. Thirty or so. Good-looking, in a girl-next-door kind of way. The other woman was older and taller and sharper. Thick, medium-length hair streaked with gray.

"I'm Jennifer McCade," the younger woman said. "Mickey sent us. You must be Grace." She gestured with her shoulder to the other woman. "This is Teresa Hollander. Teresa's an attorney with the Women's Legal Coalition."

Grace exhaled for what seemed like the first time in half an hour and then looked back over her shoulder. "It's okay," she said.

Cassie and the girls slowly unwound from one another and wandered out toward the center of the room. Scared and hopeful, at the same time.

"Oh," Grace said. "Excuse me. Come in. Come in," as she threw open the door and got out of the way, so the women could enter.

"We thought you might be able to use a few provisions," Jennifer said as she crossed the rough plank floor, set the grocery bags on the counter, and began to put things away in the cupboards. Teresa put her bags on the kitchen table and stepped back. "No need to go hungry while we figure out what we're going to do next," she said.

Grace stopped in her tracks. Wasn't until that moment, when her fear-addled brain cleared up sufficiently, that she realized who this was, and why Jennifer seemed to know where everything went in the kitchen.

"You're Sergeant Dolan's ex. Aren't you?" she said.

· · · · · · ·

Mickey was drinking Bushmills Malt and attempting to channel his mother. Emma Dolan had been one of those people who, regardless of the magnitude of the disaster, could always find something positive to say about it afterward.

You fell in a manhole and broke both legs, that woman would find some reason why it was all for the best, or how it had been God's will, or was something you'd been needing for ages anyway. Didn't matter. If it happened, she had a homespun homily on hand.

For Mickey, the question had always been whether or not she really meant it. Like . . . was it possible to actually have such a rosy outlook and not be an idiot, or did she just make up that shit as a means of getting through the night, so to speak. She'd been dead for a decade, and Mickey still hadn't figured it out.

Maybe getting suspended and, in all probability, fired would turn out to be a good thing. He had, after all, been locked in the throes of self-doubt lately. Since his split with Jen, he'd taken to wondering who he was, and how he'd gotten to this place in life, without consciously willing it so. How it had all just seemed preordained. Like he'd just been along for the ride, and wasn't necessarily the manly self-willed guy he liked to think he was.

On the way home, he'd stopped at the liquor store and picked up another bottle of whiskey. Thought he might need a spare. Good thing, too, because, for some reason, as much as he wanted to, he couldn't seem to get hammered tonight. No matter how much whiskey he poured down his throat, seemed like nothing happened. He was still working at it when the doorbell rang.

He craned his neck and squinted into the kitchen. The clock on the stove read ten after four. Last Mickey could recall, it had been a little after 9:00 p.m. Amazing how time passes when you're having fun. He set his glass on the side table, grabbed the arm of the sofa, and attempted to push himself to his feet.

Turned out to be harder than he'd imagined. Maybe he was having more luck with his getting-shitfaced project than he'd figured.

Careful now, he pushed himself upright and tottered over to the front door, like a man walking on a tightrope. He twisted the deadbolt and eased it open. A woman. Vaguely familiar. He stuck his head outside and surveyed the surrounding area. Nobody else in sight. Just the woman.

"I'm Joanna Bloom," she said. "I think we need to talk."

Mickey kept one hand locked to the doorframe, maintaining his balance. She was older than she looked on TV. And shorter too. Both of which, for some reason, made Mickey happy.

He leaned his back against the door. "Come in," he said.

She brushed past him and strode into the living room like she owned the joint. Mickey hustled over and pulled his laundry from the wing chair, dropping the disheveled pile onto the floor beside the chair. "Have a seat," he said.

She stepped over and perched herself on the edge of the chair.

"Can I get you a drink?" Mickey inquired.

"What have you got?" she asked.

"Bushmills or Bushmills and water."

"I'll take it neat," she said.

Mickey found a semi-clean glass and poured her more whiskey than he figured she could drink. He grabbed a couple of coasters off the kitchen counter and made his way back into the living room. She looked about as comfortable as . . . as . . . try as he might, he couldn't come up with a decent metaphor . . . or was that a simile? So he put the drink on the table beside her and repaired to his spot on the couch.

He raised his glass. She followed suit. "Salute," he said.

"Salute."

He watched as she took a serious pull and then set the glass back onto the coaster.

"They've been arrested," she said.

"Who they?"

"Jennifer, Teresa, the Royster family . . . all of them."

Took his numbed brain a few seconds to process the information.

"How'd that happen?" he asked.

She took another pull on the Bushmills. Shrugged. "I guess they figured it out," she said. "The cabin appears on our income tax forms . . . probably on yours too, so I'm guessing it wasn't rocket science."

"Shit," Mickey said. "I figured the cabin was good for a couple of days."

"From what I'm told, the State Police had the Forest Service do a flyover on the homestead late yesterday. They saw smoke coming out of the chimney. Troopers took them into custody a little after midnight."

"Where are they now?"

"State Police barracks in Garden County."

Mickey took a hit of his drink. "Charged with what?"

"That's where we got lucky," she said. "Teresa's an attorney for the Women's Legal Coalition. She was smart enough to know that, other than Mrs. Royster, nobody was technically guilty of anything illegal, so whenever the first Garden County judge shows up in the morning, Jennifer and Teresa and your friend . . ."

"Grace."

"They'll be free to go."

"And the Roysters?"

"Mrs. Royster is facing a number of serious charges. What they're going to do with her I don't know. The girls will end up with Family Protective Services until they get everything sorted out. As I understand it, once they get them transported back here, there'll be a formal hearing in Family Court, after which the girls will be returned to their custodial parent."

"Who just happens to be a child-molesting son-of-a-bitch of the first order."

She finished her whiskey. "We're doing everything possible," she said.

Mickey took another sip. "Cassie Royster's not going to fare well in the county lockup. They need to get her out of there as quick as they can."

"Teresa's not very hopeful about that," she said. "Mrs. Royster has been held in contempt of court. From my experience, they can keep you inside for just about as long as they want on that particular charge."

Mickey nodded. Out in the street, somebody's car alarm started going off. Things were like urban crickets these days. They could honk for a month and nobody would pay a damn bit of attention.

"How *you* doing?" Joanna Bloom asked.

"Relative to what?" Mickey said.

"My little courthouse birdie tells me you've been suspended."

"Yep."

"For refusing to tell them where to find the Royster family."

"Among other things."

"It was the right thing to do."

He met her eyes for the first time. She had eyes that looked like they'd had a lot of practice telling people things they didn't want to hear.

The car alarm stopped.

"What with everybody being in custody," Mickey said, "seems like maybe it wasn't the best idea I ever came up with."

"The right thing's the right thing," she said. "No matter what happens."

"Seems a bit ironic, don't you think?" Mickey said.

"What?"

"You and I sitting here in the middle of the night, drinking whiskey and bandying back and forth about *doing the right thing*."

"Strange bedfellows," she said.

Mickey smirked. "In a manner of speaking," he said.

"I didn't mean it that way," she said.

Mickey took a pull of the Bushmills. He wanted to say something adult sounding and non-judgmental, but "I did" fell out of his mouth instead.

She leaned forward in the chair, elbows on knees. "Does that bother you?"

"Does what bother me?"

"The thought of Jennifer and me in bed together."

Mickey shrugged. "Only when I think about it."

"Because I'm a woman?"

"Because you're not me."

She sat back in the chair for the first time, folded her arms across her chest.

"Life's complicated," she said.

"Feels like I lost," Mickey drunkenly blurted.

"Jennifer?"

He shook his head. "The game. Feels like I lost the game."

"Is that how you see it? As a game?"

Mickey thought it over. "Not while it was going on," he said. "But once it was over, I felt like that. Like . . ." He stopped himself. "Don't get me wrong," he said. "I wasn't any happier than she was. The relationship wasn't working worth a damn for either of us. But I kept hanging in there, trying to make it work, because I didn't want to lose," he said. "Didn't want to feel like I'd failed at something."

"Some things just aren't meant to be."

"You sound like my mother."

The car alarm recycled and began to bleat again.

"Could I ask you something?" Mickey asked. "Something personal."

"Seems like we crossed into personal territory a while back."

"When did you know . . ." Mickey went searching for a phrase and couldn't find it.

Joanna took pity on him. "I was a lesbian?"

"Yeah," Mickey said.

"I always knew," she said. "Even before I knew what a lesbian *was*."

"How'd you know?"

She shrugged. "Something just wasn't right," she said. "I never wanted what other girls my age wanted. I wanted to be up in the tree, not on the ground watching. I wanted what the boys had." She leaned forward. "I remember when I was about ten, my mother bought me this set of mystery books. The same ones she'd read as a girl. Nancy Drew." She smiled at the memory. "While I was reading them, I came across an ad in the back of the book for the Hardy Boys books. I think they had the same publishing company. They were sort of the boys' equivalent of Nancy Drew, and I was completely captivated by them." She spread her hands in an expansive gesture. "They had so much better toys than Nancy Drew did. Cars and boats and motorcycles. All Nancy had was her little roadster."

The car alarm stopped again. Silence filled the room.

Joanna stood up. "I've got to be to work by ten," she said. "Thanks for the drink."

Mickey tottered across the room and opened the door for her.

"Thanks for sharing," Mickey said.

She stopped in the doorway and searched his eyes for sarcasm. Not finding any, she patted him on the arm. "Hang in there," was the last thing she said.

Mickey stood in the doorway and watched Joanna Bloom fade into the darkness, about three streetlights up. For reasons he couldn't explain, he felt as if his pockets had suddenly been emptied. Like he'd been walking around with his pants full of nickels and had suddenly been relieved of the burden.

The car alarm began to blare.

Mickey closed the door.

. . . .

The official title was Civilian Review Panel, probably because Several Retired Cops and a Bunch of Guys Who Belonged to the Rotary Club was too long to fit on letterhead.

Mickey's two PBA-provided lawyers were hunkered down at the far end of the table shuffling papers and whispering to one another. Norman Beal was a local civil attorney who the union hired on a piecemeal basis. Budget-friendly, but competent. Fifty-something. One of those guys who lose all their hair except for a thick patch right up front where you don't want it.

Paul Dobbins was a full-time union lawyer. Spent most of his time doing routine administrative work for the PBA. Hadn't been in a regular courtroom since the Eisenhower administration, but was known to be a feisty little union man where a member's rights were concerned.

They'd spent an unpleasant half an hour out in the hall before the proceedings began, going over who did what to whom and why. According to Beal and Dobbins, this morning's proceedings were just a dog and pony show. They made no bones about it. Mickey was hosed. The best they could hope for was a general discharge from the department and a partial pension.

Once the proceedings got underway, things went straight to hell in a hurry. First person they wanted to talk to was Chief of Detectives Marcus T. Nilsson, who was also wearing his dress blues, almost like he and Thomson wanted to put as much distance as possible between themselves and the idiot over there in the gray suit.

They took Nilsson through all the name, rank, and serial number stuff and then got down to the nitty-gritty. "It is my understanding that Sergeant Dolan was assigned directly to you, Chief. Is that so?"

If there was any good news, it was that, like most cops, Nilsson wasn't fond of lawyers. While the cop end of the business was pretty much good versus evil, the lawyer end lived and died for the intermediate shades of gray. Drove cops nuts.

"Yes," was all Nilsson said.

"Is that standard procedure?"

"Is what standard procedure?" the Chief asked.

"For you to take a direct hand in investigations."

"No. It's not."

"Why so in this case?"

"Sergeant Dolan was coming back from a personal leave of absence. He hadn't been reassigned yet and I needed an experienced man to conduct an investigation."

"What investigation was that?"

Nilsson recounted the story of Family Court and the missing Royster kids.

"That's a civil matter, is it not?" the guy asked.

"Yes."

"Does your department generally concern itself with civil matters?"

"Not as a rule."

"Why so in this case?"

Nilsson told him how, despite repeated efforts, when the normal investigatory channels had failed to turn up the Royster family, he had been asked to see what he could do. No names. All very passive voice and vague.

"And that was Sergeant Dolan's assignment. To locate the Royster family for the purpose of turning them over to the proper civil authorities?"

Nilsson threw an angry glance in Mickey's direction. "Yes."

"To your knowledge . . . did he find them?"

"Yes."

The DA's man approached the front of the room. "Mr. Chairman . . . at this time we'd like to screen a piece of closed-circuit video."

Dolan's PBA attorneys objected most strenuously, citing the lack of authentication and such. The panel listened patiently to their legal lamentations and then told them to sit down.

The room darkened, the camera blinked and there was Mickey Dolan, stuffing Grace and the Royster family into his unmarked cruiser and driving off into the sunset.

"Did Sergeant Dolan subsequently turn them in to civil authorities?"

"No. He did not."

"And why was that?"

"You'd have to ask him," Nilsson said.

So they did. Nilsson was excused and suddenly it was Mickey Dolan's turn in the barrel. "Was that you in the video we just watched, Sergeant Dolan?" the DA asked.

"Yes," Mickey said.

"And that was the family you were assigned to locate and then deliver to Family Court authorities?"

"Yes, it was."

"And did you do so?"

"I found them."

"But you did not deliver them."

"No."

"And why was that?"

"I didn't think it was in the best interest of the children."

And that's where Mr. Rock met Mr. Hard Place. Where Mickey was either going to heed the advice of his PBA attorneys and shut his trap, or where the Royster-as-child-molester discussion began, a move which, his lawyers assured him, would prove to be a personal and financial disaster of truly life-altering proportions.

The DA must have been clued in too. He didn't want any part of it either. Instead of asking the obvious question—you know, why Mickey didn't think it was in the best interests of the children to do his sworn duty and turn them over to the proper authorities—the DA's man started flipping through his notes, looking for another line of inquiry. Something that led somewhere, anywhere else.

Problem was, Mickey didn't have the charade in him. Whatever it was going to take to sit there and listen to this guy serpentine his way to the obvious . . . Mickey just didn't have it this morning.

So he interrupted. "Stop," he said. Looked over at the panel. They looked back. "The decision to stash the family was mine. I was fully aware that I was not in compliance with the orders given to me by my supervisor, or my legal responsibilities as an officer of the court. I willfully chose to disregard those responsibilities. At the time, I saw it as an act of conscience."

"And now?" the DA prodded.

Mickey felt like laughing. Or maybe crying. He wasn't sure which. "Now I see it as a futile act of conscience," he said.

Mercifully, it was all downhill from there. Several panel members rose from their seats and huddled around the chairman, forming a tight, muttering knot of furrowed brows and pointing fingers. After about five minutes of discussion, everybody returned to their seats. The Chairman announced that they'd reached a decision. Drum roll.

Fixing Mickey Dolan with his most baleful stare, he announced that the panel had unanimously agreed that Sergeant Michael Dolan should be permanently removed from duty, and any and all appeals regarding the specifics of his dismissal would be heard next Thursday at 10:00 a.m. End o' story.

Took about two minutes of hushed voices and sliding shoes for the room to completely empty. Next thing Mickey knew, only he and a bailiff at the back of the room were still sharing the oxygen. Mickey took a couple of deep breaths, trying to calm himself.

"Sergeant," the guy said.

Mickey looked his way. "Lots of reporters out there," the bailiff said, nodding his head toward the big, oak double doors at the back of the room. He reached behind himself and opened a smaller painted door. "Probably best you go out this way," he said. "Leads down to the parking lot."

Mickey nodded his thanks. The guy patted him on the shoulder on the way by.

. · . · . · . ·

You can fool some of the people some of the time, but with Natalie Mendonhal, it was a bit harder. Mickey could make her out from fifty yards away. Only one smart enough to know he wasn't going anywhere without his car. She'd parked her orange VW with the Secrets license plates directly behind Dolan's ride, and was leaning against the driver's door, waiting for Mickey to put in a guest appearance.

"Do I still call you Sergeant?" she asked as he walked up.

"Yeah . . . like one of those Kentucky colonels."

She waved a portable tape recorder in his face. "Would you like to make a statement, Sergeant?" she asked.

Mickey unlocked the car with the push of a button, opened the door and slipped into the driver's seat. Natalie sidled her hip into the door jamb. She made a show of turning off the recorder and dropping it into her purse.

"And nobody's going to mention the talk about Edwin Royster and those girls?"

Mickey looked up at her. "What talk is that?" he asked.

"You know what I'm talking about. The sexual abuse."

"I did what I thought was the right thing," Mickey said.

"What do you think now?" she asked.

And all of a sudden, in his mind's eye, Mickey could see Vince Keenan's face.

"I think that sometimes if you *can* do something, you *have* to do it." He spread his hands in resignation. "'Cause there's no way you could live with yourself, if you didn't."

"Nice thought," she said.

"I also think you need to move your car, Natalie, so I can get the hell out of here," he said with a small smile.

She met his gaze. Put a big, knuckley hand on his shoulder. "Good luck, Sergeant," she said. She stepped aside, looked down at Mickey and shrugged. "I guess sometimes the truth doesn't set you free."

Mickey watched her move the car, then closed his door, dropped the car into drive and wheeled out of the lot. Once he got out onto the city streets, he turned right on Yonker Boulevard and just kept driving. Farther out that way than he'd been in years. Past the gypo car dealers, with their ragged pennants flapping, past the strip malls and last-chance groceries, drove it all the way to the end, out where the landscape was very much as the original hunter-gatherers must have found it. Way out in the tulles where it ran into Boundary Road. Framed by an ocean of swamp grass and bulrushes, a brand new billboard loomed dark against the afternoon sky. United Airlines. Vacations to Florida. Senior citizen couple looking like they'd just won the lottery.

The guy . . . something about the guy . . . And then Mickey Dolan realized how much the old man looked like his father. Right before he went into the hospital and never came out. He saw a brief flash of him brushing dust from his patrolman's uniform before . . . And then things got blurry.

Mickey reached up and touched his face. Water seemed to be leaking from his eyes.

Mickey patted himself down, looking for a handkerchief, but it was no go. In the pocket of his pants, however, he found a white business card, with a phone number written on the back in pen. As he gazed down at those handwritten blue numbers, pictures began to run in his mind, so he closed his eyes and waited as the pictures took shape and he could begin to see the movie. Then he picked up his phone and dialed.

4

"You never take responsibility," Grace said. "When things go wrong, you just sit there like a sphinx and make like you didn't have a damn thing to do with it."

Eve clamped her mouth shut, spun the chair in a half circle and rolled over to the window. Evespeak for she'd heard enough.

Grace went on anyway. "We had no business trying to relocate the Royster family. That's not what we do."

"Others wouldn't have had the courage to try," Eve said.

"Don't you get it, Mom? We screwed up. Those little girls will be back with their father sometime on Thursday. Just thinking about it makes my skin crawl. Cassie Royster's in the county jail on a contempt of court citation, which means they can keep her for as long as they want. A man who tried to help us is about to lose his job." She threw her hands up in despair. "We couldn't have botched this worse if we'd tried."

"The Women's Coalition is working on getting Cassie Royster released. They're doing everything they can." Before Grace could respond, Eve changed the subject. "Mr. Thurmond has been calling incessantly. Indra says he sounds frantic."

"Of course he sounds frantic. I was supposed to see his wife last night. But, of course, I was in jail. Poor guy must be going crazy by now."

"Surely he'll understand."

Grace took a deep breath. She needed to calm down.

"What if I told you he wasn't a Hollywood mogul and doesn't really have a million dollars."

Must have been some sort of record for how slowly a wheelchair could be turned in a one-eighty. The cords in Eve's neck stood out like bridge cables.

"What do you mean?" she asked.

"Just what I said. He made up all that Hollywood millionaire stuff just to get our attention. He's just a kid with a wife in a coma. He's broke and scared and probably about as far down as a person can get. He doesn't have anything. I'm betting he spent everything he owns to get his wife this far."

"Have you checked with Indra? I believe we have several other inquiries."

"He's probably got his wife stashed in some cheap clinic, and you think I should turn him down because he doesn't have the bucks?"

"We can't work with people who lie to us," Eve said.

Grace laughed. "People lie to us all the time, just like they lie to themselves all the time. Self-denial is the national pastime," she said. "How can people who are lying to themselves be expected to tell us the truth? They left the truth so far behind they don't even remember doing it."

"You can't do this," Eve said.

"I already spoke with him," Grace said immediately. "I'm seeing her later today."

"Just to spite me."

"I know this is going to come as quite a shock, but this isn't about you."

"Or some sort of perverse expiation of guilt?"

"If I was working from guilt, I'd be trying to do something for Sergeant Dolan. He's the guy ended up getting the worst of it. All he was trying to do was keep those girls out of their father's hands, and he ended up losing everything. He's probably sitting around his apartment, right now, trying to figure out what he's going to do with the rest of his life."

"You've been dewy over him since first sight."

"And look what it got him."

"He seemed like a rather resourceful man to me," Eve said.

The door at the far end of the room opened and Indra walked in holding a cell phone. "We got a call on the Transitional Center line," she said.

"Mr. Thurmond again?" Eve asked.

"No," Indra said. "There's been an incident down at the jail. Mrs. Royster has sustained some sort of injury."

. . . .

Mickey Dolan pulled the brim of the Cincinnati Reds baseball cap low over his eyes and then settled the black hoodie over the hat, urban monk style. He checked his reflection in the window, made a couple of adjustments, and then started up the hall toward the Child Protective Services office. He had no illusions. The hat, the hood, the sunglasses, and the three acres of shorts weren't much of a disguise. He told himself that knowing where the cameras were located evened the odds a bit, and all he had to do was to avoid looking directly at any of them on the way in. If he got *in* clean, he'd look like just another baggy-pants homeboy fallen victim to the system.

As he pulled open the CPS office door and stepped inside, the old Roman-numeral clock on the back wall read 12:25. A dozen or so people were milling around the office. All eyes were on a guy with a big, red face who was yelling at the young woman behind the front counter.

"This is my life," he was yelling. "You're talking about my life here lady."

"I'm sorry sir," was all he heard the girl say before the guy started yelling again.

The hostility had attracted the attention of the security guard, who was now inching toward the counter, in case the yeller got any more out of hand.

That's when the recorded message started rolling out of the overhead speakers. *"Ladies and gentlemen, by order of the mayor and the City Council, this office closes every day between 12:30 p.m. and 2:00 p.m. . . ."* Everybody in the room simultaneously looked at the clock.

Mickey kept his face averted as he slid along the back wall, down the short corridor, and ducked into the men's room, where he walked down to the last booth, climbed up on the toilet so his feet wouldn't show under the partition, and leaned his shoulders against the white tile wall.

He waited. The guy at the counter was still yelling, but the words were no longer intelligible. He tried to ignore how uncomfortable he was, while he listened to the shuffle of feet and the disjointed calliope of voices as the crowd was ushered out into the hall.

Several minutes passed before the security guard kicked open the men's room door, checked the floor for feet, and then presumably headed off for the comfort of his furlough chair in the hallway. Mickey stifled a groan as the swinging door creaked and closed. He felt like a paraplegic, but leaned back and waited some more. Waited until he was engulfed by silence and his hips had grown completely numb, then carefully put one sneakered foot on the floor. Then the other. His knees were shaky, his back in a knot. He leaned his shoulder against the wall, giving his extremities a chance to regain some feeling, then pulled a pair of latex gloves from one coat pocket and a dark blue ski mask from the other.

He took his time putting them on. Shook out his legs and took several deep breaths before stashing the Reds cap and shades in his pocket and poking his head out into the silent hallway.

This was the part he hadn't been able to envision. What in hell he was going to say if he got caught creeping around a locked city office, wearing this outfit, latex gloves, and a ski mask. Hard as he'd tried, he'd been unable to come up with an excuse that sounded even remotely plausible. Way he saw it, once you've been fired, the realms of possibility just naturally get a whole lot wider.

He stepped out into the hall and tiptoed into the main room. The place was empty and still. He checked high up the corners. The green lights of the CC cameras peered unblinkingly down on the room. The old clock clicked the passing of another minute as he walked quietly to the far end of the service counter and sidled past the Employees Only sign into the office area.

He walked directly to the nearest desk and pulled open the center drawer. He'd been expecting to find a file cabinet key. He found six, cursed under his breath, and scooped all of them up.

He was in the process of trying the fourth key when his peripheral vision caught a flicker of change. He checked the corners of the ceiling again.

Green lights out.

Cameras off.

He was still trying to wrap his head around this change when the front door clicked open. He dove for the nearest desk, crawled under it and rested his back against the modesty panel. He held his breath and waited.

A woman giggled.

Two pairs of legs walked through his field of vision, close enough to touch. One male. One female. The male was wearing pants with a shiny stripe down the pant leg. Uniform pants. Had to be the security guard.

The female sounded breathless. "We shouldn't be doing this. If Mrs. Robertson . . ."

"Don't worry, baby. Ain't nobody gonna find out. Cain't nobody get in here less I let 'em in. I got the only key."

A faint rustle of fabric reached his ears. "Got somethin' here for you baby," he whispered. Fevered rustlings ensued.

"Oooooooooooooooh," she cooed. "Yes . . . yes . . ."

Mickey crawled out from under the desk and peeked around the corner of the desk. The woman had her skirt hiked up to armpit level. A pair of lavender panties lay crumpled on the desktop beside her. She was bent over the desk at the far end of the room. The security guard was hunched up behind her with his pants around his ankles, slipping it to her for all he was worth. His butt cheeks seemed to have a life of their own, bouncing this way and that, as he thrust into her again and again.

Apparently, the young woman was big on affirmations. "Yes . . . yes . . . yes . . ." she hissed over and over again as he rhythmically pummeled her from behind. "Oh yes . . ."

Mickey ducked back under the desk and waited. The audio part of the program was moist and hard to listen to, but all he could do was try to tune it out and wait some more. The old wall clock clicked eight more times before a long, wavering crescendo finally faded to labored breathing.

He heard the tinkle of the guy's belt as he pulled his pants up. Another minute passed before their legs wobbled by his vantage point again. At the door, they shared a moment of . . . what? Tenderness? Lust? Guilt? He couldn't decide, nor did he particularly care. Then the door closed, and he was once again alone in the room.

He counted to fifty and then crawled out from under the desk. He had to stifle a groan as he stretched and rolled his neck. This time he got lucky. Found the right key on the second try. The drawer rolled out. The green lights came back on.

He picked his way through the alphabet to R and pulled out the folder labeled Royster. The file was sealed inside a blue plastic envelope. "Sealed by Order of the Court." The day, the time, the court, and the presiding judge were all listed on the label. Right next to a list of citations and penalties for the unauthorized opening or otherwise tampering with the contents.

Voices suddenly could be heard in the hall. In a burst of nervous energy, Mickey slipped the file under his arm, rolled the drawer closed, locked the cabinet, and then slipped over to the desk, where he returned the keys to their former home in the center drawer. Two voices now. Something banged against the office door hard enough to rattle the frosted glass.

He'd just made it back to the customer side of the counter, with the Royster file still tucked under his arm, when the voices again reached his ears. Louder this time. Combative. Mickey thought it might be the guy who'd been yelling earlier, maybe come back to make his point again, but he didn't stick around to find out.

Instead, he hotfooted it down the hallway, slid back the bolt on the frosted glass door opposite the men's room, and pulled it open a crack. In a single deft movement, he snatched the ski mask from his head and replaced it with the Reds cap, put the shades on and then covered it all up with the hoodie. A second later, he stepped out into the empty hallway and hurried off.

. ˙ . ˙ . ˙ .

Cassie Royster had a world-class shiner. Started over by her ear and ran all the way to her nose, which at this point was stuffed with bloody cotton.

Jennifer McCade and Teresa Hollander perched on the edges of their chairs, leaning toward the scuffed-up piece of reinforced plastic that separated them from her. All professionally concerned and sisterly, and of exactly no help whatsoever.

Grace, who'd arrived last, stood behind them, leaning against the wall. She hadn't seen Jen or Teresa since they'd been taken into custody together. "Detained" was what the state cops had called it. They were being detained for everyone's safety, until the legalities got sorted out. Not arrested, mind you. Merely detained.

They'd been trying to sort out what to do with Gus. On one hand, he had a criminal record from here to Poughkeepsie, and, not coincidentally, had spent major portions of his adult life as a guest of the state. Not only that, but, to make matters worse, he was presently out on parole. The Relentless Technology mouthpiece claimed that Gus had wantonly attacked his duly appointed agents and should be held pending further charges.

On the other hand, the attorney who'd shown up to represent Gus and Grace had not only proclaimed his client's innocence, but produced a dozen local citizens, all of whom had been present at North-haven Mall at the time of the fisticuffs, and all of whom swore up and down that Gus had been the victim of the attacks rather than the instigator. In the end, local color won out. They'd decided to keep the Relentless employees locked up and to let Gus and the women go.

Cassie Royster was an emotional wreck. She'd spent the past fifteen minutes trying to relate the story of how she'd come by the shiner. The story arrived piecemeal, between sniffles, shredded tissues, and intermittent bursts of tears. Seems a couple of other inmates had simply walked up and taken her breakfast tray. When she'd protested their lack of manners, they'd beaten her down. Pulling her off the bench by the hair, and kicking and punching her repeatedly, as both the guards and other inmates stood by and did nothing.

"They saw what was happening," she bawled. "They just stood there."

"We're filing a complaint with the city," Teresa said.

"No," Grace said, bumping herself off the wall. "That'll just make things worse. Filing a complaint will make her a snitch, and, as far as these people are concerned, *snitches get stitches.*"

Jennifer and Teresa looked at Grace as if she were speaking in tongues.

"Excuse me?" Jennifer McCade said.

Grace stepped forward, looked down at Jennifer. "Would you mind?" she asked. "I'd like to have a few words with Cassie."

Took Jennifer a full five seconds to figure out that Grace wanted the chair. She seemed amazed. Apparently, Teresa agreed.

"Oh." She shot Teresa a sideways glance and pushed herself to her feet. "Of course."

Grace plopped down onto the worn seat beside Teresa and then leaned as far forward as possible, resting her forehead against the scuffed plastic separating them. She made eye contact with Cassie Royster. "Listen to me now," she said. "There's three kinds of people in jail. There's predators, there's victims, and there's people just doing their time. Nobody's going to take your side until they find out which one you are."

Cassie went all purple-faced and started to cry.

"You can't be a victim in here," Grace said. "If you don't stand up for yourself, nobody's going to do it for you. They'll just kick your butt and take your stuff every day."

"Are you advocating violence?" Teresa asked.

"I'm just telling her how it is," Grace said. Again she pinned Cassie with her eyes. "It won't stop with food. If they make you to be an easy mark, then sex will sure as hell be next. You'll be taking some of the most unpleasant showers of your life." She waved a hand. "There's no end to it, Cassie. It's not like they're going to leave you alone if you lie on the floor and cry. To these people, that's just blood in the water. When you're inside, it's real simple . . . you have to make it so it's not worth anybody's while to be messing with you." She tapped the plastic shield. "Are you listening to me?" she asked Cassie. "You have to make it hard for them."

Cassie nodded, clearly without meaning it. Her eyes said *beaten dog*.

Grace lowered her voice. "You knew what was going on, didn't you?" she asked.

"Huh?" Cassie frowned.

"With your husband and the girls. You can't live in the same house with something like that going on and not have a clue. It's just not possible. I know . . . I've been there . . . on the girls' end of it."

For a second or so, Cassie tried to find the moxie to deny everything, but instead, after a frozen moment, her shoulders began to shake.

"Next time they mess with you, take all the anger you've collected over the years, the blame, the hate you've aimed at yourself for not doing more. Think about that husband of yours and that judge who awarded him custody of the girls, roll it all into a ball, and then go nuts on them. Even if you don't win . . . they'll start looking for somebody easier."

"Please . . . Grace . . . you can't . . ." Jennifer sputtered behind Grace.

Grace stood up. "Listen, I don't want you to think I don't appreciate everything you guys do for women . . . because I do." She threw a thumb back over her shoulder. "But what's going on in there isn't women's politics, or gender neutrality, or any such Sunday-morning talk show shit. What's going on in there is something neither of you know a damn thing about. It's just not part of your worlds . . . and you know what. I were you, I'd keep it that way."

By now, Jennifer and Teresa had the astonished-look thing down.

Grace turned back to Cassie.

"You've got to be your own hero in here. The cavalry's not coming to the rescue. You've got to do it for yourself."

Cassie blew her nose.

Grace nodded at Jennifer and Teresa and headed for the door.

. . . .

The car was right where it was supposed to be. A shiny blue Buick, with dealer plates, sitting there under the elm trees in the two hundred block of Westminster Avenue. From a block away Mickey could see that they'd either stuffed a polar bear behind the wheel, or that was Gus Bradley in the driver's seat. The passenger got out and held the door for Mickey. The immediate question for Mickey was whether or not to let on he knew who the passenger was. He was thinking it might be best to just play dumb and let it ride at that.

Teddy Hicks's piss-yellow eyes were the last thing quite a few guys had ever seen. He'd spent twenty-five years as Sean Keenan's crew chief and personal button man. You saw Teddy coming up your front walk, you knew the talking was over, and it was time to make out your will.

Teddy looked Mickey over like a dessert menu. "I knew your old man," he said.

So much for anonymity. Mickey nodded, but didn't speak.

"Far as cops go, he was a good man," Teddy said. "Just did his job. Treated everybody the same. Didn't take it personal."

"Thanks," was all Mickey could think to say.

"Whatcha need?"

Mickey told him.

"Happens I know a guy."

He bent down, stuck his head in the car and spoke to Gus. "Take him to Sketchy and wherever else he needs to go. We're along for the ride here."

Teddy straightened up and ran those yellow eyes over Mickey again. "I put you with Gus 'cause you two already know each other from that little party out in the sticks with the Roysters." He leaned in close. "Today's different," he said. "Anything you see today, doesn't exist," Teddy said. "Right?"

"Right."

"Not now, not ever. Don't matter whether it's cop business or not."

"I understand."

He moved aside and let Mickey slide into the passenger seat. Mickey dropped an athletic bag onto the back seat and then buckled up. When he checked the mirror, Teddy Hicks was gone.

"What's in the bag?" Gus asked.

"Change of clothes."

"You got a date?"

"When I'm done today, this stuff I'm wearing is going to need to disappear from the face of the earth."

Gus smirked. "That saggy-ass ghetto prince outfit oughta disappear," he said.

"And here I thought I was the very soul of sartorial splendor."

"I could get in them pants with ya," Gus joked.

"Let's not dwell on that thought," Mickey suggested.

Gus turned off the car, pulled the keys from the ignition and handed them to Mickey. "Put the bag in the trunk," he said.

Mickey did as he was told. As he buckled himself back into the passenger seat, Gus pulled an illegal U-turn and started west toward the river.

Three minutes later, Mickey found himself looking down into the black water of the Parker River as they crept across the Yale Street Bridge into Coaltown.

As they slowed to a crawl and squeezed through a serpentine series of lanes, he wondered how many bricks they'd used to build all of this. Millions, maybe trillions. Every damn thing was made of bricks.

What seemed like thirty-five turns later, Gus pulled the Buick to a stop under a stout brick arch. He looked over at Mickey and said, "Sketchy isn't real talkative, but he's the best there is. He did the paperwork for the Royster girls. You just tell him what you need, and he'll take care of it."

Gus popped the door and stepped out into the street. Mickey followed him down a flight of stone stairs, through a dank passageway and down to a serious steel door at the far end. Gus didn't knock or ring or anything. He stood there until the door buzzed and then stepped inside.

Talk about stereotypes. Mickey had been picturing the classic forger dude from the movies. Three foot six, pasty complexion, green eyeshade, and sleeve garters. Except that Sketchy was an enormous red-headed biker type, damn near as big as Gus, and wearing a Hawaiian shirt that was undoubtedly visible from the space shuttle.

Apparently, Gus was right. Sketchy wasn't big on greetings and salutations.

"What?" he said.

Mickey pulled the blue plastic bag containing the Royster file out from under his coat. "I need two copies of everything inside. Then I need it put back together so nobody can tell it's been opened."

"Is it clean? No prints."

Mickey showed a latex-gloved hand. "There'll be prints, I suppose, but none of them are gonna be mine."

Sketchy nodded and then stalked off toward the door at the back of the room.

Gus wandered over to the nearest couch, sat down and started playing *Angry Birds* on his phone. Mickey turned the wooden chair around and sat on it backward.

Twenty minutes later, Sketchy reappeared. He handed Mickey a brown envelope.

"Two copies," he said. And then the blue plastic envelope containing the Royster file. Mickey turned it over in his hands. Brought it up close to his face. The court seal was unbroken and the bag showed no signs whatsoever of having been tampered with.

"The wonders of polymer chemistry," Mickey joked.

Sketchy shook his big head. "Seal-a-Meal," he said.

Mickey thanked him.

"You gonna rain on that baby-raper's parade?" Sketchy wanted to know.

"I'm sure as hell going to try," Mickey said.

Sketchy looked over at Gus, who was reaching into his pocket.

"It's on the house," he said and walked off.

. . . .

Grace was on her second latte when Roberto finally put in an appearance. A sweaty sheen lit his face. He was breathing through his mouth as he weaved between the tables and chairs and sat down beside her. "Sorry I'm late," he huffed. "My wife . . . I . . ."

He looked up and checked the clock on the wall.

"Is something wrong?" Grace asked.

"No . . . no . . . nothing wrong. I was just . . . Could we go now?"

Grace got to her feet. "Where?" she asked. "Where we going?"

Roberto was moving now. Toward the door. "Come on . . . it's not far."

Grace moved in his direction. "Where's the car?" she asked.

"It's not far," he said again, as he backed out the door.

Grace set her coffee on an empty table and stepped outside. In the half hour she'd been inside, the breeze had freshened and changed direction, coming in now from over the river, swirling the tops of the trees like ghostly dancers.

Roberto was halfway across the parking lot by then, waving her forward. She watched as he sidestepped between parked cars. "It's not far," he called again.

Grace walked out onto the sidewalk and looked around. Outskirts of town, anywhere USA. A Wendy's burger joint, an auto body shop with a big impound yard, a plumbing supply house, and Crazy Terry's Discount Tire City.

Half a block down, on the other side of the street, the Lucky Seven Motel sign flickered. VA NCY. Then further on down, an IHOP jabbed its blue spires into the threatening sky like daggers.

Roberto beckoned her forward and started across the street.

Grace stopped walking. "No," she said.

Roberto came hustling back to her side. "Please," he said. "I had to leave her alone."

"Alone?"

"Last time . . . when we met . . . the old lady next door . . . she stayed with Sophia till I got back," he said.

"Where's your wife?" Grace demanded. "I'm not moving another inch until I get some idea where we're going."

"The old lady's drunk. Passed out. So Sophia's alone."

"Where?"

He pointed across the street and the Lucky Seven Motel.

Grace's jaw dropped. "That motel? You've got your wife in a roach motel?"

He nodded.

. . . .

Child Protective Services was jammed to the rafters. The wretched refuse of our teeming shores was stacked six deep at the counter. Anger and frustration floated on the air like cannon smoke. Mickey picked his way through the writhing throng, got himself situated between the empty water cooler and the wall, and waited for the melee to thin out a bit.

About the time an entire Spanish-speaking family of five vacated the area directly in front of him, Mickey slid forward, like he was on wheels. The crush of the crowd pinned him in the corner, over by the empty box of tissues and long-dead pens.

Mickey checked the area. Waited and then checked it again. Picked a moment when Miss Goodbody had just finished up with a customer and everybody in the joint was trying to make eye contact with her so they could be next.

That's when Mickey made his move.

He slid the blue bag out from beneath his coat and slipped it onto the counter. As he turned to leave, a big black hand latched onto his wrist like a Rottweiler. Mickey froze. Then looked to the right. The security guard was right up in his face, using his hip to cram Mickey deeper into the corner. Same guy, with the D. Williams name tag.

"You'll have to come with me sir," the guy said, pushing harder. His eyes were hard. His voice was low. Big pissed-off crowd like this wasn't something you wanted to get excited, so he was trying to handle the situation with great discretion.

"I don't think so," Mickey said.

The guy's eyes widened. He leaned on Mickey harder. Reached for his pepper spray.

"Sir . . . don't make me . . ."

"Howsabout I don't tell anybody about how you bang Miss Tight-bottom on that desk over there every lunchtime."

The eyes flickered. "No idea what you're talking about," he tried.

"Sure you do. How you turn off the CC cameras and take her over in the corner for a little poke in the whiskers when the place is shut down."

Mickey took a chance. "And I'm betting Mr. D. Williams got a wife and a couple of kiddies stashed someplace, and I'm also betting his old lady *really* don't want to hear he been doggin' around on her."

They stood there, leaning hard on one another, having a staring contest. That's when the same guy started yelling again. "Hey . . . hey . . ."

Williams's cheek twitched. Mickey watched a single bead of sweat form above his mustache. When he exhaled hard, Mickey knew his guess had been right.

The grip on Mickey's wrist began to lessen. The guard checked the room, then glanced down at the file.

"How'd you get that?" he wanted to know.

"Question's not how I got it, question's how we can get it back where it belongs," Mickey said, leaning closer. "When you close up tonight, you put that file back in that second file cabinet over there. Keys are in your little friend's desk. Top drawer. The brass-colored key." He nodded in that direction. "That way I get out of your life, and you get to keep on keeping on with your little cutie there."

The guy let go of Mickey's wrist. Checked the room again.

Mickey reached up onto the counter and pulled a dog-eared *LIFE* magazine over the file. Then threw a couple of *Outdoor Life*s on top of the pile.

"I can't . . ."

"Sure you can. Leave your gloves on. Under R."

"No . . . I . . . no . . ."

Mickey pointed up at the nearest camera's unblinking eye. "And it might be a good idea if this little piece of CC tape had an accident, too. Really no point in anybody seeing you and me chatting here, is there?"

He maybe wasn't the fastest thinker in the world, but D. Williams wasn't feeling suicidal either. Images of his wife changing the locks on his house and spending his pension check on Italian shoes did wonders for his moral pliability.

"Okay," he said finally. "Nothing gets said. Ever."

"My lips are sealed," Mickey promised as he bumped himself off the wall.

D. Williams grudgingly stepped aside. His eyes were hard as gravel.

"The lavender drawers were a nice touch," Mickey said as he passed.

. . . .

Old-time cabins. Ten little separate units built in a U-shape, office at one end, coffee shop at the other. The Lucky Seven Motel's office was open, its windows lined by green and red Christmas lights. The coffee shop was dark and still. The cabins looked mostly empty except back at the right rear, where it looked like somebody had rented adjoining units and was throwing a party.

Couple of beat-up Camaros, one of those mud-scarred pickup trucks with tires so tall you needed a ladder to climb into the driver's seat. Three or four buttrockers with mullet haircuts and black rock-band T-shirts, stumbling drunk, milling around one of those barbecues with the big round lid, drinking beer, hooting and hollering, trying to convince themselves they were having a good time.

Over on the opposite side of the U, a gigantic food truck was parked diagonally across half a dozen parking spaces. Not the modern kind of food truck, where you could get a nice dollop of duck confit on a locally sourced brioche. The old-fashioned kind of truck. The kind that made a living showing up at construction sites every day, dispensing week-old egg salad sandwiches and pastries hard enough to pound nails. Known, in the vernacular of the trade, as "The Garbage Wagon."

Thirty feet in front of her, Grace watched as Roberto ducked behind the truck, pulled out a key and opened the door to unit two. A soft yellow light spilled over the cracked concrete step. He motioned for her to follow.

"Hey baby," somebody shouted from across the way.

Grace sighed and kept her eyes straight ahead.

"Hey Blondie," another voice shouted. "Do the carpet match the drapes?"

A chorus of wild laughter echoed around the U. Somebody repeated the line, and another round of merriment bounced around the cinderblock walls.

Grace began to move toward the cabin door. The only window was festooned with thick burglar bars. Must be a lot like sleeping in jail, Grace thought.

"Got a cold one for you baby," the first guy shouted, holding out a dripping can of beer and stumbling in her direction.

"I got a hot one," the other guy yelled, sending the drunken throng into yet another frenzy of knee-slapping jocularity.

Grace followed Roberto into the room.

"Hey baby," a voice shouted. "Doangoway . . ."

Roberto reached around her, bolted the door and set the chain.

. . . .

"Get that thing outta here," Gus growled. "I could pull fifteen for just being in the car with that thing."

He was talking about the high-output electric lock pick Mickey had retrieved from the bag in the trunk, and he was right. This was an anti-private property device. Even a guy with a clean record like Mickey's would probably do a bit of time for just having it on his person. America might be a free country, but you weren't free to walk around with one of these babies in your pants. No siree.

Mickey'd liberated it from a professional car thief a couple of years back. Told himself he just wanted to see if the thing worked. Took a little practice, but after a few tries Mickey was able to open just about any lock other than a Medeco in ten seconds or less. Told himself it was the sort of thing that just might turn out to be handy someday, and decided to spare it the disconsolate life of the police property room.

Mickey stuffed the pick in his jacket pocket and got out. He could see her car from where he stood. Looked like a rusty pumpkin sitting there with the Secrets license plate seriously askew.

Mickey dodged traffic across four lanes and a landscaped center strip, and then stepped between a pair of low shrubs and strolled into the *Morning Standard* parking lot. Everybody had their own little sign, saying this was their parking spot and nobody else's. All nice and white-man like.

Mickey approached from the rear, keeping his head as far back inside the hoodie as he could. The afternoon light was fading, but Mickey left the hubcap shades in place as he eased the pick into the driver's side door lock and pushed the button. Paranoia amplified the whirring noise to chainsaw proportions. He checked the surrounding area. People were coming out of the *Morning Standard* building now. Dribbling out in ones and twos, heading home for another night of *Dancing with the Stars*.

Mickey could feel the pick raking the disc cylinders, feel them turning, separating and reaching the shearline. Then it stopped on a dime. He pulled on the handle and the VW door popped open.

Mickey pocketed the pick, dropped the sheaf of papers onto the front seat, and then reached in and relocked the door.

A Bekins van blasted its angry air horns at Mickey as he matadored his way back across the street. The blast separated Gus and the pissed-off birds. He quickly lost the phone and started the Buick.

"I want to see her get it," Mickey said as he got in.

Gus turned off the car. *Angry Birds* again.

Must have been a hot news day. Natalie Mendonhal stayed late. It was a full fifteen minutes after everybody else had headed home before she came rolling across the lot to her car. "There she is," Mickey said.

Gus looked up as Natalie Mendonhal opened her car and plopped down into the seat . . . and then immediately got back out, frowning down at the seat, as she picked up the paperwork and set it on the roof of the car. She craned her neck and looked around. And then scanned the area again.

They watched as she got her glasses from her purse, stuck them on the end of her nose, and then started fingering her way through the stack, pressing the pile of pages to the roof with her free hand as the wind tried to scatter them like dry leaves.

Two minutes passed. She stopped and looked around again, as if in disbelief, then, in rapid succession, hugged the pages to her chest, slammed the car door with her foot, and started jogging back toward the newsroom like she was on fire.

"Shit's about to hit the fan," Gus said with a grin.

"About 6:00 a.m., when the morning edition hits the street," Mickey said.

Mickey got out of the car. "I'm going to change my clothes," he said to Gus. "Then we need to get rid of this stuff."

Gus started the car as Mickey climbed in the back seat.

"Sure gonna miss that ghetto getup," Gus said as they pulled out into the street.

"Let's remember him as LaMichael," Mickey said as he pulled the sweatshirt over his head.

. . . .

She was tiny. Maybe ninety pounds with rocks in her pockets. He had her wrapped up, like a swaddled baby. But that wasn't what left Grace speechless. It was the rest of the stuff in the room that had her jaw resting on her jacket.

He had one of everything, piled over in the corner. A ventilator, an ECG, an ICU monitor collection, oxygen tank, leg bag, Posey vest. The whole ball of wax. Head trauma central. Virtually none of which was currently in use.

From where Grace stood, it looked like the nasogastric tube in her throat, the catheter running out from under the covers, the IV stand, and a standard blood pressure monitor attached to her arm were the only pieces of equipment she was actually connected to.

She turned to Roberto. "Where'd you get this stuff?" she asked.

He shrugged and looked away.

"What's that mean? she demanded. "You've got half a million dollars' worth of medical equipment here. You telling me this belongs to you?"

"It was in her room," he said.

"What room?"

"At the hospital place."

"And you took it?"

He nodded again.

Grace walked over to the side of the bed and looked down. Sophia was beautiful. Something about her affect reminded Grace of a renaissance Madonna, something Spanish maybe, serene and lit from within.

"How'd you get her here?"

Roberto threw his eyes toward the door. "The truck," he said.

Grace was unable to disguise her astonishment. "That truck?" she said pointing at the door. "You brought her all the way from LA in a food truck?"

"It's self-contained," he said. "You could plug it in, or it's got batteries."

Grace sat down on the edge of the bed and looked up at Roberto. "This is insane. We can't do this," she said. She swept a hand over the ICU equipment. "They'll come looking for you, Roberto. You can't walk out of a hospital with stuff like that and expect them to let you get away with it."

"I'm gonna bring it back . . . soon as . . . you . . . when Sophia . . ."

Grace held up both hands. "Don't you realize . . . I mean, even if Sophia awakens . . . I mean, best-case scenario, she's going to need months, maybe years of physical therapy before she can begin to lead anything like a normal life."

"I hadda do something," Roberto said. "They was gonna kick her out."

"Kick her out?"

"My insurance expired. They said I hadda put her someplace else. And then I saw this magazine thing about the Silver Angel . . . you know . . . and I thought . . ."

"Jesus, Roberto."

"They gimme a list of places where I could take her. They all had long waiting lists. I went to one." His eyes nearly rolled in his head. "You shoulda seen it. People stacked like animals . . . I couldn't . . . I just hadda do something. She was pregnant when this happened. They hadda take the baby . . . some kind of tubal thing. They said it was her or the baby."

BANG. Somebody hit the door. "Come on out and play, baby . . ." a voice slurred. "Come on, Blondie . . . ve vill not harm you." Shitty German accent.

Grace ignored him. "Roberto . . . we've got to call an ambulance. Sophia needs professional care. Much as I'd like to be able to help you . . . both of you . . . I just can't."

BANG. The whole front wall of the cabin shook from the impact. The door lock exploded. The door cringed inward, stopped only by the flimsy gold chain.

An arm inserted itself into the breach, holding a dripping can of beer.

"Come on, baby," he crooned. "Poppa got a brand new bag."

Grace launched herself at the door, hitting it in full stride, shoulder first. Sounded like someone had snapped a broom handle in two. An agonized roar raced into the room. The beer can dropped to the floor. The arm snaked back out. Grace slammed the door. A high-pitched keening noise seemed to be everywhere at once. BANG. BANG.

"Bitch . . . you fucking bitch!" he was screaming. Trying to kick in the door.

Grace looked over at Roberto. "Slide the dresser over here," she said.

Roberto began to drag the dresser over toward the door. The sticky shag carpet made it heavy going, but he stayed at it, moving it two feet at a time.

"Turn it the other way," Grace said as she heaved against the door with her shoulder. Roberto slid it around so it sat lengthwise against the back of the door, leaving only about four feet between the edge of the dresser and the wall.

The rest of it he figured out on his own. He dropped to the floor, put his back against the wall and his feet against the end of the dresser. As long as he kept his knees locked, nobody was coming through the door.

Grace stepped back, huffed several deep breaths while she patted herself down, looking for her phone. "I'm calling the cops," she announced, when she found it.

BANG. BANG.

"Oh . . . please, please . . . they'll take me away from her. She'll die without me. Please. Don't . . . don't . . ."

Grace started to dial 911 but stopped. The banging had stopped. She listened. Other than the faint passage of traffic, it had suddenly grown quiet.

In her mind's eye, Grace could see her mother's face, smug and sleek and stainless as her chair, saying "I told you so. You can't deal with people like this."

Grace wandered over and sat on the bed next to Sophia. She knew from past experience that the comatose often were completely aware of what was going on in their surroundings. They just weren't able to respond to any of it.

She reached out and put a hand on Sophia's forehead, then laid her own brow on the back of her hand. Somewhere in the universe, music was playing.

"It's alright," she whispered. "It's alright."

. . . .

Coaltown again. All the way out to the north end of the island this time. Out to where the darkening sky was ruled by an enormous stone smokestack. The kind they'd never let you build anymore, standing against the horizon like a giant *screw you* finger, pointing up at the ocean of airborne sludge it released every night, saying *here it is fool, whatcha gonna do about it?*

Used to be an old lead smelter, back in the days before they'd noticed that lead exposure was about as healthy as smallpox. Same folks who'd wanted to make the island into a park wanted to tear the stack down, wanted to remove the blemish from their horizon, they'd said. That lasted until the state environmental impact study came back saying that pollution abatement alone was going to cost the city the price of a new library, and that, depending on the method of demolition and the prevailing winds at the time, a major evacuation of a three-county area might well be required. So much for demolition.

Biosystems turned the old blast furnace into a giant incinerator, and used it to get rid of anything they couldn't save, sink, or sell.

Gus pulled the Buick to the curb in the big circular drive.

"Bring the bag," he said, as he unbuckled his seatbelt.

Mickey felt it the minute he got out of the car. It felt as if a hand were pushing against his chest. Like he was walking up a steep hill, working his legs like crazy, but not making any progress.

Gus picked up on Mickey's discomfort. "Place gives me the willies," he said.

Mickey followed Gus around the side of the building, where the giant overhead conveyer belt snaked up from the water, screeching and groaning like a gored animal as it rumbled along, bristling with the carcinogenic rubble of post-industrial society.

The closer they got to the open doors, the heavier the bag seemed to get. From twenty yards away, Mickey could see the terrifying red glow seeping out into the night. His cheeks could feel the fire. Felt like his skin was crackling and his hair was about to burst into flame. His will forced him forward, but his legs had their doubts.

The glare was so bright now that Mickey had to look away. When he peeked again, somebody in a flameproof suit was shuffling in his direction. Big square head, backlit by the unholy orange glow, holding out his hand . . . reaching.

Mickey's feet stopped moving altogether. His arm trembled as he held out the bag. Soon as the guy took hold of the handle, Gus grabbed Mickey by the shoulder and pulled him back. Took everything Mickey had not to stumble into a run.

Wasn't till they rounded the corner of the building, and the back of his neck began to cool, that Mickey realized he'd been holding his breath the whole time. He stopped, put his hands on his hips and gulped air.

"You okay?" Gus asked.

"Yeah," Mickey said. "I'm fine."

Gus pulled out a handkerchief and mopped his face. "I don't know how those guys work there."

"Must be Catholics," Mickey said.

. . . .

Grace could feel her presence. Sophia was floating, becoming less herself and more everything else, minute to minute. When she was younger, Grace had come to picture the process as a Creamsicle floating in warm water, the little orange wisps spreading slowly toward the edges, getting thinner and thinner, until the vanilla ice cream began to show and the ripples turned to white.

The deep throb of an engine pulled Grace's head up. She tiptoed over to the front of the room, cocked her head and listened. The steady thump of the exhaust was getting closer. She reached over and peeled back the filthy curtains covering the front window.

"Damn," escaped her lips. They were backing the monster truck up to the front window. One of the drunks was walking along beside the truck swinging a thick chain, with a hook on the end.

She watched in horror as he ran the chain through the burglar bars and hooked it back on itself. She looked over at Roberto, wedged tight, keeping the door closed.

"Go cover Sophia, Roberto. Cover all of her."

"But . . ."

"The door's not a problem. Go cover her."

Grace found her phone and dialed.

"Doan call the cops. Please . . . doan call the cops," Roberto chanted, as he hurried to his wife's side.

"No cops," Grace said. "Gus . . . I need help," she shouted into the phone. "Lucky Seven Motel on Willis Avenue."

A shout from outside. Grace looked toward the window just at the moment when the entire front wall of the room exploded in a hail of airborne debris. She threw herself to the floor, shielding her eyes from the maelstrom of broken glass.

When she pushed herself to her knees, she was amazed at the extent of the damage. They'd hooked the monster truck up to the steel burglar bars and floored it. Instead of wrenching the bars from the window, they'd pulled down most of the cabin's front wall and dragged it out into the center of the U, where it was now tangled up in the truck's rear tires. The driver was out of his seat, pulling and kicking at the enormous piece of rubble that had brought his truck to a shuddering halt.

Beneath where the window used to be, an electrical line was twirling in the air, arcing and sparking, like some deranged pinwheel. Grace picked a piece of broken glass from her palm and got to her feet.

"Bitch," somebody screamed. "You busted Petey's fucking arm."

. . . .

They'd dropped the Buick off at the Wagner Brothers Cadillac-GMC dealership, way the hell out on Beckman Boulevard. Gus went inside the office, carrying the dealer plates and the second copy of the Royster file, and came out a few minutes later empty-handed. Mickey didn't bother to ask any questions.

The Hardwig PD had returned the white van that Gus had been using for Demolition Derby the other day. Gus and Mickey climbed in.

Gus asked, "Where you want me to leave you?"

"I live over on the West Side," Mickey said. "Bartley Street."

Gus nodded. As they pulled out into the street, a guy on a chopped Harley blew by them at a thousand miles an hour, all ape-hangers, peeled-back lips and bugs in the teeth. They watched in silence as the chopper's taillight faded to black.

"Trying to remember if I was ever that young," Mickey said, as the bike's throaty roar faded to a whisper.

Gus chuckled. "Know what you mean," he said. "Lately I been thinkin' about packing it in and maybe going back home. Figure I got enough stashed to spend the rest of my days fishing."

"Where's home?" Mickey asked.

"Pensacola."

"Weather's sure as hell better there," Mickey said.

"Got a sister still lives there too. Rest of 'em's gone. Died . . . moved away."

"I've never lived anyplace but here," Mickey said. "Spent my whole damn life in about a hundred square miles."

"Better that way," Gus proclaimed. "Gives a guy a sense of belonging . . . you know . . . of being part of something bigger than just him."

Mickey pointed out to the left. "Maynard Avenue," he said. "That's where my grandfather used to live. Forty-seven years in the same house. Smoked these cigarettes with a little brown coupon on the back of each pack. You collected enough coupons you could redeem them for merchandise. He had piles of them all over the damn house, wrapped in little blue rubber bands. Old guy had a couple hundred thou in the bank, and he smoked himself to death trying to get a free toaster."

"People are crazy that way," Gus said, a second before his phone began to ring. He fished it out of his jacket pocket and squinted down at the face. He frowned and brought the phone to his ear. Listened. "Where?" he asked.

Mickey could make out a woman's voice, rapid-fire . . . excited.

"Comin'," Gus said as he floored the van. He looked over at Mickey, his face set hard as concrete. "Gracie got a problem," he said. "I'll leave ya at—"

Mickey shook his head. "I'm in," he said.

They were doing seventy in a thirty. Gus thumbed a single number into his phone.

"Gracie got a problem," he said. "Lucky Seven Motel over on Willis Avenue." He hung up, stood on the brakes, and power slid them around a corner, tires screeching, every nut and bolt in the van threatening to shake loose as they cut a reaper swath through the intersection. Mickey sucked air through his teeth. Watching as a bright blue BMW burst a tire, bouncing up onto the sidewalk, trying to escape the van's erratic path. An angry horn began to blow. Gus clicked the high beams on.

Mickey reached up and grabbed the *oh shit* handle.

. . . .

"Turn off the oxygen," Grace shouted above the roar of the engine and the snap of sparks. Shards of shattered glass and masonry had fallen like sleet. Roberto's back was covered with debris. Beneath him, Sophia appeared to be uninjured. But . . . if the sparks got to the oxygen tank . . .

"No," Roberto shouted. "She doan breathe so good. She needs her—"

Grace didn't wait to hear the rest. She crunched through the debris, kicking things aside, as she threw herself across the bottom of the bed and began to turn the wheel on the top of the oxygen tank as fast as she could.

Outside, somebody let loose a drunken rebel yell. Grace looked up to see the motel manager grappling with two of them. She winced as the one in the filthy John Deere hat swung the chain like a medieval mace. The sound of the impact was sickening. The manager dropped to his hands and knees on the pavement. They began kicking him as he crawled along the blacktop, trying to escape. The one in the cap kicked him hard in the ass, sending him sprawling forward onto his face, breaking his glasses and bloodying his nose. Fueled by terror, he ignored the pain and kept crawling forward, scratching across the asphalt till he managed to throw himself inside the office door.

When they got through whooping it up, they turned Grace's way. Three of them, shitfaced drunk, their faces etched with the kind of blind anger that self-haters can't help but spread around. The one with the chain twirled it as he moved her way. "Comin' to get you, bitch," he shouted. "Gonna get your skinny little ass."

Despite the jagged six-foot hole decorating the front wall, the three stooges opted to kick in the cabin door and come in that way, stumbling over the rubble as they made their way through the shattered doorway.

Grace rushed to meet them, screaming now. "Get the hell out of here," she shrieked and launched herself at the one in the green hat. The force of the impact drove him backward into the old TV. They went down in a heap. She was trying to remove his eyes with her thumbs when an arm slipped around her throat and lifted her from the carpet. She kicked her legs, catching the first guy under the chin, sending him pinwheeling back to the floor. Her head felt as if it might explode. She was gasping for breath, clawing at the arm, flailing haplessly against the brute force crushing her throat.

Grace threw her head back with all the muscle she could muster. Her attacker grunted and reached for his face, and the pressure on her throat lessened just enough for her to slip beneath the arm. She wrenched herself free with enough force to send her staggering, banging into the cabin wall, trying to catch her breath.

"Bitch," one of them shouted.

Roberto was down in the doorway, with the guy with the broken arm trying to stomp him through the shag carpet. His face was a mess, but he wouldn't stay down. No matter how many times the guy kicked him, he still tried to struggle to his feet.

The other two were on her now, smelling of new sweat and old piss. Green Hat grabbed her in a bear hug and lifted her from the floor. They were face to face. Two inches apart. He opened his mouth to speak. Grace spit in it. He roared like an animal and swung her heaving body toward the doorway. That's when the guy with the chain grabbed her legs and they went lurching across the room.

She felt the cold air wash over her face and knew they were outside. And then she was down on her hands and knees in the parking lot. They were tearing at her clothes. The buttons on the front of her blouse exploded like a machine-gun burst. A hand reached over her head, grabbed the back of her brassiere, and tried to pull it over her head, but the angle was wrong and it wouldn't go.

Somebody was clawing at her waist now. Dragging her jeans down around her ankles. "Get her on the ground," somebody shouted. "Get her down!"

And then . . . the screeching of tires rose above sounds of struggle and the rumble of traffic. A hand tore her underwear, just as a new voice began to shout.

She heard the tinkle of the chain followed by a collision of bodies as she tried to gather the remnants of her clothes around herself. When she looked up, the chain was whirling in the air. She watched open-mouthed as Mickey Dolan stepped inside the arc, avoiding the lethal hook, allowing the chain to wrap around his body, pistoning his knee upward at the guy's crotch as he hurtled forward. She heard Mickey gasp as the hook finished its wrap and made contact with his back. He brought the knee up again and this time made solid contact. Green Hat dropped the chain and staggered backward, his eyes squeezed shut, his mouth a black hole.

Over by the cabin's door Gus had polished off the guy who had been kicking Roberto and was now running in their direction. When Grace turned back, Mickey had dropped to his knees on the asphalt, hugging himself and gasping for breath.

She turned again toward Gus. And then . . . the shot went off. The God-almighty roar of a rifle tore the air to pieces. Grace watched in horror as the force of the slug not only stopped Gus in his tracks, but actually lifted him from the ground and threw him backward, like a cardboard cutout.

Grace began to crawl in his direction. "Gus," she screamed. "Gus."

"Kill the motherfuckers," Green Hat shouted.

The driver lifted a scoped rifle up to his shoulder. Grace watched as he worked the bolt, sliding another round into the chamber. On her left, Mickey Dolan had managed to push himself to his feet.

The driver swung the rifle in Mickey's direction. Sighted down the barrel.

Grace held her breath.

Somewhere in the distance several sirens could suddenly be heard.

"Kill 'em, Coy," Green Hat shouted again.

Grace opened her mouth to scream, and, just like in the movies, the world seemed to go into slow motion. Green Hat arched his back and crumpled to the ground in a loose heap. The one with the rifle frowned and straightened up. He took his right hand off the weapon and tried to reach behind himself, like he wanted to scratch the middle of his back. The rifle clattered to the ground. He wobbled for a second, took an awkward step forward and fell onto his face.

Mickey Dolan staggered across the pavement and dropped to his knees beside Gus. A moment passed before his chin dropped onto his chest.

Movement in her peripheral vision brought Grace's eyes back toward the parking lot, where a pair of dark shadows stepped from between cabins. She stifled a moan, as they bent at the waist and shot each of her attackers behind the ear.

The one on the left turned and melted back into the shadows. The other took a step forward. He looked over at Dolan and Gus. Motioned with the gun.

Dolan gazed down at the massive hole in Gus's chest and shook his head. Somewhere in the darkness, an engine started.

The remaining shadow made the sign of the cross, and then turned and walked away. Grace began to cry.

· · · · · · · ·

They took Mickey's cellmate away just before nine in the morning. Crazy bastard hadn't eaten a bite or said a word in fourteen hours, just sat there staring at the wall and rocking back and forth on his tailbone. Then when they came and told him he was being moved to another cell, he went completely apeshit. Before it was over, it took four burly COs and a spit mask to get him strapped into a restraint chair and wheeled off.

They left Mickey standing in the hallway with the cell door open, so he had a pretty good idea what the score was. He went inside the cell and sat on the steel bench, running his hands through his hair, combing out pieces of debris with his fingers, feeling the various cuts and craters in his scalp, when he heard the sound of shoes and looked up.

Marcus Nilsson stood in the cell doorway. Mickey started to rise, but Nilsson waved him back down. "Forchristsakes siddown," he growled.

The Chief of Detectives stalked over and sat down on the bench next to Mickey. "Don't suppose you've seen the morning papers," he asked.

"Delivery's spotty down this end of the cell block," Mickey said.

"It's a hell of a mess out there."

Mickey kept running his hands through his hair and staring at the growing pile of hairborne debris on the floor between his feet.

"Always is . . . isn't it?" he said.

"Not like this," the C of D said. He sighed, as if he didn't know where to begin. "Gus Bradley's dead," he said. "But of course, you know that."

"Dumbass redneck shot him with a deer rifle."

"Got one of them with a broken neck. Somebody turned the guy's head all the way around backward. Docs say he probably isn't going to make it, and if he does he's gonna do it sitting down, with somebody spooning his porridge for him."

"Gus was defending himself," Mickey said.

"That's what I figured," Nilsson said. "It's the other two stiffs I was hoping you could help me with."

Mickey kept his eyes on the floor. "What other two?" he asked.

"What they say was the rifle shooter and another guy." When Mickey didn't say anything, he went on. "A double tap. Both with one in the torso and then another in the back of the head." He looked over at Mickey. "Small caliber . . . looks like professional work."

"I didn't shoot anybody," Mickey said. "Last time I saw my piece, you had it."

"I know. We ran your hands and jacket for gunpowder residue. They came up clean. Likewise with Gus Bradley and the Pressman woman."

"Sounds like a real mystery," Mickey said.

"The skell who can still talk says it was a couple guys came out from between the cabins and capped both his buddies and then just walked off." He leaned over close to Mickey. "Sound familiar?"

Mickey kept his mouth clamped shut.

"And you didn't see a thing."

"No sir," Mickey said.

"A seasoned police detective, and you didn't see a damn thing?"

Mickey looked away.

Marcus Nilsson snorted and folded his arms over his chest. The air was thick as tapioca. "Where's everybody else?" Mickey asked finally.

"Bradley's in the morgue. Last I heard they're gonna ship him back to his sister in Florida someplace. Pressman . . . that woman's got a way of disappearing. Soon as we took her statement and swabbed her for gunshot residue, she just sort of evaporated."

"The woman in the coma?"

"She's over at Memorial. Still comatose, but otherwise okay."

They sat in silence for a time. Then Nilsson got to his feet and looked down at Mickey. "Then there's still the matter regarding theft of public property and violation of a court order."

"What property is that?" Mickey asked.

"The Royster Family Court file," he said.

"It's missing?"

Marcus Nilsson sat back down and cocked his head. "Now that's the funny part of this whole thing, Mickey. It's not missing. It's right where it's supposed to be. Locked up in the CPS offices."

"So what's the problem?" Mickey asked, with as much faux wonder as he dared to run by Nilsson.

"The problem is that *the Morning Standard* printed the entire contents of the Royster file in this morning's edition."

"No kidding."

He looked up at the ceiling. "Some of the worst shit I ever read." He choked up. Rubbed the bridge of his nose as a diversion. "Terrible stuff. Heartbreaking. You read that stuff and . . . I mean . . . how does anybody justify giving those kids back to an animal like that?" He threw a hand in the air. "Hell, the *Standard* excised the worst parts of their testimony and put a warning on every page, and I still damn near puked." He pinned Mickey with his fiercest glare. "Heads are already rolling over this. This is the biggest shake-up in seventy-five years. City Council's meeting at six tonight for the purpose of expelling Edwin Royster from their ranks. The DA's office is preparing indictments for enough sexually related charges to keep Royster in prison for the rest of his stinking life."

"And how they *do* love their baby rapers in the joint," Mickey mused.

"The forensic accounting guys started running Judge Nalbandian's finances first thing, and as you well know, Sergeant . . . first thing the number crunchers do is slap a hold on everything. I mean . . . you can't buy a bean burrito, when they get through freezing your assets."

The C of D had a gleam in his eye. He leaned closer to Mickey.

"Except . . . they can't find any assets. Every dime the Nalbandians own was moved offshore yesterday. The Caymans they think. The house was signed over to the oldest daughter. The cars were donated to their church."

"Busy day yesterday."

Nilsson waggled a thick finger, as if to say wait there's more. "Just so happens that Dorothy and Charlie Nalbandian left for an extended trip around the world. Yesterday! Their attorney assures us it's been planned for quite some time. Their travel agent says they made the reservations yesterday. The mouthpiece swears he's as stupefied as we are, and has no idea when to expect them back."

"Rats abandoning ship," Mickey said.

"Royster's attorney went on TV this morning denying everything. Threatening to sue everybody in town, especially Natalie and the paper."

"Depends on how Natalie came into possession, doesn't it?" Mickey asked.

"She says she found the file on the front seat of her car."

Mickey sat up and rubbed the back of his neck. He could feel where every link of that rusted chain had made impact with his spine. He stifled a groan.

"You think she's telling the truth?" Mickey asked.

"*Standard* ran her by their own polygraph expert before they printed it. She passed. So we ran her by ours . . . and she passed again."

"That changes everything," Mickey said.

"Yeah," the Chief said. "Turns her into the champion of the people's right to know. She'll probably win a Pulitzer. Better yet, it makes her eligible for whistleblower protection. Nobody's suing her or the paper for anything."

"Amazing how that worked out," Mickey commented.

Nilsson pinned him with an iron stare. "That where you want to leave it, Mickey?"

Mickey thought it over. "Am I under arrest?"

"No."

"Then I'm gonna walk over to city hall, sign some paperwork, and then come back over here, pack up my stuff and hit the road," he said.

. . . .

Roberto looked like he'd been to war. One side of his face was the color of an eggplant. He'd lost a front tooth and had a bandage the size of a waffle covering the dent in the back of his head. He struggled into the upright position as Grace walked his way.

"They won't let me see her," he said as she arrived at his side.

"They're stabilizing her condition," Grace told him. "From what I hear, she's doing fine."

"I gotta see her . . . I gotta . . ."

Grace heard the hiss of the elevator door. She looked back in time to see her mother and a junior attorney from the firm of Spearbeck, Scott and Reynolds emerge from the elevator and begin moving in their direction.

"Roberto . . ." She turned halfway around. "That gentleman is going to be acting as your attorney."

"What? I—"

"Don't worry about Sophia. She's in good hands. The Women's Transitional Center is going to be covering her hospital costs, until we get everything figured out, so you don't need to worry about that."

"Why do I need a lawyer?"

"Because there's a couple of LA detectives downstairs who want to talk to you about some missing medical equipment, and what is apparently a stolen food truck."

"It used to belong to my brother-in-law."

"They don't seem to feel that constitutes ownership," Grace said.

Eve turned the wheelchair left, over toward the nurses' station. Probably delivering the financial responsibility paperwork, Grace figured.

The young man in the good suit arrived a second later.

"Roberto . . . this is Mister . . ."

"Fain," the attorney said. "Robert Fain."

"Mr. Fain is going to represent you. See to your rights and if necessary post bond for you, so you don't have to worry. I don't know how long any of this is going to take, but by the time you're finished, and back here, they'll probably let you see Sophia."

"I don't . . . are you . . ."

"I've got to go," Grace said. "A friend is waiting for me."

. · . · . · .

Mickey knocked softly on the office door.

"Yeah."

Mickey poked his head inside. "Wanted to say goodbye," he said.

"I wish you luck, Mickey," Marcus Nilsson said. "I really do."

"And I want you to know I appreciate the kindness and understanding you've always thrown my way, Chief. Without that, I sure as hell wouldn't have gotten this far."

"You're a good cop, Mickey. Lately . . . seems like things had gotten a little out of hand for you. Maybe it's for the best you take a little time and regroup."

"Been feeling like the job is doing me lately, instead of the other way around."

"It's a tough job," Marcus Nilsson said. "Lots of ambiguity. Kind of thing wears on a person. You get to feeling you gotta make things turn out the way they should, which, unfortunately, ain't what we get paid to do." He got to his feet, walked around his desk and extended his hand. "Take care," he said. "You need a reference, gimme a call."

Mickey got the message. Nilsson still thought he was cop material, but not in *his* department. That wasn't possible anymore. Not after all of this.

He clapped his hand onto Mickey's shoulder and walked over to the door with him. "One last thing, Mickey."

"Yes sir."

"I'll bet over the years I've known thirty, forty guys who could have figured out how to get the Royster file out of the CPS office." He leaned closer. "But I've only known a couple guys smart enough to put the damn thing back."

Nilsson's pale blue eyes were drilling holes in the side of his head.

Mickey kept his mouth shut and his eyes averted. The Chief clapped him on the shoulder again and then disappeared into his office and closed the door.

Mickey stood there for a moment and then started across the room, over to the borrowed desk he'd been using. He went through the drawers. Same stuff that had been in there when he got the desk.

A brown evidence envelope rested on the blotter. From the look of it, Joseph's diary, back from the lab. Mickey slipped it under his arm. As he turned to walk away, he noticed the clear plastic bag under the desk. Joseph Reeves's personal effects.

His first instinct was to leave them there, and walk out. He took a step toward the elevator, but stopped, went back and picked up the bag. Just in case anybody ever wanted the stuff. At least that's what he told himself.

He took his time leaving the building. Walking slowly. Making it a point to take it all in, savoring the sounds and smells one last time. He traded two-fingered salutes with the Duty Sergeant, pulled open the door, and stopped dead in his tracks.

They were halfway up the stairs. Holding hands. Jen and Joanna.

"Oh," they said in unison.

Mickey let go of the door. "Yeah . . . oh," he said.

"We were over at city hall . . . they said . . . you'd . . . that you were . . ." Jen said.

"I'm done," Mickey said.

"You resigned?"

"Nope. I was fired."

"Just like that?" Joanna asked. "Don't they have to . . ."

"There's a process," Mickey said. "They'll have a couple meetings with the union. Work out how much of my pension I'm going to get, that sort of crap. But I'm definitely out of here."

Jen reached out and put a hand on his arm. "Oh Mickey . . . I'm so sorry."

"Don't be," Mickey said. "Tell you the truth, I'm ready to move on with my life. I don't know where I'm going or what I'm gonna do. I just know it's gonna be better than how it's been for me lately."

Nobody spoke. Jen had one hand entwined with Joanna's and the other on Mickey's arm. Out in the street, a Metro bus disgorged a load of passengers and then went roaring off down the street.

Mickey cleared his throat. "Listen . . ." he began. "I've had all this crap floating around in my head about the two of you and what the whole thing said about me, and what people were thinking about me." He cut the air with his hand. "All of which pretty much turned out to be bullshit."

They both looked astonished.

"Turned out I was just feeling sorry for myself." He shrugged. "Wish I'd handled it better, but it is what it is."

"You did fine," Jen said.

"You know what I think?"

"What?"

"I think love is hard to find."

Jen removed her hand from his sleeve. "Good luck, Mickey," she said.

Mickey nodded and headed down the stairs.

. . . .

He looked smaller, lying there on the steel table, waiting to go home. A profound sense of loss numbed Grace's chest like polar ice as she walked around the table, taking in Gus Bradley for what would surely be the final time.

Dead bodies had always affected her that way. Never seemed to Grace that a person's mortal remains had much to do with the being she'd known in life. Always seemed like the body was just the vehicle they happened to be driving when they ran out of gas, and that whatever it was that made a person a person had managed to slip out of the driver's seat and disappear without a trace.

She thought back to the story Gus had told her, about losing his daughter and how his marriage had fallen apart, and realized that sad tale was virtually all she knew of his life, and how, despite all the hours they'd spent together over the past few years, they had somehow managed to remain strangers.

She held her breath, reached out and put her hand on his broad forehead. He was cold. His skin felt thick and rigid, like chicken skin. She swallowed a sob, pulled her hand back and stuffed it deep into her pocket.

Behind her, the door opened. She didn't look. Didn't want to see them coming for him. Didn't want him to go. Some childish instinct was telling her that it couldn't be real if she didn't look at it.

"How you doing?" a sudden voice asked.

Mickey Dolan was standing there by her side.

"I'm okay," she said. She looked his way. "How's Cassie doing?"

"She'll be out later today. She'd have been out already if she hadn't tied a can of cream soda into a sweat sock and used it to beat the hell out of a couple of women who'd been harassing her."

Grace almost managed to grin. "My mother says the Royster family is going to go back to Hardwig when this is all done." She shrugged. "The rent's paid on the duplex for the year. The girls really liked that school they were going to, so you know . . . why not. Hardwig's a nice enough little town."

"Sounds like a good idea," Mickey said. "I think sometimes it's better to leave everything behind and just start over from scratch."

He looked down at Gus. "In his own way, he was a real good man," Mickey said.

"I thought cops and robbers were supposed to be like cats and dogs."

"Me too," Mickey said with a sigh. "I guess things aren't as black-and-white as I once figured they were." He ran a hand over his face. "A lot of things," he added.

Behind them, the gleaming double doors burst open, and a pair of blue scrubs— coroner's orderlies—wheeled a gurney into the autopsy room. Grace and Mickey slid into the corner, giving the orderlies plenty of room to maneuver Gus into a black rubber body bag and then onto their cart. They were graceful at their work, almost as if they'd known Gus in life, and were aware of the degree of physical respect he would have required of them.

As they started off, a fresh pair of shadows appeared in the doorway. Teddy stepped aside and let Vince Keenan precede him into the room. Vince stood with hands folded in front of him as the cart came abreast of him, then raised his right hand.

The cart squeaked to a halt. Vince reached down and slid the body bag zipper down a couple of feet. He stood for a moment gazing down into Gus's lifeless face and then pulled the zipper back up and nodded at the orderlies.

"Seems like I've known Gus all my life," Vince said, as they wheeled him out the door. "Like he was my uncle or something."

"I remember when he used to come to our Little League games," Mickey said. "Had one end of the bleachers all to himself, because the other parents were all so shit scared of him they wouldn't sit down there."

Vince nodded. "My old man somehow could never find the time. Said he wasn't about to spend a couple of hours every week watching me sit on the bench like a loser. But Gus . . . he made it more often than not."

"Funny. I didn't know him that well, but for some reason I'm gonna miss him," Mickey confessed.

Vince raised his gaze and looked over at Mickey. His eyes were hard as gravel. "Like you said, Mickey . . . sometimes shit like this is just the price of doing business."

Teddy followed Vince out through the double doors, and the silence of the dead settled over the room.

Grace leaned her shoulder against Mickey's. He could feel her swallowing her tears, trying to be brave like she imagined Gus would have wanted. He slipped an arm around her shoulders. She hiccupped once and covered her mouth with her hand. Mickey patted her back. She put her head on his shoulder.

"It's my fault," she said.

"No," Mickey said. "No it wasn't. You didn't shoot anybody. All you were doing was trying to help somebody out."

She cried for a while. Somewhere in the bowels of the building another motor started, adding to the underlying hum of technology that flowed around them like an unseen stream.

"Gus and I were talking about how weird people are," Mickey said, remembering his grandfather again. "How they're more than willing to take the blame for stuff that couldn't be helped, and absolutely unwilling to shoulder the responsibility for the stuff that could. Almost like if they plug up all their guilt holes with bullshit, there won't be any room for the real stuff to get in."

"If I'd just walked away," Grace whispered.

"My grandmother used to say, 'If wishes were horses, beggars would ride,'" Mickey said.

"And . . . she was so close."

"Who? My grandmother?"

"Sophia," Grace said. "She was right there. Wanting to come back to us."

Mickey hugged her closer. "Maybe you ought to finish it, then," he said. "Maybe if somebody comes back, you won't feel so much like somebody's gone."

Grace thought it over. "She's in Memorial Hospital," she said finally. "They'll never let me . . ."

"Yeah," Mickey said. "They will. I've got friends in low places."

. . . .

Mickey was someplace else. Out on Whitefish Lake with his mom and dad, splashing water on each other and yelling at the top of their lungs. The squeak of the chair next to his dragged him back to Memorial Hospital. He sat up and looked over.

"You're cured," Pamela Prentiss said.

"Of what?" Mickey Dolan asked.

"Whatever erectile malaise you claimed to have when I hit on you the last time."

"How do you know?"

"All a body's got to do is watch *you* watch *her*. That and the fact that I'm a nurse, of course." She cut the air with her hand. "It's an airtight diagnosis."

Before Mickey could work up a blanket denial, Sophia Salazar's door opened and Grace appeared. Pamela Prentiss jumped to her feet. Grace started walking their way.

"She's coming out of it," she said, when she got close.

Prentiss went into nurse mode, jogging across the gleaming floor and disappearing into the room. "That was quick," Mickey said. He checked his watch. "You been in there what . . . an hour."

Another nurse and a pair of orderlies came sprinting down the hallway and slid into the room.

"I helped her find her edges," Grace said. "After that, it was easy. She wasn't ready to leave us yet. It's like Roberto told me . . . they had a lot of plans, a lot of things they wanted to do. Start a business. Have some babies. She was ready to come back to us."

. . . .

The wind had slacked off. This morning's clouds had been blown to the western horizon, leaving a bright neon sky glowing overhead.

Mickey opened the car door and lifted the pile of Joseph's things from the passenger seat. When Grace slid in, he handed her the pile.

"What's this?" she asked.

"Joseph's stuff," Mickey said, starting the car. "I'll stick it in my garage, in case anybody ever wants it."

He looked over at Grace, who'd pulled Joseph's diary out of the evidence bag and was slowly leafing through it. The lab had inserted clear plastic sheets between the pages, giving the charred bundle the appearance of a small spiny animal.

"You hungry?" he asked.

"Starved."

"Want to catch a bite?"

She seemed surprised. "You and me?"

"Yeah."

"Sure . . . I guess. Celebrate my new life among the leisure class." She pinned him with those icy eyes. "Is this a date?"

"If you want it to be," Mickey said with a smile.

"I want it to be," she said, and went back to leafing through the diary.

They were halfway up Strander Avenue, headed for Scott's Bar and Grill, when Grace suddenly sat back in her seat. "Have you read this?" she asked.

"The diary? No."

"It's not a diary."

"What is it?"

"A long love note."

"To who?"

"Somebody named Brian."

Without willing it so, Mickey lifted his foot from the throttle. The woman in the car behind tapped her horn and swerved out around them.

"You sure?" he asked.

"No doubt about it," Grace said. "He was in love with a guy named Brian." She flicked her fingers at the pages. "This is all *my life was nothing before you. You're everything to me* stuff."

"Unrequited, maybe?"

"No way," she said. "Thing's full of times and dates. Brian liked so-and-so movie and he didn't. This restaurant was really romantic. These two had a thing going."

Mickey eased the car into a Metro Park and Ride lot and jammed it into park.

He looked over at Grace. "You thinking what I'm thinking?" he asked.

"The pissed-off Mrs. Reeves," she said.

He pointed to the bag containing the rest of Joseph's effects.

"Lemme see that," he said.

She handed it over. Mickey went in armpit deep, all the way to the bottom where the cell phone had come to rest. Brand new phone. Still had juice in it. Something like two dozen calls, all to the same local number. Nothing longer than twenty seconds.

Mickey dialed the number. "*The number you have dialed has been disconnected and is presently out of service. Please check the—*"

Mickey hung up and called Dispatch, figuring it would take a few days for his departure to make its way around the grapevine. "This is Sergeant Michael Dolan." He recited his former badge number. "Connect me to Technology please."

Click. Click.

"Technology. Yester."

"Got a number I need to run." Mickey read the number.

"Disconnected."

"Who had the number the last time it worked?"

"Brian Price. 4311 Shannon Terrace."

"He leave any kind of an emergency contact?"

"Didn't have enough credit to satisfy Ma Bell. Needed his grandma to cosign for the service." He read the grandma's phone number. Mickey pulled out his pad and wrote it down.

Mickey broke the connection and then gave Grace the short version.

"So . . . where is he?" she immediately asked.

"Brian?"

"Yes, Brian! Your friend and lover has an accident. He's in a coma. You never bother to get yourself on his visitor list? Never once show up to see him? Instead of being there for him, you suddenly move and change your phone number?"

"Explains the phone calls Joseph made," Mickey said. "Twenty calls over two days. I wondered about that. You know . . . you call and get the same recording three or four times and most people are going to stop calling. It was like Joseph couldn't believe it. Like it just had to be some kind of terrible mistake."

"And then he killed himself when he realized it wasn't."

Grace plucked Joseph's phone from Mickey's fingers and dialed the number he'd written down. "May I speak with Brian, please?" she asked.

Mickey could make out a woman's voice on the other end. Probably the grandma, he figured. Whoever it was sure liked to talk.

"How wonderful," Grace said, after a while, and then listened some more.

"When was this?" she asked.

Two minutes later, Grace said. "Yes . . . yes . . . thank you. I will. Yes."

She pressed the phone against her chest and closed her eyes.

"You're not going to believe this," she said.

"Try me."

"Brian's attending art school in Atlanta. He was planning to go to school here, you know, like community college, because he didn't have the price of tuition, but guess what?"

Mickey waited for the punch line.

"He won the lottery. Twenty thousand bucks."

"Do tell. When was this?"

"Four days before"—she made imaginary quotation marks in the air with her fingers—"Joseph's accident."

"And to think . . . you've been blaming yourself."

"To think."

"I'm thinking maybe we should return Joseph's things to his mother."

"It's the least we can do."

· · · · · · ·

She was standing on the second step of an aluminum ladder, planting pink begonias in a pair of window boxes over on the south side of her condo. She was decked out for a Beatrix Potter movie. Big white English garden hat. Flowered apron, elbow-length gloves. The whole Mr. Toad's-coming-to-lunch look.

Whatever transient joy she might have been deriving from planting flowers evaporated the second she looked their way.

She set her jaw like a bass. "What do you want?" she demanded.

Mickey held out the plastic bag. "These belong to Joseph," Mickey said, setting the bag on the grass. She looked down at the bag as if it had teeth.

"This too," said Grace, putting the book on top of the bag.

"Get out of here," she said.

"You bought him off, didn't you?" Grace blurted.

Her spine stiffened. She untied the sun hat and took it off.

"I have no idea what you're talking about," she said.

"Brian Price. Joseph's lover."

Roberta Reeves shuddered at the sound of the words. Almost as if she'd been slapped in the face.

"You paid Brian's art school tuition just to get him out of town," Grace added.

"Get away from me," she growled.

"Joseph and the pool. Was it really an accident?" Mickey asked.

Her lower lip began to quiver. She pointed down at the bag and the book.

"Get off my property and take that filth with you," she said.

"Did he tell you? That day by the pool? Is that what happened? He told you he was gay? Hoping to maybe get a little love and support from his mother?"

Her body began to shake as she climbed unsteadily down from the ladder.

"He was an abomination," she whispered. "A disgusting pervert."

"He was your son," Grace said. "Your son."

She was shaking her head. "No son of mine . . ." She trailed off.

"So you bought off his lover," Grace said.

Mickey jumped in. "That's why you wanted to pull the plug on him, wasn't it? And why you were so angry when Grace woke him up. You didn't want him awake. You didn't want him around at all."

"I wanted him dead," she screamed. Her face was bright red. A thin line of spittle had escaped her mouth. "Dead," she screeched again. "I wanted that disgusting creature dead and in hell with the rest of them."

She threw the sun hat to the ground and stalked off. Ten seconds later the sound of a slamming door boomed through the yard.

Mickey threw an arm around Grace's shoulders. "That went well," he said with a hint of a grin. "Still up for lunch?"

She shook her head and looped her arm around his waist.

"Me neither," Mickey said.

. . . .

"I used to fish down here when I was a kid," Mickey said. "Those days there were actually fish in here."

"What kind?"

"Mostly perch," Mickey said. "Maybe a sea bass, once in a while."

They were seated side by side on a pair of granite boulders, beneath the Yale Street Bridge. The tide was all the way in. The river was black and slack, and no matter how hard they tried to change the subject, the conversation kept coming back to Joseph.

"I don't understand people like her," Grace said. "How could she have so much hate for her own flesh and blood?"

"That's the kind of thing you need to know going in," Mickey said. "You need to vet these people you work with. You need to know everything there is to know about them. Keep the surprises to a minimum."

"You volunteering?" Grace asked.

He looked over to see if she was kidding. She wasn't.

"Maybe," he said. "I could at least show you how to go about it."

"There's a bunch of things you could show me."

About the Author

Photo © 2004 Skye Moody

G.M. Ford is the author of eight other novels in the Leo Waterman series—*Who in Hell is Wanda Fuca?*, *Cast in Stone*, *The Bum's Rush*, *Slow Burn*, *Last Ditch*, *The Deader the Better*, *Thicker Than Water* and *Chump Change*. He has also penned the Frank Corso mystery series and the stand-alone thriller *Nameless Night*. He has been nominated for the Shamus, Anthony, and Lefty awards, among others. He lives and writes in Seattle, Washington.